JOHN CREED

The Day of the Dead

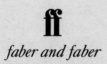

faber and faber

First published in 2003
by Faber and Faber Limited
3 Queen Square London WC1N 3AU

Typeset by Faber and Faber Ltd
Printed in England by Clays Ltd, St Ives plc

The right of John Creed to be identified as author of this work has been asserted in accordance with Section 77 of the Copyright, Designs and Patents Act 1988

A CIP record for this book
is available from the British Library

ISBN 0–571–21677–3

PART I

One

It was a dry day for a change, the wind had veered to the west, and I had spent the day trying to repair some of the winter wear and tear on my converted trawler, the *Castledawn*. It was low-key, satisfying work, and I was looking forward to the fresh scallops that were sitting on ice in my small croft. As I walked up the path from the little pier, I was feeling pleasantly tired and about as at peace with my surroundings as a man at my age and in my career is likely to be. There is a Russian proverb which states that we are born in a clearing but we die in a forest. I knew that the trees were closing over me. I woke at night sometimes with the faces of dead men almost visible in the darkness. But it was spring and the sun was shining, and the shiftless branches of those dark trees had not yet blotted out the light.

Such moments are made for irony. Peace and a degree of peace offered and then snatched away. It may have been a trick of the declining sun, but when I turned the corner towards the croft, the figure sitting on the doorstep momentarily seemed a small crabbed thing, harbinger of evil to come. A fancy perhaps, but when I looked back later, it didn't seem so far off the mark. I found myself wishing I had brought a gun with me and almost simultaneously felt a kind of weariness at the return of the survivor's instinct, the visceral need to feel the weight of a firearm in your hand.

As I moved a little closer, the man stood up and held up a hand in welcome. Six feet tall, olive complexion and black hair, Prada suit and Gucci loafers. Thankfully, Paolo Casagrande bore no resemblance to the haunted creature of my imagination. It had been a few years since I had seen him, but we spoke frequently on the phone, trading in art sometimes and in information frequently. Paolo was as close to a friend as you got in this business and I was glad to see him. As I approached him, we surveyed each other for signs of damage, the way that men of our age do. Paolo looked good, but there was a grimness in his eyes and dark shadows under them which didn't bode well. Even in the worst of times Paolo had a way of looking at the world which allowed that good and bad could coexist as long as you took the good where you found it. It seemed to keep him healthy and happy. But this time there was something wrong.

I reached out to shake his hand, but as usual he embraced me and kissed me on both cheeks.

'Still the Anglo reserve, Jack,' he said, laughing.

'Celtic reserve, please,' I said, 'and it beats the hell out of your over-the-top Latin exuberance.'

'It's good to see you, Jack,' he said. 'You look fit.'

'And older,' I said.

'Fuck older,' he said, and laughed. Paolo liked English swearwords and was fairly indiscriminate about where and when he used them. I'd seen him reduce a nun to stunned disbelief when he told her cheerfully that he'd be fucked if he would let her stand on a crowded train while he sat.

'You're right,' I said. 'Fuck older. Come in and have a drink.'

We went into the croft and did all the usual things that old friends did. Opened a bottle of the good Bardolino that Paolo had brought with him, asked about old friends, summed up the previous few years in a few inadequate sentences, remembered a few old times, opened another bottle. Before long, it was eight o'clock and the scallops were being seared in a pan that had been used for

4

frying good bacon, to give the seafood the tang it needed to lift it to the sublime. Still Paolo hadn't got to the purpose of his visit, but his unease of spirit was starting to flood the room. The only real sign I had seen of the old Paolo was the enthusiasm he showed for some new paintings by young artists that I had bought. I was in the middle of striking a deal for one when he frowned and a shadow passed over his face and he looked around the room as if he no longer knew where he was. I poured him a large Redbreast and put it in his hand.

'The sun's setting,' I said, nodding towards the immense conflagration of colour that suffused the land and sea. 'Go watch it while I do the dinner.'

I knew he would tell me what was wrong when he was ready, and I wasn't going to ask. People in the intelligence trade share a trait with courtroom lawyers engaged in cross-examination. They never ask a question unless they already know the answer to it.

It was an hour and long gone dark before Paolo came back. The scallops were cold but he ate them with salad and mopped up the juices with bread. He drained his wine and refilled the glass, pushing his chair back from the table. He sighed. He was ready.

'You remember Alva?' He said. His daughter. Even in his dark mood you could feel the faint lift of a parent's pride in his voice.

'Of course,' I said. I remembered playing with her, carrying her home on my shoulders after a long walk, fireflies scattering in the Fiesole dusk, her little voice piping out into the darkness. I also remembered with a pang that that evening was a long time ago.

'She must be eighteen now,' I said.

'Nineteen.' He slid a photograph across the table to me. Paolo's speciality and great love was fine art photography. This was only a holiday snap but it was clear that you didn't have to be Robert Mapplethorpe to bring out her beauty. She had long black hair and green eyes, and she was looking directly at the camera, the corners of her mouth turned up in a wry, easy smile. I had never met her mother and Paolo seldom talked about her. She had been a photographer who had been killed in a plane crash in Eritrea when Alva was a child.

'I don't know where to start,' Paolo said. 'Suddenly I feel foolish.' I waited.

'She's in New York,' he said, 'with a man.' He held up his hand as if to silence me, although I had no intention of speaking.

'I'm not being an old-fashioned father about this,' he went on. 'We always had – what would you call it? An open relationship. But this is different.' He sighed. 'This is difficult. Perhaps if I show you what he looks like, you will know what he is.'

He passed another photograph across the table to me. A photograph with the grainy, long-range look of a surveillance photograph. The man in the photograph was in his early forties. He looked as if he had some South American blood in him, indigenous blood. He had high cheekbones and deep hollows in his cheeks as if he was sucking them in. His hair was dark and straight and he was expensively dressed. But it was the eyes that held you. They seemed almost colourless and filled with . . . filled with nothingness, if that is the right word. But not quite nothing. Some ancient cynicism lurked there, a sense of the grave. I had a painting of a Venetian woman by an unknown hand. She was beautiful, dressed in dark velvet, jewels at her slender neck. But her eyes fixed you. They stared out at you, ageless and corrupt, with a disturbing air of arch amusement. She would have been a fitting partner for this man, I thought, not the open and grinning nineteen-year-old I had been shown earlier.

I handed the photograph back to Paolo.

'Who is he?'

'A Mexican. Goes by the name Ricardo Xaberra. I met him through the market. He bid against me for a photograph, a Man Ray. He got the photograph . . .'

Once again Paolo's voice tailed away. I was beginning to pick up

6

something, I thought. Paolo collected people the way he collected art.

'You invited him to Italy,' I said. Paolo nodded miserably.

'I invited him into my own house, *mia casa*!' he said.

'You didn't check him out?' I asked.

'Not as much as I should,' Paolo said. 'His – what do you say? His credentials look good.'

'But not his real credentials,' I said gently. Paolo's currency had always been information, and it was starting to look as if he had not attended to his own trade, and that inattention had cost him the most precious thing he had.

'He had such a passion for the Man Ray,' Paolo said, looking off into the distance, his eyes hard as though he had for the first time realized that art was about the hard things as well as the good things and that the corrupt could love it as much as the righteous.

'Who is he really?' I said gently.

'A bad man, Jack, a very bad man.'

Over the next hour, Paolo told me stories. Of a Mexican boy, son of a provincial university lecturer. Of a man grown rich in the trades of misery. Drugs, prostitution, extortion. There were stories of retribution exacted, and of terrible, gratuitous cruelty. Mexican girls forced into prostitution and runaway girls being chained together and thrown into the sea. Of torture overseen by those same pale eyes. If Paolo's nose for information had let him down first time round, then he had compensated for it since. Xaberra seemed endlessly wealthy and endlessly well-connected. He had friends among the anglicized New York élite, but he also had friends outside that effete bunch. Names known to Paolo and myself, but perhaps not to very many others. They were men of immense power and influence. It is almost a cliché that the influential men of our time are virtually unknown. It took a lot to penetrate their circles. Not just money, but intelligence and the power to shape events. I was impressed.

'What do you want me to do, Paolo?' I said.

I thought I knew the answer to that question and felt a faint sense of dread as I awaited his answer. He got up and stood at the window, not looking at me. The silence stretched on until I felt compelled to break it.

'If you want me to kill him, Paolo, you should say so.'

He turned to me with a look of mild surmise in his eyes. But he didn't answer my question immediately.

'Do you not think of your soul when you ask such questions?' he asked.

I almost smiled. As young men we had debated questions of ethics and morality long into the night. But those were questions posed in the abstract. This was different. These were real issues, where you ended up standing over a man, watching his blood drain into the earth and the life fade from his eyes.

'I have thought about my own soul in this,' he said deliberately, 'and I want my daughter away from this man. By whatever means it takes. All my resources are at your disposal and I will pay a gratuity in advance.'

He laid a banker's draft on the table. I made a certain amount of money buying and selling art, but the market was bad and buyers were waiting for better times. I wasn't broke but I wasn't wealthy either. I was no longer employed in the field of full-time spookery and income was sporadic. I thought about killing this Xaberra. He was a bad man and I had killed bad men before. And there was the life and well-being of a friend's beautiful young daughter at stake. But the money changed everything. It was a contract on Xaberra's life, and I hadn't sunk that low yet.

'I will find your daughter and take her home if I can,' I said. 'I won't kill Xaberra.' There was a long silence.

'You may have to kill him,' Paolo said. 'You may have to, my friend. One of us may.'

'There's always that,' I said. 'You're coming?'

8

'I would not ask such a task from anyone,' Paolo said, 'but you know New York better than I do. I am . . . I am old enough to be able to say this, Jack. I am afraid of this man. I need someone I can trust with me.'

He lifted the draft and put it in my hand. I hesitated, then took it, placing it on the top shelf of the dresser, as somehow it distanced me from it.

We talked then as if a burden had been lifted from us. As old friends talk, long into the night, drinking the Redbreast. But there was a poignancy there that I could not put my finger on, a sense of something coming to a close. At the time, I thought it was because the money had somehow changed our relationship. But perhaps it wasn't that. Perhaps it was because it was one of the last times I was to see that proud, handsome man sitting intact in front of me. His daughter was not the last thing that Paolo was to lose to Richard Xaberra. The affair was about family and love. Paolo loved his daughter and wanted her back. But things were to take a different direction, to sink to a more primitive level of blood and honour, and the first blood to be spilled was to be Paolo's.

Two

I always remember the first time I saw mercury as a child in the school lab, the quicksilver stuff slipping along a steel tray, unable to find any purchase, inherently unstable. Dangerous stuff. Frictionless and deadly, because mercury is a metal. And metal conducts electricity.

I arranged to meet Paolo in London three days later. I met him in Hazlitts Hotel in Soho, an ancient, charming, half-askew affair and the only hotel in Soho, unless you counted the ones you booked by the half-hour. Paolo knew that I liked to be close to the Soho restaurants and we spent several well-fed but oddly melancholy days while he finished off some business. He spent hours over his espresso, trying to formulate a plan. Sometimes he said he would go down on his knees to his daughter and plead with her to come home. At other times he swore to leave the streets of New York littered with corpses. He didn't know what to do and this infuriated him. I tried to calm him down. I liked to improvise situations.

In any other circumstances, it would have been a good time to go to New York. There was a Hopper retrospective at the Whitney. And it was years since I had visited the Guggenheim. And it was autumn, which is the best season in New York. But I shut out the attractions. Almost unconsciously, I was working myself into the right frame of mind for the job ahead. Working on the instinct for trouble. Working on my mental reactions, honing everything down: something I thought would become harder with the years, but was worryingly easy. And the final thing, which always slid into place of its own accord. A kind of moral deadness, the killer's pitiless single-mindedness, clanging into place with a dull, echo-less sound.

I made some calls to New York. Liam Mellows was there, and Paolo was glad to take him on board, although there was a wild-ness in Liam which mystified and sometimes worried Paolo. For my part, I couldn't imagine anyone more suitable for the kind of game we were playing. Liam accepted the offer of a job almost without asking about it. There was a wistfulness in his voice. Liam had been part of the war in Ireland for many years, but his faith had been shaken and a year ago he had taken off to New York and started a small construction business.

'Missing the action, Liam?' I asked.

'You're joking,' he said. 'The SAS is child's play compared to New York sub-contracters.'

He didn't mention his sister, Deirdre, which worried me. Deirdre was working for the UN in Manhattan. She had left Europe and left a lot unresolved between us. Things had been bad before, but Liam had never left her name unspoken between us.

But I put it out of my mind. I was going to New York to do a job.

We were due to leave on Thursday morning. On Tuesday evening I used the hotel system to check my e-mail. There was a message from Marie Regan. It said to ring her. It said something about old times. Deliberately casual, the message for that very reason suggest-ed need. I didn't know her well enough to be sent a chatty e-mail. She was the widow of Paddy Regan, a border smuggler, crook and reluctant friend who had died in a fight of my making a long way from home. I owed Paddy and I owed his family. I wondered if there was a payback involved. I remembered Marie from Paddy's funeral. Unexpectedly tall and beautiful, she had walked behind the coffin with her two little girls, her head high, the epitome of dignity. But I knew that she came from tough border stock, people who liked to make a bargain and hold to it. I picked up the phone and dialled the number. Paddy was dead and a bargain was a bargain. I was apprehensive, though. I understood that the spilling of Paddy's blood was a matter of honour and demanded an honourable response. But I'd bent my own rules to breaking point and beyond.

One of the little girls answered the phone straight away. She had given me the home number, not a business address. After a little suspicious probing from the little girl, I heard Marie's soft Mullaghbawn accent on the phone. An accent so soft you thought about a gentle, bookish seventeen-year-old. It took an effort to summon up the stern beautiful mask that I remembered. I asked about the girls. She asked about Deirdre Mellows, a faint tone of amusement in that soft voice. I countered with a bit of semi-embarrassed male bluster, a sense of the formalities of such exchanges being observed.

'We could always meet,' I said, 'catch up on a few things.' I knew that she wouldn't talk over the phone.

'Where are you now?' she asked.

'London, but I'm going to New York on Thursday.'

'Hold on a minute.' I heard her speak to someone in the background, then she was back on the line. 'I'll get an early flight,' she said. 'I'll see you in the morning.'

That evening, I made a few phone calls to New York. I hoped that this wasn't to be the kind of job where guns were required, but it was handy to have the hardware in place. Paolo joined me for dinner. We agreed that Paolo would remain in the background. I would arrange to meet Xabarra. According to Paolo, he was a regular in the New York art world. I would assess the situation, what his hold appeared to be on Alva, and then we would decide how to act. Alva would of course recognize me, but it wouldn't be all that unusual for an art-dealer friend of her father's to be in New York.

Looking back on that night, we seemed naïve. For all our talk and experience, we had made the basic mistake of underestimating our opponent. I suppose New York seemed a long way from London and we had forgotten that rich and cunning men will maintain a presence in any part of the world if it is in their interest to do so. And we knew nothing about mercury.

Marie Regan was sitting in the lobby of the hotel next morning at ten o'clock. She didn't look as if she had got up at dawn to catch a flight from Belfast. She didn't look like the widow of a border smuggler either. The suit was Joseph. The bag was Armani. But perhaps they're breeding a more stylish border smuggler nowadays. She stood up as I approached her and kissed me coolly on both cheeks. The hair was long and dark, the hazel eyes carried a permanent look of faint amusement and the glances of men passing in the lobby slid off her like rain off a granite boulder. I asked after the girls. Her look softened, giving way to something more girlish, as she described them and their exploits.

'They're proud of their father,' she said. There was a hint of defiance in her voice which puzzled me. I was fairly sure she knew how much I had liked and admired her husband. She caught my look.

'They were always proud of him,' she said. 'They knew what he did for a living and they sat through many a raid on the house. Not a word from them. Wouldn't even look at the policemen. This is different.'

She handed me a newspaper cutting. There was a photograph of Paddy at the top, looking furtive as he ducked away from the camera. The headline described him as a drug smuggler, bringing heroin into Ireland. The customs had raided one of his sheds and found twenty kilos of uncut heroin. If I was the whistling type, I would have whistled at that. It was worth a lot of money. And would have cost a lot of money from men who don't send you a stiff letter when you don't pay up.

13

'My husband was many things,' she said angrily, 'and some of them were bad things. But he was no drug smuggler. Those drugs did not belong to him. And my girls will not be exposed to this nonsense.'

I studied the article. The usual tabloid blend of lurid speculation and downright lies.

'What do you want me to do, Marie?'

'I want you to find out who planted these drugs in our shed.'

'You realize,' I said, 'that even if you find whoever planted the drugs, these stories will probably go on. It's good copy.'

'I don't want my girls to have to listen to this stuff in school,' she said again. There were tears in her eyes. I put my hand on hers. It was an unthinking gesture and I wasn't prepared for the shock of recognition as my skin touched hers. I don't think she was ready for it either. I took my hand away cautiously. She looked up at me. There were depths in those eyes that I hadn't seen before, depths that I could lose myself in.

'I'll do what I can,' I said, the phrase coming out softer and hoarser than I intended. I meant to go on to say that her husband had saved my life, but for some reason I found I wasn't able to say Paddy's name.

'I don't want anything I haven't paid for, Jack.' I realized it was the first time that morning that she had used my name and it gave the moment a curious intimacy. I shook my head. I could see Paddy lying on his back in a filthy shed, his blood pumping from a hole in his chest.

'It's already been paid for,' I said. I meant it. I wouldn't be able to take her money. I was glad in a way. When you pay for something, it gives you control, and I wanted to be able to do things my way, take them as far as I wanted to go, and pull out on my own terms. I shook off the feeling that had rushed through me when I touched her hand.

'I'll find out what I can, Marie. I don't want to make any

promises. I still have some contacts in Ireland, but I haven't been over for a while. And my contacts here are a little rusty.'

Rusty wasn't the word. Seized solid more like, since I had left the covert business. My calls weren't returned any more. My old boss Somerville was behind it, I suspected. If it wasn't for his latent thriftiness, I probably would have found myself lying in a ditch with a bullet in my head. Somerville wasn't a man to waste a bullet. Still, I wasn't without resources, and I had twenty years' experience to draw on. Long runs the fox, as Liam Mellows used to say.

We were interrupted then as Paolo came down the stairs. He saw Marie first. He was on his way over before he saw me. I got a look that implied he didn't think I had it in me, then he swept past me.

'So you are Marie,' he said. 'Jack mentioned your name . . . but I had no idea.' He seemed so genuinely lost in admiration that she laughed and got to her feet and shook his hand. I don't know how he did it, but somehow, by talk and laughter and force of personality, he propelled her into the bar and within five minutes they had a bottle of Pouilly-Fumé open on the marble top in front of them and me standing behind them with a stupid grin on my face and a glass of wine in my hand. Paolo played the Italian male to the hilt, attentive and charming to the point of parody, and I had yet to see a woman of any age, half-laughing and half-beguiled, who did not come away from an hour with him glowing like a teenager. The taste of good wine early in the morning made us all giddy and we talked and laughed for over an hour.

It was one of those spontaneous gatherings, the kind of thing you bring up and ask each other if you remember it, even if ten years pass between meetings, as though each time you have to reconfirm that the other's recollection is still as sweet as yours. It was one of those moments that was meant to be carried intact through your life as proof that life can sometimes near perfection.

15

It was not meant to end the way it did, in terrible pain and blood and evil.

After the hour was up, Paolo had to go. I stood with Marie on the steps of the hotel to wave him off. He was to return that evening for the following morning's flight. Meanwhile, he had to travel to Birmingham and he had hired, at great expense, a 1958 Maserati. A beautiful thoroughbred car with nothing practical about it in any department. We watched as he got into it and started the engine. He grinned as the beautiful engine note filled the street, and put the car into gear.

A mercury tilt switch is fundamentally a sealed glass tube containing a small globule of mercury. At either end there are two live electrical contacts with an empty space between them. Once the device is armed, the slightest movement will send the mercury sliding rapidly towards either end of the tube, filling the space between the contacts. Mercury conducts.

The experienced bombmaker will take half a kilo of explosives and mould it into a cone. The cone shape focuses the blast on to the target area.

If you had had a camera on Paolo's car and were able to watch it in slow motion, you would have seen an area of intense orange flame under the wheel arch, spreading upwards, showing in the doorsills and the space between the bodywork and the bonnet. Then you would have seen the metal of the door buckling outwards, the flame now visible through the driver's window as the blast tore through his flesh, rending and cauterizing as it went, the windscreen blowing outwards, metal shards filling the air, the roof of the car buckling upwards, Paolo's lungs at the point of collapse as the vacuum effect of the bomb sucked the air out of the interior of the car, all the time as the car rolled incongruously slowly across the road, all gear and engine linkages blown apart. And then smoke overtaking the flame. Heavy black smoke billowing from the windows. And then finally, seemingly a long,

long time after the detonation, the sound came, a crack and a boom almost together, as the car came softly to a rest against the opposite kerb, a gentle motion made almost obscene by the violence of the explosion.

For a moment, we stood there. I could feel the fugue of shock threatening to overwhelm me. I forced one foot in front of another towards the car, fighting the shock, forcing my mind and body to respond. Move towards the car. Make your mind check for danger. Black smoke billowing from underneath the bonnet. It wouldn't be long before the flames started. The driver's door was still closed, but buckled. Bad news. A buckled door would be hard to open. I couldn't see Paolo for smoke. I reached the door and tried to open it. It seemed to be jammed solid. The smoke swirled for a moment and I saw Paolo's face momentarily, streaked black, his eyes closed. I rolled over the back of the car and opened the passenger door. It was then that I realized that Paolo was still alive. I heard him moan through the smoke and terror and terrible, debilitating pain.

'Hold on, Paolo,' I said, 'hold on.' The words people always say in these situations. As if holding on can repel the terrible damage that such an explosion does to a body. I looked into the drivers footwell where Paolo's legs would have been. There was some terrible carnage down there, and the flames were flickering upwards. I was choking on the smoke. I got my hands under his arms and started to haul but I couldn't shift him. There was a loud hissing sound and I realized that someone was using a fire extinguisher on the flames. It was helping a little, but the fire had got a firm hold. I tried again, kneeling on the seat, my face almost pressed into Paolo's face, my lungs seared by the fumes as I tried again. I felt rather than saw Paolo's gaze on me. When I turned my head, he was looking into my eyes and he seemed to have drawn on some deep well of inner calm for there was none of the fear and mounting urgency that I felt.

17

'You're going to have to help me.' I said, almost whispering the words. 'You're going to have to help me, Paolo.'

In the end, he did help me. Levering himself up with his arms and whatever remained of his shattered legs. And as he did so and I pulled him from the car, the flames leaping from it and following us as though angry at being deprived of their prey, he let go of a cry, a primal sound of terrible pain and effort and loss.

It was Marie who had been working the fire extinguisher. She came to us with the extinguisher dangling forgotten from her right hand. I tried to speak but my breath wouldn't come. I touched my lips and my finger came away black with the soot from the fire. I tried to lever myself upwards to see Paolo and I didn't remember anything from that moment until the moment I woke again, still lying on the pavement with an oxygen mask over my mouth, but this time on my own, Paolo and Marie both gone.

Three

It was a long, draining night. In casualty they insisted on giving me a chest X-ray and I had to sit through the indignity of a young intern telling me that 'we're not as young as we were'. My chest and throat felt as if they'd been seared with a blowtorch, so when he refused to tell me anything about Paolo's condition I told him to find somebody else to patronize and that I was still young enough to snap his spine. That and a few other remarks made sure that they discharged me there and then. Discharged me, in fact, with a warning that if I ever came back they would call the police.

I found Marie in intensive care. Paolo was in surgery. The surgeon had told her that if he had been in a modern car, he would certainly be dead. The sturdy bulkheads of the old car had saved his life for the time being.

'What about his legs?' I asked.

She shook her head.

'It was just a mess down there, Jack.' She didn't add any more, and I didn't ask. We sat in sombre silence for an hour, then I felt her nudge me. Two men with the unmistakable air of plain-clothes policemen were coming down the corridor towards us. I was surprised they hadn't found us before now.

'Move,' I said urgently to Marie. 'They don't know that you have any connection to Paolo.' She didn't need to be told twice. There was no other exit from the waiting area, but she solved that by placing herself in front of one of the windows looking in on a young man almost invisible behind the machines that were plugged into him. As the two detectives approached me, she was staring at him with her features composed in an expression of wifely anxiety, and they barely gave her a second glance.

The interview took three long hours and only ended when I persuaded them to let me phone the head of CID in Belfast. They smelled a rat. They knew there was something wrong about me, but they couldn't put their finger on it and they didn't wear my story of having met an Italian businessman in the hotel, and my feigned amazement that he could have come to such a terrible pass. In the end, the younger one foolishly tried to break me down with threats. I came back at him with all the verbal brutality I could muster and left him silent and running his finger around the inside of his collar. His older colleague watched the display quietly. Then he agreed to the phone call. The man in Belfast was an old ally, a former border policeman. We had fought for our lives side by side and that gave us a connection. The policeman spoke to him first, then handed the phone to me.

'Don't do this again, Jack,' he said softly.

'Thanks, Ronnie,' I said. I heard the phone being replaced.

'You're free to go,' the older policeman said, without looking at me. The younger man looked as if he was capable of shooting me there and then. As I walked down the corridor, I heard his voice raised in argument. I didn't care. I ran outside and hailed a cab. I was back at the hospital within ten minutes.

Paolo was out of theatre. You could look at him through the observation window, although you couldn't see much for the metal arch that supported the blankets over the place where his legs had been.

'He lost both legs,' Marie said. 'One above the knee, the other below.'

'Jesus.'

'He had a message for you.'

'You talked to him?'

'I pretended I was his wife. They let me in for a minute.'

'He was conscious?'

'He seemed to know I was there. I knew a man once blew his stomach open with his own bomb. He forced himself to stay alive long enough to tell his friends what he had done wrong, so they wouldn't make the same mistake. They called him an iron man. Your friend is an iron man, Jack, for all his fancy Italian ways.'

'What was the message?'

'He said two things. He wants you to go to New York. Do the job for him. Those were his words.'

'What was the other thing?'

'He said it was the Mexican – he used a name . . .'

'Xabarra?'

'I think so. He said to tell you it was him who did the bomb.' I saw her hesitate a little.

'Did he say anything else?'

She bit her lip and shook her head as if laughing at some private joke.

'He asked me to ask the nurses a question.'

'What?'

'He wanted to know if, he wanted me to ask them if his . . . God . . . his balls were still there.' I was surprised at the way she reddened.

'Kind of important,' I said. 'Particularly for a Italian, I suppose. Were they?'

'The nurses were busy,' she said firmly, 'so I looked for him. All present and correct.'

'What did he say?'

She shook her head, half-laughing.

We were quiet in the taxi on the way back to the hotel. The receptionist's eyes opened wide when we walked in. I realized that my clothes were covered in blood and small burns. I could see the dark shadows under Marie's eyes. I waited while she booked a room.

'Go and have a shower,' she said. 'I'll see if they can manage a sandwich or something.'

I felt a little better after the shower, although my chest still felt tight and burned and my eyes felt gritty from the smoke. As I was dressing, the phone rang. It was Marie. She had soup and sandwiches in her room. When I got there, I saw that she had taken the penthouse and I realized for the first time that Paddy had left her a very wealthy woman. She had showered as well and was wearing simple white cotton pyjamas which had probably cost a king's ransom. It sounds strange, but I didn't really notice at the time, nor the way she had loosened her hair so that it flowed over her shoulders. I was wondering what kind of a man Xabarra was. An under-car device on the streets of London is a very extreme way of ensuring that your lover's father doesn't bother you, even if that father is as dangerous as Paolo. There was another thing. An incident like this normally attracts a lot of attention: grim-faced men with flak jackets and sub-machine guns, the media, questions in the House. This time, there was nothing like that, just two very low-key detectives. But Paolo was convinced that Xabarra was responsible. It left me with a very uneasy feeling.

Marie watched me while I ate, saying nothing. When I had finished, she went to the sideboard and poured two glasses of brandy. We touched glasses. It was vintage Napoleon and very good.

'Were you scared?' she said.

I nodded.

She drank thoughtfully and I had the feeling that I had confirmed something that she had suspected about me. She finished her drink and put the glass on the coffee table. Then she took my hand and placed it on her breast through the opening of her pyjamas.

It would be true to say that trauma leaves you emotionally vulnerable, in need of confirmation that you are still alive, still vital. It is also true that trauma generates bonds that are longlasting and intimate. But we both knew the truth here and the truth was that the first time our hands had touched we had felt that electricity that we had not expected. We stood without moving for a moment. I savoured the feeling of her skin under my hand, then our lips met.

She wanted to take the lead and I allowed it to happen. I thought momentarily about Paddy and then the thought faded. You can't betray a dead man and it's the worst form of presumption to imagine that you can. We made it to the bedroom. Marie luxuriated in her physicality, but I felt the undertone of urgency as she sat astride me and pulled me into her body, almost immediately emitting a cry like a wounded thing.

After that, things slowed down. She allowed me to set the pace and a deeper intimacy counterpointed the wildness of our first touches. In the end, it was all slow and holding back, one deferring to the other's pleasure until we could defer no longer.

At last we lay there, holding each other sleepily.

'That was good,' she said sleepily. 'Slow, nice.'

'I'm kind of built for comfort, not for speed,' I said ruefully, surveying my spreading waistline.

'You did the speed bit OK too.'

I looked at my watch. It was just after three. Ten o'clock in New York. I lifted the phone and dialled Liam's number. He answered after a few rings. He listened in silence as I told him what had happened to Paolo.

'It seems a crazy thing to do,' I said, 'on the street in London.'

Liam was silent for a few moments.

'It was meant to seem crazy,' he said, 'and it's meant to send a message. This Xaberra telling the world that he's crazier than anyone else, that he's prepared to go over the top and that he is confident he can get away with it. I'd say if you look back through his career you'll find a lot of the same stuff.'

I thought about what Paolo had told me. Runaway girls chained together and thrown into the sea. Keep that image in your head, I told myself.

'Are we prepared for all eventualities?' Liam asked cautiously, not willing to ask about firearms over the phone.

'I hope it won't come to that, but yes, we are.'

I made arrangements to meet Liam and hung up. Then I called Jesus. Jesus had been a street heroin dealer in the East Village when I met him. Now he didn't deal on the street any more and he didn't deal heroin, only cocaine and ecstasy. He lived in a restored apartment building in Alphabet City and all his dealing was done through intermediaries over the phone. I knew I was supposed to disapprove but I had seen the place that Jesus came from, and I wasn't sure that I was entitled to be judgemental when an intelligent, resourceful kid takes the only route open to him to get out of the slum. I was aware that heroin kills people. I was also aware that drugs are a favourite medium of intelligence agencies when they want to play games with large sums of money without letting their paymasters know what they are up to. Jesus wasn't Mother Teresa, but he didn't stand outside school gates selling it to children. Besides, necessity had forced Jesus into drug dealing. I had chosen my own dirty trade through nothing more than a misplaced sense of romance. I dialled the number of his cellphone in New York – old street-dealing habits die hard, and I had never seen Jesus without that phone.

'Jesus,' I said.

'Hey, Jack,' he answered, 'you still flying in tomorrow?'

'Yes. Looking forward to seeing your mother.' I was old friends with Irene, Jesus's mother.

'Yeah, her too.' I sensed a hesitancy in his voice.

'What's up?'

'Listen, man, I got the things you asked for, but I got a worrying

24

situation on my hands. Could be I won't be able to give you much help.'

'How much trouble?'

'Ah, some guys.'

Jesus was being casual, but I could sense that things weren't good. He wasn't easily rattled.

'Listen, I'll see you tomorrow, Jack, all right.' Jesus hung up.

I must have looked worried.

'Hey,' Marie said softly, 'you need to get some sleep, mister.' She was right. I lay back down on the bed. I saw her looking at me. I got up and took my clothes into the other room. I pulled on trousers and shirt. When I looked up, she was standing in the doorway.

'I'm sorry,' she said.

'That's all right,' I said. I meant it. There are different kinds of intimacy. I knew that the time we had spent together wouldn't cause Marie any guilt, but the weight of a man sleeping in the bed beside her might awaken too many lonely memories. There was that strange mixture of the chaste and the truly lewd. As I went out of the room, she grinned at me and gave me a look of such open indecency that I could barely restrain myself from leaping across the room like a seventeen-year-old.

But she was right. I needed sleep. I shut the door behind me and stumbled down the corridor, dragging myself along it until I got to my room.

I pulled off my clothes and fell on to the bed. But there was to be a postscript to that longest of days. As my mind started to drift off, I heard the phone. I lifted it. The voice on the other end sounded very, very old, and very, very far away and it was a moment before I recognized it. It was Paolo. God knows what effort he had to expend to fight the pain and the drugs long enough to make that call. At first I couldn't make out what he was saying.

'Say it again, Paolo,' I urged.

The voice came again, stronger this time.

'I don't want her to know,' he said, 'I don't want Alva to know about this.'

'I hear you,' I said.

The line went dead. Some part of me understood. He was afraid that she would come home and find him in that hospital. That she would see the ruined body before he had time to come to terms with it himself. Before he could teach her the courage to deal with it. And I suppose somewhere in the back of his mind he saw Xabarra standing with her at his bedside, in possession of his daughter as he looked helplessly up at him. I realized that when I thought about Xabarra, I felt a certain amount of fear. I don't know what it was, but it felt like some ancient, dormant instinct being stirred, as if there was something of the occult about the man. I tried to convince myself that the fear was a good thing, like when I was trying to get Paolo out of the car, that it kept you sharp, honed, alert to danger. But when I shut my eyes, the fear was still there, strong and irrational, like the fear of the terrible things that prowl in the dark when the light is out and the wind is howling like a thousand demons.

But in the darkness and fear of my dreams that night, I conjured an image of beauty and decadence, dark and light colliding and neither winning. And that image gave me the germ of an idea – not to get close to Xabarra, but to bring Xabarra to me.

Four

I looked down into the night as the Airbus banked towards JFK. The glitter of a million lights that never failed to stir you. And the realization that a few thousand of those lights had gone out for ever. I wondered whether I was returning to the same city.

But later that evening, as I walked down Tenth Street with a cold, fresh wind razoring down the avenues and passing the old buildings which used to house Polish and Ukrainian and Lithuanian migrants, I felt that somehow the city had engaged with the melancholy that those exiles felt during the long winter that fell on their countries after the war. New York was the most European of American cities and now you were more than ever aware of the blood and sorrow that underpinned that experience. I thought of Berlin, Moscow, Warsaw, Budapest; cities drenched in sorrow and death, but rebuilt and reformed, the burden of their history shouldered into the future. And you had the sense that New York was still the same place, but with a gravitas and self-knowledge that it hadn't possessed before, as if it had come of terrible age.

I met Liam Mellows in Devines, one of the new Irish bars that had sprung up in the East Village, where the beer was still Guinness but the soundtrack ranged from Shane McGowan to John Cale and the clientele were young, fashionable and Irish. Liam was nursing a Jameson at one end of the bar. When he saw me coming, he called for a Redbreast, then stood and shook my hand. If he looked a little less honed, and a little greyer around the temples, he had also lost the hunted look that had worried me the last time I had seen him in Ireland. He took a long look at me as well. I wasn't sure what he saw, but his expression turned from welcome to concern.

'I have a funny feeling about this one,' he said quietly. 'Like it's dark all the way through.'

I looked at him curiously.

'You know the way you can usually guess at outcomes, that a situation might go this way or that. But there's nothing like that here. You get a feeling that anything could happen.'

'If you aren't easy, Liam . . .'

He laughed and clapped me on the back.

'Don't worry, Jack. I'll come along just to see which way it turns out. Curiosity if nothing else.' He looked up. 'I suppose this is your Puerto Rican friend?'

I looked round. Jesus was light-skinned and light-boned, almost feminine in the lithe way that he walked. I also knew that he was as tough as nails. He shook my hand warmly. He looked prosperous. He also looked anxious. I introduced him to Liam. Jesus grinned.

'Jack told me about you. He thinks a lot of you. And your sister apparently . . .'

I cut across him.

'How's your mother doing, Jesus?'

'She's great, Jack. You're having dinner with her tomorrow night . . .'

I started to object. I had a lot to do, but he ignored me.

'Bring Liam as well. As for now, we need to do our business. I got the car outside.'

There was an urgency in his tone which brooked no argument and we started to shoulder our way through the crowded bar. I started to ask him about the trouble he was in, but he silenced me.

'The less you know about it, Jack . . .'

I was relieved. I had enough on my plate, and I didn't probe any further. If Jesus needed help, he would as for it, I thought. Although as events developed, asking turned out to be unnecessary.

It was a cold night, with winter not far off, and our breaths steamed in the freezing air as we gathered round the boot of the car, looking, I thought, worryingly like men waiting to inspect something illegal. Which of course we were. Jesus opened the boot and flicked the catches of a solid Samsonite case to reveal a selection of firearms, ranging from a slim Beretta to the solidity of a pump-action shotgun. As far as I could see, he had assembled a small arsenal. I was about to say something along the lines of not being in the business of starting wars when I saw Liam glance up. I followed his gaze to the black saloon gliding towards us down the narrow street.

Then everything happened very fast, but in a way that seemed contrived, and I couldn't escape the feeling that we were on a film set, with the black saloon gliding towards us and suddenly a man with a narrow moustache leaning out of a window, aiming some kind of a Saturday night special in our direction. I remember Liam lifting the pump-action from the boot and I remember thinking this was stupid, that there would be no way that the gun would be loaded. I remember Jesus having something in his hand which made a flat, cracking noise. Then, suddenly, it seemed as if things became real again. Liam switched the shotgun into his right hand and slung it underhand at the windscreen of the car. The heavy stock of the weapon hit the windscreen hard. Suddenly the windscreen went opaque. The gunman in the car opened up, multiple shots with a muffled, silenced sound. But the driver veered left and the saloon collided heavily with a parked car, throwing the gunman's face into the window pillar with a sound that you could feel in your own bones.

There seemed to be a moment's lull, everyone gathering their thoughts, then a man stepped from the passenger side of the crashed saloon. I was aware that the car had stalled and that the driver was trying to start it. The man who had stepped from the car was firing in our direction in a languid fashion, then the car 's engine caught and he stepped back in. The car was slewed across the street so it couldn't go backwards, and it sped towards us. But the driver had obviously lost it. He struck two parked cars and almost stalled again, so the car wasn't moving at much more than walking pace when it drew level with us. Liam was watching from behind a parked Jeep, which seemed sensible as he had no weapon. Jesus was struggling to insert a cartridge into his pistol. There was a sense that everyone wanted the whole thing to be over and only the driver's incompetence was getting in the way. But as the car drew level, the languid man in the passenger seat saw me through the open window and raised his weapon. Instinctively I stepped forward and drove the heel of my hand into the base of his nose. Neither of us were aware of the increased force produced by the forward momentum of the car. I don't think he particularly wanted to shoot at me, but he did. I didn't particularly want to kill him, but I did. I could feel the shock through the heel of my hand as the bones of his nose splintered, driven back into the nasal cavity, back into his brain, the whole structure giving way like something rotten. And then the driver found his courage again and the car roared and leaped forward and was gone. I was aware that Jesus was looking at me anxiously.

'Did you kill him?' he asked.

Liam was leaning against the wall, looking at us with the kind of half-grin you put on your face when something isn't really funny.

I looked at my hand. I could still feel the skeletal framework of his face collapsing under the impact. It had happened so quickly that it seemed almost a trivial thing. I nodded. Jesus turned away.

I had intended to spend my first night in New York catching up on old times with Liam, having a few drinks, something good to eat. Instead I had just killed a man, having stepped into some kind of drug situation I didn't know anything about. But we were all professionals in our own way. Jesus was in the driving seat of the car, Liam had the Samsonite case in his hand. Within thirty seconds of the car turning the corner, we were walking swiftly in one direction and Jesus had taken off in the other direction, driving smooth and fast.

When we had covered five or six blocks, Jesus pulled up alongside us. We stepped into the car and drove another few blocks in silence.

'Turn right here,' Liam said.

Jesus swung the car around. Five minutes later, we pulled up outside an Irish bar, one of the old-fashioned ones this time, with the shamrocks and Bob Hope crooning 'How Are Things In Glockamora' on the juke-box. It was dark and homely and Liam pointed out that it was an off-duty cops' hangout, so we were reasonably safe from anybody that might be following us. We ordered drinks and took a booth.

'So these were the men you were talking about, the ones you had the trouble with?' I said, mentally cursing him for getting us into the situation.

Jesus looked at me for a long time.

'The only thing is, Jack, I don't know who they are. I have no idea.'

'Are you sure they were after you?'

He made a gesture with his hands. Without thinking, I looked at Liam. It wouldn't be out of character for people to be shooting at Liam. I got that half-amused look again and he shook his head.

'The building-permit people might want to shoot me. The IRS maybe. But not the Puerto Ricans.'

'Maybe, Jack, they were shooting at you?' Jesus said.

'No reason to,' I said. Without adding that my troubles were of

31

the Mexican variety, not Puerto Rican. I was starting to feel removed from my surroundings, their voices coming from a great distance, a terrible weariness settling on me. I had just killed a man and the only effect that it had on me was a dull pain in the wrist where I had hit him. I didn't know who he was, or why he was there. Killing somebody is something that should be reflected on with all the rigour at your disposal, put in some kind of spiritual and psychic context where you can live both with yourself and the shade of the dead man. I felt Liam's eyes on me.

'He was trying to kill you,' he said softly, 'would have killed you if you had done nothing.'

I knew the argument. I had used it before. Somehow it didn't satisfy me the way it used to.

A man in his fifties, drunk and red-eyed, with a beer belly that looked like it should be on wheels, stumbled past the booth and looked in. Some third-generation Kelly or Dolan working on an early coronary. He looked in at us and muttered something about fucking spic faggots and wandered on.

My first thought was surprise. I realized I had never seen Jesus with a girl. When I caught his eye, he was looking at me with a faintly mocking look. My second thought was to groan inwardly as Liam got to his feet. I didn't want a bar brawl to round off the night. I didn't have to worry. Liam put his arm around the man's neck in a sympathetic way. I don't know what he said to him, but the man reddened and put his head down and walked past without looking at us on his way out of the bar.

'Thanks,' Jesus said when Liam returned to his seat.

Liam shrugged.

'I don't like bad manners,' he said.

I didn't say anything. Liam had killed people for what he regarded as bad manners, in a place and a time when bad manners included firing live rounds at people. He had a broad definition of bad manners.

Jesus left, refusing the offer of another drink and arranging to meet me the following evening.

'This is not good, Jack,' he said. 'This dead man is not good. I'm going to try to find out who he is.'

After he had left, Liam called for another drink.

'Don't look so mournful,' he said.

'I can't help it,' I said, 'I just killed somebody, and I don't even know who he is.'

'If you knew who it was, would it make things better?'

I couldn't answer that, so I drank my Redbreast and ordered another, and refrained from saying that I didn't like the sense of things being out of control, the unknown cropping up in the form of under-car bombs and mystery gunmen, and sudden violent death.

At 2 a.m., we were standing on First Avenue eating slices of pizza and drinking hot coffee. The wind had got stronger. It was cold and exhilarating, and it seemed to sweep the face of the dead man out of my mind, the remorse disappearing with an ease that should have worried me but didn't.

Five

The little doorway in the meat-packing district had been there for a long time. The district was now trendy, but the doorway had been there before, when the district was dominated by Teamsters and Mafia and the streets groaned under the weight of beef and the gutters ran with offal and ordure. It was a nondescript door. Nothing was written on it, and the battered intercom box could be seen on a million doors in the city. If you looked closely, you would see a tiny fish-eye lens above the door, that was all.

It was a bright morning and I'd walked from the apartment Paolo had rented for us in Christopher Street. I loved the West Village in the morning and, despite everything, I felt my mood lift. In a few minutes, I was standing in front of the little door, with, despite myself, a tremor of anticipation. I knew what lay behind that door.

Before I had a chance to buzz, the door opened and a taciturn little Scotsman in overalls opened the door. He barely nodded at me and I barely nodded back. It was a routine we had developed over the years. Our shared nationality meant nothing to him. I suppose he came to New York to get away from Scotsmen.

I followed him down the shabbily carpeted stairs and then along a long corridor, poorly lit. When we got to where we were going, he nodded at me gloomily and disappeared. I knocked on Eddie Mack's door and went in.

The contrast with the corridor was startling. Eddie had

designed the place himself, and had managed to build an astonishing underground living space. It was almost a small cathedral, built from pre-stressed concrete material I had never seen anyone use to any effect, but Eddie had managed to make it both soaring and intimate.

Eddie himself came towards me with his hand outstretched. He was wearing dark glasses and cotton gloves.

'Jack,' he said. He was a big man but the voice was curiously soft, a certain beguiling quality to it. Eddie had a reputation for being a womanizer in his youth and you could understand it. He had started out in Montana, running the huge herds of sheep you found out there, and had worked his way towards New York, where he had risen to become one of the foremost fine-art photography dealers in the world. If you knew how to find him. But the legacy of those days on the hungry Montana trails had never stopped working on him. He had been exposed to deadly organophosphates – a nerve-gas constituent they used in sheep-dip. It had got into his system and had worked on his immune system, breaking down his immunity to most man-made things. He was allergic to perfumes, exhaust fumes, cleaning fluids and eventually even sunlight. So he came down here and started building underground.

'How are you, Eddie?'

'You know what?' he said. 'I think I'm turning into Howard fucking Hughes down here.' His expression turned serious. 'How is Paolo?'

I didn't ask how he had heard about the bomb. Paolo and Eddie had known each other for years, friends through their passion for photography. I told him. Eddie looked grim.

'You know who did it.'

'Paolo gave me a name,' I said, watching for Eddie's reaction. 'Richard Xabarra.'

Eddie gave a low whistle.

35

'Paolo knows how to pick his enemies. Is this to do with the daughter? She's with Xabarra now, isn't she?'

'It started like that. It's got beyond it now.'

Eddie nodded.

'I fucking hope you don't want to involve me in this, my friend. Xabarra is a dangerous man.'

'Well, I was kind of hoping you might be able to assist.'

Eddie shook his head.

'No direct involvement, Eddie, just setting up a deal.'

Eddie took a bottle from a drawer and poured us both a brandy, a Torres Reserve. I didn't need it but I sipped at it anyway. Eddie drank his down and poured another. He turned to face the photograph on the wall behind his desk. It was a Helmet Newton, monochrome, a woman in high heels and basque, night-time wear but captured in the full glare of the sun, so that she half-tottered like a tormented mannequin. It was a cruel image. He contemplated it for a long time, then turned to me.

'What the fuck,' he said. 'Life gets boring down here. But first let me show you some new acquisitions.'

Underneath Eddie's buried apartment there was a large, temperature-controlled room with storehouses off it. In it Eddie stored a treasurehouse of twentieth-century American photography: Robert Capa, Annie Leibowitz, Warhol. Favoured items were displayed, the rest were kept in storage. He owned many of them; others he bought for investors and stored. Sometimes he said he was ashamed of keeping them in darkened rooms, that the photographs were made to be seen.

As we looked at some new work by young photographers, Eddie told me what he knew about Xabarra. He was a big player in the photography scene, as I already knew. He had a knack of getting in with the right people.

'For a Mexican, he has an aristocratic air about him,' Eddie said. 'And you know how much they love that shit around here.'

'He had a bad name with women,' Eddie went on. 'Especially young ones. Of course, that gives him an edgy thing that people like. There's a whiff of droit de seigneur about it. He wears them out and moves on. Paolo might find that his little girl isn't the same as the little girl who left home.'

I thought of the Helmet Newton piece. A woman constrained and tormented, with nowhere to go in the burning sun.

I asked Eddie if Alva was likely to recognize me, explaining I hadn't seen her since she was five.

'I doubt if she would even recognize Paolo now,' he said. 'Xabarra takes her to openings. He keeps her close. She goes everywhere with him. She's likes a robot, Jack. A beautiful, sad robot. What age did you say she was?'

'Nineteen.'

Eddie sighed.

'Tell me what you have in mind.'

I told him. Eddie didn't say anything for a long time. He poured another brandy. He either ignored my glass, or he was too deep in thought to notice that it was empty. He took a cigar from his desk and carefully lit it, then he looked at me through the smoke. There was none of the *bonhomie* in his face. His eyes were clear and cold.

'Tell me something, Jack,' he said. 'What the fuck do you think you're doing? Coming out here like some half-assed Galahad, your butt itching for action. The girl is nineteen years old. She can do what she likes.'

'Paolo thinks there is duress involved.'

'He's her father. He has to think that. I think that bomb blew your brains clean out your ass.'

I didn't say anything.

'Hang on a second,' Eddie went on slowly. 'I guess Paolo is paying you. That makes it different. That makes it OK. Just don't start mixing business and pleasure.' He gave me a long look. 'Forget about little girls corrupted by bad men. Forget about your friend with his legs blown off. Keep your head clear and collect the cheque.' He snorted, half-laughing. 'Sometimes it's even more moral that way. Come on. Let's get this business started.'

I knew Jesus was doing well, but I didn't realize how well. You walked down from First Avenue into the area they called Alphabet City. As you walked towards the river across avenue A and B and C, the streets got rougher, the white faces became more rare. It wasn't as rough as it had been, but it wasn't a place for a stranger after dark. I did that city thing, walked fast, throwing a bit of swagger into the walk, a hard-nosed local with places to go. Liam wandered along, taking everything in, for all the world like an elderly tourist in Trafalgar Square. Liam didn't need to act hard. There was a deadly streak in him that went right to the core. He wasn't conscious of the aura that he projected, the sense of a man who wore the mantel of violence and nihilism as easily as he wore his charm and insight.

Jesus's building was the opposite of Eddie's place. Eddie was discreet, but the building that Jesus lived in said money. Not that it was over the top. It was an old twenties warehouse building, with subtly ornate detail, common enough down here, but whereas the other buildings were decrepit and begrimed, this had been restored, the sandstone beautifully sandblasted, the wrought iron stripped down to the metal and repainted, the woodwork spotless. Down here, it bespoke money and power. There was graffiti everywhere else, but there was no graffiti on Jesus's building. Inside, it was the same: discreet and bare and well-designed. Jesus welcomed me with a glint in his eye which said 'Look at this, Scotsman, look where this street dealer ended up'. But my eyes were on the distinguished-looking elderly woman sitting at the end of an exquisitely balanced ash and walnut table. Her eyes were warm with recognition and with amusement. As Jesus and Liam exchanged greetings – and there was an empathy between the two of them that I hadn't expected – Irene stood to greet me and her eyes were warm.

I had met Jesus through Irene. I had been living in their building, a young man just out of college and wondering what to do with himself. I knew there was a heroin shooting gallery in the basement of the building and I knew to stay clear of it. One day, I had got stuck behind an elderly lady with shopping on the stairs. As much out of impatience as manners, I had carried the shopping for her. She nodded and clucked and thanked me in Spanish as I left the bags at her hall door.

I was working in a restaurant on Seventh Avenue, working late shifts, which meant I was never home before three. The streets around my apartment building were lonely and dangerous at that time. One night, as I turned the corner, I saw a small crowd of Puerto Rican junkies outside the building. I decided to walk through them. It was the wrong choice. As I started towards the door, they bunched around me wordlessly, blocking the doorway and closing me in. I tried to turn back towards the street, but they wouldn't let me.

It was the way it was done, without words, that frightened me, the sense that some junkie telepathy was working amongst them. I felt something prick my arm and looked down to see blood on my sleeve, but I couldn't see who had knifed me. I decided that I wasn't going to wait for the next knife thrust. I picked out the biggest one and hit him hard in the neck. He went down gagging and I saw the knife swinging through the space where he had been standing. I jumped back and felt it slice through my jacket. I hit another one and kicked someone hard on the knee. I felt a blow on the side of my head that left me momentarily dizzy, allowing them to get in another few hits. I dived to the ground and rolled through their legs into the hallway, where they could only come at me one at a time, or so I thought. I hadn't considered the stairs. As the knifeman moved warily towards me, a thin, pock-marked man swarmed up the stairs until he was above me and started clawing at me from above, one of his long nails catching me in the eye before I grabbed his finger and broke it. Half-blinded with tears, I backed further down the hallway, still dragging the scrawny man by his broken finger, when I felt his hand being jerked from my grasp and his yelps of pain being replaced by a sickening series of thuds. I looked up to see Jesus standing at the top of the stairs, a stubby Colt revolver in his hand, having just kicked the scrawny man down the stairs. He barked something in Puerto Rican and the junkies backed away sullenly. Jesus nodded to me to get up the stairs. I didn't need to be asked twice. But as I passed him, I started to feel lightheaded. I looked at my arm. The blood was pumping from it in great gouts. The lightheadedness increased, and the last thing I remember was slithering to the floor at Jesus's feet.

I woke in an apartment. The little old lady whose bags I had carried was bandaging the wound on my arm with some kind of field dressing. I had the feeling it was something she had done before. I started to speak, but she hushed me.

'You've lost some blood,' she said, in perfect, almost unaccented English, 'but you will be all right. Just rest.'

I slipped out of consciousness again and woke several hours later, lying on a small sofa. Jesus was sitting at the kitchen table, drinking coffee and watching me with an ironic half-grin on his face, which was his usual expression, as if irony was the only possible response to the world we lived in.

'Here,' he said, pouring me coffee. 'You're a lucky man.'

'How?' I said, feeling lightheaded and nauseous and not very lucky at all.

'Firstly because people getting killed in my building is bad for business, but mainly because my mother told me you helped her. For that, you get my protection.'

'I only carried her groceries up the stairs,' I said.

'That's what I said, but Mama said he is a good-mannered boy and you must look after him, Jesus. So now you are alive.'

He said it flatly, as if it was a matter of no consequence to him one way or another.

I got to my feet. I could just about stand if I held on to something. Jesus watched me make my way towards the door. I wondered where his mother was. As I struggled with the door catch, my eye caught a photograph on the wall, an old monochrome image of a young girl. She was wearing combat gear and carrying a rifle, half-squinting into the light with a determined expression on her face. With a shock, I realized that the girl in the photograph and the little old lady were the same person.

Jesus saw me looking. He laughed.

'You're right, that's my mother. That's Irene.'

At the time, I didn't know what war Irene had been in, or how that war would come to haunt her fifty years on, but now I greeted her and kissed her on both cheeks and spouted some gallant nonsense until she told me to shut up and sit down.

The evening started well. Jesus and Liam circled each other for a while until they discovered a mutual interest in fishing. Soon they were sitting to one side while Jesus waxed lyrical about bone-fishing in the Gulf and Liam tried to persuade him of the delights of his native cold mountain streams.

Irene told me that she still lived in the same apartment building.

'The only difference is that Jesus owns it now.'

I could see the pride in her face. I didn't know if she knew how Jesus earned his living. It was impossible for someone as shrewd as her not to know, I thought, but I wasn't going to start moralizing.

Dinner was bluefin tuna with Jesus's special tomato and lime salsa and plenty of Coronas to try to douse the fiery chilli sauce. Jesus liked his food hot. I had forgotten how hot. I knew that Liam didn't particularly like hot food. Despite this, he was in good form

41

and hit Irene with his usual line of roguish patter which had her laughing despite herself.

But there was one thing about Jesus's salsa. It didn't just hit you straight away. It took its time to build to a fiery crescendo. While Jesus and his mother were arguing over dessert, I looked over to see that Liam was red in the face. He gave me a small rueful grin and excused himself, heading for the bathroom.

Later, he told me that he could feel his whole face on fire and opened the bathroom window to feel the cool night air on his face. It helped a little and he stood at the window breathing for a few moments. It was then that he saw a slight movement on the roof of the building across the street. He turned off the light and crouched at the windowsill, letting his eyes become accustomed to the light. He saw the movement again, a figure silhouetted against the night sky that glowed a faint orange over New Jersey. He waited and saw the figure again, a man's figure standing up momentarily, a man's figure holding a rifle standing against the roofline and creating the perfect sniper's profile before ducking back into the shadow. From what Liam could see, the man was working his way round to Jesus's side of the building. Jesus may not have been the target but, as Liam said, you wouldn't have bet against it either. Liam made his way swiftly back to us. As soon as he came in, I saw his eyes sweep towards the window and I knew there was trouble. I was in the open-plan kitchen with Jesus, which left only Irene in the line of fire. Liam told us swiftly what he had seen, then instructed Irene to get up and walk naturally towards the kitchen. She took him at his word, taking the time to gather up some empty dishes before walking towards the kitchen. Jesus started towards her as if to grab her and haul her to safety, but Liam held his arm.

'Better find out who's trying to kill you,' he hissed, 'because your mother's in danger as well until you do.'

It wasn't a great argument, but it kept Jesus thinking while

42

Irene crossed the remaining few yards. He grabbed her and almost pushed her into a corner.

'Stay there, Mama,' he half-ordered and half-pleaded.

'I've got a better idea,' Liam said. 'I want Irene to stay here, put up a semblance of normality while we get across on to that roof and see if we can put our hands on this man. Can you do that Irene?'

'No!' Jesus said.

Irene smiled easily.

'That's no problem,' she said, with a smile on her face.

'If anybody's going to act as a decoy, it should be me,' Jesus said.

'We need three.'

'Go on, son,' Irene said, 'I know what I'm doing.' Then, as he hesitated, she spoke with a flash of steel. 'Go!'

Jesus seemed to come to a decision. He reached into a drawer and pulled out three Luger pistols. He handed one to Irene, who popped the magazine, then slammed it back into the breech like a pro, something in her seeming to come alive when she handled the weapon. Liam looked at me with raised eyebrows. I grinned. Irene could handle herself.

Within forty seconds, we were in the basement boiler room, running. Jesus popped a well-oiled lever and an old delivery hatch swung open on small hydraulic rams.

'Every rat has got more than one hole,' Jesus said, grinning.

The hatch opened at the rear of the building. We ran up the alley behind the building for a block before cutting across the street, our progress hidden from the sniper by the metallic mass of the fire escape. By the time we hit the rear entrance to the sniper's building, I could feel the blood pounding in my ears and my breath rasping. I looked around for the elevator. Jesus shook his head.

'You know these buildings, man. No elevators for the poor people.'

I looked up into the stairwell. It seemed to last for ever. But

Jesus and Liam were already on the second flight. Grimly, I started after them.

If the residents of the building thought there was anything strange about us, they didn't comment. Two men with drawn guns running flat out, and another man puffing along two flights behind them, cursing with a Scottish accent which got broader the more he sweated. I thought about Irene in the kitchen. The other two were well ahead of me by now, so I thought I'd take a look. I'd seen several abandoned apartments on the way up and on the next flight I came across one that faced the front. I scanned the room quickly before I stepped in. Nothing except two filthy mattresses and a corner which stank with unnamed human ordure. Sometimes you hear fashion editors talk about heroin chic. There is no equivalent for crack cocaine. No chic in their lightless dens.

I made my way to the window. I was looking slightly upwards. The sniper would be looking down. I could see Irene's arm gesturing as if she was in the middle of a conversation. I saw her raise a glass in a toast. There was a bit of the ham actor in Irene, I thought, hoping that the sniper couldn't see too much of her performance.

I turned towards the stairwell again, forcing my tired legs upwards. I was near the top of the building when I heard the flat, deadly crack of a rifle, one single shot. Suddenly I had the legs of a man twenty years younger. I covered the last flight of stairs without my feet touching the ground, hit the roof door and emerged, gun at the ready, into a strange tableau. Liam and Jesus were standing stock still at the back edge of the roof. There was a metal beam stretching between the building and the block next to it. A metal girder about one foot wide. In the middle of the beam, a middle-aged man was edging his way across. Beneath him was the street, fourteen floors down. The surface of the beam looked slick and uneven. Liam and Jesus had their guns trained on him, but I knew that neither of them was capable of shooting him off the girder. Wordlessly, I edged up until I was standing beside them. The man was moving with great deliberation, lifting one foot and then the other in a curious, high-stepping kind of way, placing each foot with precision. There was almost a fastidiousness to the way he did it.

The man's back was to us, but there was something about him that took a moment to figure out. His hair was black and slicked back. He wore a black suit, the jacket long and almost to his knees, seeming cinched at the waist. When I looked again, I realized the reason for his odd gait. He was wearing high-heeled Western boots. It must have been almost impossible to walk on the metal with boots like that, but he was managing it and, even though he had sneaked up on us with a sniper's rifle, we were all willing him to get across. And he did it, running the last four feet, running lightly, then leaping from the end of the beam and disappearing into the shadows. Jesus put one foot on the end of the beam, as if he was going to give pursuit, but Liam put his hand on his arm.

'We'd better see about Irene,' he said.

Jesus's face turned white and he bolted for the stairs. Liam followed him.

I hesitated. The man had no gun in his hand when he crossed the girder. I saw a dull glint on the parapet. I went over. It was an old Martini Henry sniper's rifle with telescopic seats and a wooden stock, polished with use. An old gun and one obviously cared for. I squinted down the sight. I could see through the window of Jesus's apartment, but I couldn't see Irene. I hid the rifle as best I could and started down the stairs.

When I got to the apartment, Irene was sitting on an Eileen Gray sofa with a large brandy in her hand. She smiled at me as I entered, but her face was grey and there was a nitroglycerine inhaler on the sofa beside her. There was also a small bullet hole on the other side of the sofa.

Jesus was on the phone, talking loudly in Spanish and gesticulating angrily. Liam was at the window, trying to work out the angle of fire.

'We must have disturbed him just as he was squeezing off the first shot. I just can't figure out how he could see her from there . . .'

He spotted something. I watched as he examined a ventilation grille. The bottom part of the grille had come loose and was hanging down the outside wall. The sniper had fired through the five-inch gap.

'He's a hell of a shot, that's for sure,' Liam said.

When I told him about the rifle, I could see his admiration increasing. It would have been a good shot with a laser-guided weapon, never mind the vintage rifle I had seen. Jesus put the phone down. His eyes were blazing.

'No one knows nothing!' He turned to his mother. 'You have to go. Tonight!'

Irene looked at him tiredly.

'Where would I go, son?'

'Europe. Rome. Paris. It's not safe here.'

Irene shook her head.

'I couldn't go to Europe. What would I do in Europe? This city is my home, Jesus. I won't go anywhere.'

He opened his mouth to argue, but I think he knew it was futile.

'I have to see some people,' he said. 'Can you and Liam stay here until I get back?'

Before we had a chance to answer, he was gone. Irene shook her head ruefully. I thought about calling a doctor for her. I didn't like the slight blueing on her lips. But Liam had other ideas. Before I could say anything, he had Irene on her feet.

'Come on,' he said, 'I'll wash, you dry.'

I was about to protest but he winked at me.

'Domestic therapy,' he said.

Within minutes, he was chatting away to Irene about the benefits of handwashing over dishwashers. In a while, she was laughing. I felt very tired. Jet lag and the pace of events over the previous weeks were catching up with me. Not to mention the stairs in the apartment building. I closed my eyes. Before I fell asleep, a picture went through my mind of the man on the girder. There was something old-fashioned about him, almost a courtly look, as if he had come from another time.

When I woke, I was lying on the Eileen Gray sofa with a blanket covering me. I had a vague memory of waking during the night and seeing Liam and Irene sitting together at the kitchen table. It seemed to me that Liam was remonstrating with her. I couldn't remember whether it was a dream or not, but I knew I wasn't dreaming the smell of bacon and eggs and fresh coffee. I sat up, and as I did so, Irene put a cup of espresso at my elbow, the good Illy coffee. It was after nine o clock. Irene must have seen me checking my watch.

'I don't care what you have to do,' she said. 'You got to have breakfast.' I was about to protest, but the smell of bacon was overpowering by now. I allowed my protests to be silenced.

Liam had gone to his apartment and Jesus had not returned since the previous night. I rang my apartment and checked my messages. There was one from Eddie, telling me that there was a big opening that night and that Xaberra would be there. It would be an opportunity to get a look at him. Again, I felt the faint dread that his name aroused. Eddie also told me that our other plan was in full swing and that 'the goods are in transit'. Bringing an important piece of art across the Atlantic, even if it had originated in the States, was something which came with a lot of paperwork. I wondered how Eddie had bypassed the process. I decided I wouldn't ask: Eddie's fee would reflect the difficulty of the task at any rate. Irene fussed over me, asking me if the bacon was hot enough, if the eggs were cooked enough, if I had enough coffee. In the end, I held up a hand to stop her.

47

'All right, Irene,' I said. 'What is going on here?'

'Going on? There is nothing going on . . .'

'Come on, Irene. I know you. You're overdoing the mother-hen routine.'

'I swear . . .'

'It can only really be one thing, Irene. It can only be this shooting business. You know something and you're not telling Jesus. I can see it in your eyes. He could see it too if he wasn't so worried about you.'

She wouldn't look at me. She turned to the window, but I could see the remnants of an old anguish in her eyes.

I thought she might have confided in me, but then the door opened and Jesus came in. He looked tired and drawn. I knew what he was going through. The sense that you are being hunted, but not knowing who your pursuers are or why they are after you. The mind starts to construct wild scenarios. You start to distrust those closest to you. I watched Jesus carefully. If he put the thing together logically, he might decide that his life had changed most in the last few days since my arrival. He wouldn't have to be paranoid to start wondering whether my arrival was linked to what had happened.

As if turning away from whatever accusing eye was fixing her from her past, Irene descended on Jesus, scolding him for the state of his clothes, for looking so tired; all the things that a mother gathers from one sweeping glance. With a warning look at me, Irene went into the kitchen to get breakfast for Jesus.

He slumped on a chair. I looked at him. He shook his head.

'Nothing,' he said wearily, 'nobody on the street knows anything. Maybe I just got too far away from all my old people, they won't tell me things, but I don't think so. It's something new. One thing I did, I got twenty-four-hour guys on Irene's apartment. She'll be safe anyway.'

I went back to the apartment on Christopher Street and showered

48

and changed my clothes. Then I picked up the phone, looked at it and put it down. I picked it up again and asked the operator for the number of the United Nations. Once I got that, I put the phone down and took a deep breath. Two minutes later, I was talking to the operator at the United Nations building. I was put through to the UNHCR. It took a lot of talking and explaining to various operators, but after ten minutes the phone was picked up and Deirdre Mellows was on the other end.

'Deirdre,' I said, not really being able to think of anything else to say. Or perhaps not feeling that I had the right to say anything. I was indirectly responsible for a terrible injury to her, and there were complicated feelings on both sides that, on the face of it, could never be reconciled.

There was a long silence.

'Hello, Jack.' The words were infused with a terrible mixture of gladness and regret and caution and melancholy. All emotions I had expected to hear, but I had been hoping for anger. I had always been able to work with her anger, let it break over me. I think I knew it was hopeless then.

'Liam told me you were in New York. I thought you might ring.'

I had the feeling that this was a rebuke, that she expected me to have the courage to leave her alone.

'I'm sorry, Deirdre. I know I shouldn't have called, it's just that . . .' I could feel the panic in my voice, the unseemly babble waiting to get out, but she cut me off.

'It's all right,' she said, almost sharply, then more gently. 'It's all right, Jack. I understand. I want you to understand something too. That it is good to hear your voice, really good, but it's not a good idea for us to see each other. It's just not a good idea.' There was a firmness in her voice that brooked no contradiction.

'I'm going into a meeting now, Jack. I have to go. But it is good to talk you.' There was only sadness in her voice now.

'Goodbye,' I said.

She didn't answer. I heard the click and then the buzz.

I sat in Washington Square for an hour, watching the old men play chess and contemplating the woman I had been talking to, thought of her as an aid worker in Somalia, commandeering an armoured pick-up to raid food aid from a closed warehouse. I could see the light in her eyes then and thought I had had some part in dimming it. Now she was essentially a middle-ranking civil servant in the UN bureaucracy. I told myself to stop it. There were clever people in offices who still had the light in their eyes, who spent their time trying to undo the damage wrought by people like me. I looked downtown towards the spot where the Twin Towers had been and tried to consign my self-pity to the small, mean place it deserved. I got to my feet and hailed a cab.

I had only seen the paintings in books before, and, as always, I was unprepared for the impact. Hopper might not have had the *élan* of a Jackson Pollock, but he understood what he was doing. A man alone in a bar. A deserted gas station at dusk. An unknown woman alone in a hotel room. Essays on those solitary interims. Moments to illustrate both the insignificance and towering worth of unknown people alone in unknown places. I lost myself in the paintings for an hour. The Whitney on a weekday afternoon was as quiet as one of Hopper's deserted corners. I heard showery rain rattle against the windows and the light changed, darkening as the squall passed overhead.

I felt a presence beside me. I turned to see Deirdre. She was wearing a raincoat and she had her hair tied up in a scarf. She wasn't looking at me. She was looking at the painting.

'I thought I'd find you here,' she said with a sideways glance containing a small plea to accept the moment, not to ask any more of her than being there.

'There's a style of blue-grass singing, a kind of a falsetto,' I said, 'they call it "high lonesome".'

'High lonesome,' she said, savouring the phrase and smiling. I felt her arm link mine. We moved quietly from painting to painting, talking about each one less and less, because we were both picking up the same things, until in the end we weren't talking at all.

We went to a bar down the street afterwards and sat in the front, looking out on the street because we both loved the falling light and the paintings had put us in the mood for it. She told me about her new job. The same passion for the poor was still there, but the battles were with the middle managers and funding agencies now. I remembered that Liam had been a shrewd strategist when he had let his head rule his heart and I realized that Deirdre would be the same. Looking at her, I realized that she had grown and I felt diminished as a consequence. I felt worse when I told her what I was doing in New York. At first she was inclined to be angry, but she replaced the anger with a feeling which was too close to pity for my liking, as if this was something I had been reduced to.

'You can't just ride in and snatch the girl,' she said. 'This isn't the eighteenth century, Jack. It sounds like a big mistake, but it's her mistake.'

'I'll just talk to her,' I said, wondering what the hell I was going to do when I saw her.

'And why isn't Paolo here?' she said, in a tone which implied I was doing his dirty work. So I told her what had happened in London. She was quiet for a long time after that. I wondered if her mind was travelling back to the terrible journey we had made across the Irish Sea and the bullet that had ripped through her own flesh. When she started talking again, her conversation was distant, as though she already saw herself walking away. I didn't push it. Rather than wait for her to make the move, I looked at my watch.

'I've an opening to go to,' I said apologetically.

'Work or pleasure?' she asked. 'I suppose you always had a habit of mixing them.'

On the street outside, her lips were light and cool on my cheek. I watched her until she reached the end of the street, walking with her head bowed, then, at the very end of the street, she turned and waved and smiled and I could almost see her the first time I had met her. But that had been in the springtime.

It was one of those openings that bring out the big guns. Henri Cartier-Bresson at the Met. You could barely get a look at the photographs for the acres of expensive clothing on display. I had brought Jesus with me and I was surprised when I realized that he was much more at ease than I was. But I suppose he wasn't raised in a household of stiff-necked Glasgow socialists. He spent the evening pointing out people to me – the wealthy, the famous and the notorious. He accompanied his commentary with a steady stream of malicious gossip which had the effect of making me laugh and relaxing me a little. Then the reason for his ease in this milieu became clear. A young man came over to him. The elegant clothes, the flop of hair over the forehead and the languid bearing suggested that he was born to this, the effete heir of some vast fortune, but the glance he cast over me was shrewd and searching and suggested that there was a mind behind the effete exterior. He kissed Jesus lightly on the cheek and they turned away slightly, exchanging small private signals the way that lovers do when they haven't met for a while. Then Jesus introduced me.

'This is Paul,' he said. Paul shook my hand.

'Jesus told me you were coming to town.' The way he said it suggested that he held baronial rights over Manhattan. We talked about the photographs for a while. It was obvious that Paul knew a lot about them, not just aesthetics but technique, and it didn't surprise me when Jesus told me he was a photographer.

'I'd like to see,' I said. Sometimes I thought it was the one thing in me that kept its newness and eagerness, the desire to see new art, discovering a young artist.

I still hadn't seen Xabarra.

Paul shrugged.

'He usually arrives late,' he said.

Paul and Jesus stopped to talk to a girl in a long, white strapless dress and I found myself on my own. There were trays of wine circulating and I drank too many glasses. I found something appalling about the arch and wrinkled dowagers in exquisite gowns, the men in evening suits, sleek and puffed with the privileges of wealth. The more ill at ease I felt, the more I drank. The conversation around me seemed too loud, the voices harsh and braying. It was then that I caught sight of Xabarra. Sensed, rather than saw, I should say, because in the hubbub of the packed gallery he seemed to create an area of stillness around him, dominating and subduing it.

I moved closer. He was tall, black hair sleeked back. His olive skin was pockmarked. His face seemed elongated, the cheekbones higher than they should have been, so that they seemed to push his black eyes upwards into a slant. He was wearing a white linen suit and was moving slowly through the crowd, exchanging greetings as he did so. Then I saw Alva at his side, her hand through his arm. She had her hair up and was wearing a black silk dress, made dramatic by the exquisite pallor of her skin. She was poised and exquisitely beautiful and I found myself thinking of Japanese art, of technique and beauty refined and refined again until it seemed beyond nature. I was aware of Jesus and Paul beside me.

'She really is beautiful,' Paul said, almost reverentially.

'She's a user as well,' Jesus said. 'She's smacked out of her head.'

'You mean heroin?' I said, feeling naïve.

'I haven't seen her eyes . . .' Paul said. 'Yes, she is, you know,

Jack. And needing a fix as well. See her swallowing? Her mouth's getting dry. Dry as an old bone. Her nose is going to start running if she doesn't get a hit soon. Not very elegant really.'

Somewhere from the past, I felt the pressure of a five-year-old's knees on my shoulders, steering me through the Italian dusk, laughing and calling out to her father to hurry up. And as the thought passed through my mind, she seemed to hesitate and look around, so that Xabarra almost pulled her off her feet as he walked on. He turned and looked at her. Another man might look annoyed but Xabarra just looked. I saw her blanch, put her hand to her throat and start to apologize. He cut her short with a gentle smile. For some reason, she seemed to find this even more disconcerting.

It was probably the wine, but I swore afterwards that I could actually feel the weight of that five-year-old on my shoulders, her voice getting more insistent and turning to fear. Something in me raged against the scene in front of me. Afterwards, Liam suggested a rage against the loss of innocence, but this didn't feel like that. It felt like a rage against that one child's loss of innocence and I found I didn't care who first put the needle in her vein, or whether she put it there herself. I turned blindly away from Paul and Jesus and stumbled out into the night.

They found me sitting on the steps of the museum. I got up and fell into step and we walked downtown without talking much. At midnight I found myself sitting on a step in St Mark's Place, drinking espresso from a paper cup. Paul seemed to know most of the people walking past. Some of them sat down to talk to us. The conversation was pleasant, but I couldn't shake the gloom which had followed my anger. In the end, Paul motioned to me.

'Come on,' he said, 'I want to show you something.'

We walked to the bottom of St Mark's Place and went down steps into a dingy basement. There was a battered coffee machine in the foyer and the air was thick with cigarette smoke. When my eyes stopped watering, I could see that there were eight or nine people sitting in battered chairs, ranging from fresh-faced young women to grizzled old East Village veterans in battered black leathers. A young woman was on her feet, talking about her life. It was a squalid tale told with humour and provoked groans of recognition from the audience. A story of prostitution, hepatitis, prodding your arm with a dirty needle, trying to find a vein that had collapsed a long time ago, and finally of HIV.

'Where are we?' I whispered to Paul.

'NA,' he said. 'Narcotics Anonymous.'

As he spoke, the girl finished talking and there was a round of applause. Then another young woman got to her feet. This one was much shakier, even to my untutored eye. She had to try several times before she got her name out, and then the big words: 'I'm an addict.'

There were murmurs of encouragement from the audience, but that was as far as she got. She sat down again, wrapping her arms around her shoulders as if the room had suddenly got very cold. Again there was warm applause and I had the feeling that she had just done the hardest bit.

We sat for an hour, listening to stories of degradation and fortitude. When I came out, I found that if my view of the human race hadn't improved, my view of the human spirit had.

Paul turned to me on the way out.

'By the way,' he said, 'I am a recovering junkie, and I do know what Jesus does for a living.'

'And it's all right with you?'

'You learn not to judge.'

I left Jesus and Paul on the steps at St Mark's Place. As I walked towards Broadway, my cellphone rang. It was Eddie.

'Did you enjoy the opening?'

'I got a look at our man anyway.'

'What do you think?'

'Formidable, I would think.'

'I'm glad you're impressed, Jack. It slightly improves your chances of staying alive. Now. Down to business. The merchandise will be arriving tomorrow. I've contacted Xabarra's office and expect him to contact me personally tomorrow. He'll want to inspect it immediately.'

'Ring me when you know.'

I put the phone away. I was the only person on the street as I walked towards the apartment. I pulled the collar of my jacket around my ears against the cold. As Liam used to say, the game was on.

Six

The next afternoon, I went to Eddie's. The miserable Scotsman led me down into Eddie's world. Eddie was at his desk when we entered. I wondered if he ever left the desk. He got to his feet and hurried round.

'My God, Jack,' he said. 'You said it was a good piece, but it really is something else. And unique?'

'All negatives were destroyed,' I said. 'There is only one piece left.'

'For a collector,' he said, 'irresistible.'

'We'll see,' I said. 'Have you made contact with Xabarra?'

'He's coming tonight. I think he heard the enthusiasm in my voice.'

'Good,' I said. 'Can I have a look?'

'Of course Jack. Of course.'

Eddie had cleared the gallery and displayed the photograph in the middle of the floor with a single spot on it. It was a late Robert Mapplethorpe, a male nude photographed with such precision and attention to light that it seemed almost abstract. Yet there was a brooding carnality about it, something feral and uncompromising. And for all that it was a celebration of physique, there was a darkness to it, a hint of corruption. Just the right bait for someone like Xabarra. I knew that a man of his wealth could buy a hundred pieces of a similar stature. But this was the only print of this particular work.

'It's beautiful.'

I could hear the covetousness in Eddie's voice. I turned and he gave a small self-deprecating grin.

'I'd love to be able to help you, Eddie, but . . .'

'I know, I know.' He looked defeated. 'If you ever come across another one . . .' He stopped. He knew there would never be another one.

As I was leaving Eddie's, I got a call from Liam. I met him in a bar on Sixth Avenue.

'It's getting harder to find a bar that's just a bar,' Liam complained. I took this as homesickness. He looked at me for a moment.

'Have you worked out a plan yet, Jack? Or are we going to just ask that nice Mr Xabarra to give us his girlfriend?'

'I don't want to snatch her in Eddie's place. That way, Eddie's implicated. I think we should take her as they're leaving the building. If he has a driver or a bodyguard, then we neutralize them first.'

'What then, Jack?' There was a gentle mocking tone in his voice. 'What then?'

'Well, we have a nineteen-year-old on our hands, probably an extremely cross and frightened nineteen-year-old. Also, if Jesus is right, she's a junkie. These things are problems, Jack. Maybe you're rushing things.'

'Or maybe Xabarra will get sick of her tomorrow and send her down the East River with a bag over her head,' I exploded. 'Or maybe she'll get just one hit too many of bad smack, or a dirty needle, or . . .'

'OK, OK,' Liam said, holding up his hands in surrender. 'But you don't mind if I look into some options? Like what to do with a sick junkie?'

'Jesus's boyfriend, Paul, he might know how to help,' I said.

'And you need a place to stash her.'

'I know, I know,' I said impatiently, although the germ of an idea had formed in my mind.

We found Paul sitting on the steps of St Mark's Place. We sat with him and had a coffee while I rang Jesus. St Mark's was always busy. Every ten minutes or so, another five subway carriages would disgorge a crowd of New Jersey teenagers hoping to buy a little sensimilla grass or coke and feel edgy and dangerous for a while. It was cold and sunny and the old steps weren't the worst place in the world to kill some time. When Jesus arrived, I told them what Liam had said. Paul looked thoughtful.

'You know,' he said, 'there's nothing in the world is going to stop an addict finding heroin if they don't want to kick it. They have to have the desire. After that . . .'

'You need somebody who can help her and be discreet. Somebody who knows the score,' Jesus said. 'Billy E is probably your man.'

'And Tonto,' Paul said. 'Wait here.'

Ten minutes later, he was back with a big, heavyset man in a leather jacket. A patchy beard barely concealed what looked like an acid burn on one side of his face. On the opposite cheekbone was a jail mark. He looked big, burned-out and mean. The man with him was tall and thin, almost cadaverous. He was wearing a Nico T-shirt and chinos and if he noticed the cold, he showed no sign of it. Jesus introduced the first man as Billy E and the thin one as Tonto. Billy looked us up and down, then smiled and shook our hands. The smile had the authority of a man who'd been to the far side of life and back and was entitled to a little serenity. Tonto nodded at us and sat down. He took a copy of Kem Nunn's *The Dogs Of Winter* out of his pocket and started to read.

'Billy here is a main man in NA around here.'

'Jesus speaks highly of you,' Billy said with a grin. 'So does Irene, which is more important. Paul tells me you're going to snatch a junkie.'

There was amusement in his voice, but there was an undercurrent of sadness which I hadn't picked up before.

'The daughter of a friend of mine,' I said. And then for some reason I told him about the night in Fiesole, of carrying the little girl on my shoulders. The whole episode seemed to have acquired a dreamlike quality, but Billy E listened solemnly with his head bowed, nodding every so often like a battered and suffering street priest hearing a strange confession. At the end, he sat with his head bowed for a moment, then straightened briskly.

'We'll do whatever we can do, which may not be much. She won't kick until she hits the bottom, the very bottom of the pit. The addict is a strange, self-obsessed beast, untrustworthy and self-absorbed in a way you have probably never experienced before. You might have loved the child, Mr Valentine. You may not love the woman very much. However, we'll see. You haven't got her yet anyway.'

He stood up. Tonto shoved his book in his pocket and stood at his shoulder.

'We'll keep in touch with Jesus,' he said. He put his arms around me and hugged me. I had seen the NA people do this. It felt strange. Men of my working-class Glaswegian background didn't hug, and when they talked about a Glasgow kiss, they meant a headbutt.

We watched the two men walk off down the street, Billy E greeting people as he went.

'I think your story talked to him,' Jesus said quietly. 'About ten years ago, Billy was in a bad way. Had his kid daughter shooting him up in this lousy project dive he had. She gets into the gear as well. One day he brings home some bad smack. He shoots up. While he's out for the count, the daughter cops some. Difference is, he survives it, she doesn't. Fifteen years old, man. Death wrote her name in his book the day she was born. Sometimes I think the only reason Billy is still alive is that he's too brave to release himself from the pain of it. He feels he owes her that.'

I watched the big man go. I had a lot of death on my conscience, things that kept me awake at night, but I'm not sure if I could have borne the weight that bowed his big shoulders.

I spent the rest of the afternoon with Liam, trying to work out a plan for that evening. Now that we had decided what to do, the irrationality of my thinking was even more pronounced, but Liam kept his own counsel.

'You can't just snatch the girl,' Liam said. 'She's here of her own free will, as far as we know. You need to talk to her.'

'How do I do that?' I snapped.

'Did you try the phone?' Liam asked. 'You know, before you start shooting at people?'

I started to open my mouth, then shut it again. I had seen the way Alva had reacted to Xabarra at the opening. There was fear there all right. But a lot of people find their way into dependencies on others through what we call free will. And fearing someone can become as much of a dependency as anything else. I wondered if I was developing my own dependency. Something in me wanted to get Alva out of the way so that I could have a free run at Xabarra. I wanted to get close to him with a gun in my hand. I could rationalize the feeling by telling myself that he was an evil man who had hurt people close to me, but in truth, one part of me wanted to see fear in his eyes, his blood on the ground. Liam handed me his cellphone. I dialled information and asked for Xabarra's office number. To my surprise it was listed.

The phone was answered by Xabarra's secretary. It was a suave man's voice, speaking perfect English but with a mechanistic tone, like someone who has spent too much time perfecting a language from books. I asked for Alva.

'May I ask who is calling?'

Liam pointed at his chest.

'My name is Liam Mellows,' I said. 'I'm an old friend of Alva's family. I'm in the city for a few days, thought I would look her up.'

'I'm afraid Alva is not available to come to the phone right now,' he said smoothly. 'May I take a number and have her call you back?'

'That's OK,' I said, making myself sound disappointed. 'Maybe I'll call later.'

I thanked him and hung up before he could say anything more.

'So what?' Liam said. 'Proves nothing.'

'I know, I know.' I threw up my arms. 'I don't know what to do.'

'Then listen to me,' Liam said. 'Use tonight to talk to her. Hold off on the photograph. Pretend to be reluctant to part with it, fight over the price so that there has to be another meeting. We can snatch her then, if snatching is what's called for, which I personally doubt. You say she goes everywhere with him. Get your friend Eddie to take Xabarra off, make an excuse. You talk to the girl. Then we know where we stand.'

I was reluctant to accept it, but it made sense. In the end, I agreed. I looked at my watch. Six o'clock. We had two hours. I had time to get over to the Second Avenue Deli, grab something delicious which I could wolf down in the apartment, then stroll over.

Then my phone went off. It was Jesus. His voice was calm.

'Jack,' he said, 'would you mind coming over here? Mama just shot someone.'

There was a dead man on the floor of Irene's apartment. He was a heavyset man in his sixties, perhaps older, wearing Western boots and the same cinched jacket as the sniper. He had been shot in the chest. There wasn't very much blood. The bullet must have killed him immediately. Beside him on the floor was a shotgun. I bent to examine it. It was a huntsman's weapon, finely chased in silver on the stock, a beautiful gun. Irene was sitting in a corner of the kitchen as if she had sought to put as much distance as possible between the dead man and herself. The pistol that Jesus had given her was lying on the table. Irene was shaking and her face had that grey pallor again. Liam went over to her and took her hand. The gesture seemed to help. Jesus was leaning against the wall. There was a funny look on his face. And there was a smell of death in the apartment which would reach out and snag Irene every time she walked through the door from now on.

'You made arrangements?' I asked Jesus, meaning had he arranged for the body to be moved? He nodded. I didn't like the expression on his face. There was something dangerous in it. I lowered my voice to a whisper.

'For Christ's sake, Jesus, you've got to find out who is behind this. Look at your mother. She can't take this.'

Jesus ignored me. He straightened.

'I heard something,' he said quietly, 'I heard something a little while ago. I came up the stairs to check on my mother and I open the door very quiet in case she is sleeping and I hear voices.'

'Jesus . . .' Liam began. There was a warning note in his voice.

'So I take out my gun,' Jesus said, 'and I walk very softly into the room and I find myself overhearing a very strange conversation. A conversation between two people who know each other, or at least know of each other. They're talking about something that happened a long time ago. The man is very stern, very judgemental. The woman is trying to make him see something, but the way they talk, it's very old-fashioned and I can't follow it much. The woman is crying and I hear one word over and over again, and that word is 'sorry'. I don't hear much more because I walk through the door and the man turns and raises his gun and my mama shoots him.'

'You have to tell him, Irene,' Liam said, adding to my confusion.

'Yes, Mama, tell me,' Jesus said, turning to his mother, 'what was it that you were so sorry about?'

Irene didn't answer immediately. She got unsteadily to her feet and walked over to the dead man. Slowly and clumsily, she knelt beside his head. She stroked his head gently.

'He was a boy the last time I saw him,' she said, 'a fine boy. He had two sisters and a brother, all much older. They loved him very much but it never spoiled him.'

She looked at Jesus.

'Turn him over for me.'

Jesus hesitated, then did as he was asked, turning the man on to his back. She put the back of her hand against his cheek and held it there, then she gently closed his eyes. She started to fumble in her pocket, then turned as Liam held out two coins. She placed them on the dead man's eyes, then blessed herself and started to pray. Liam also blessed himself and bowed his head. It was a strange moment, two of them praying gently in a crime scene that could have got us all life without the possibility of parole. I used the moment to get my mind around the basic premise of the situation, which was that the men had been after Irene all along, not Jesus. And Irene had not told Jesus this, for some reason. But she had obviously confided in Liam. This didn't surprise me. People often saw something in Liam that invited confidence. When they had finished praying, she took a bottle of brandy from the shelf and poured four glasses and started to tell us why these strange, old-fashioned men were trying to kill her.

Irene had been brought up in a small village in Puerto Rico. One of those villages you still find all over Asia and South America, places that exist only by the grace and favour of others. A place rich in social bonds but ultimately vulnerable. Her father had worked in the city and had come into contact with ideas of equality. When he came home to get married to Irene's mother, he had books sent to him from the city. He learned words like internationalism, read about freedom struggles, although in the end his own ambition was simply for some fairness in the way his own small society operated.

According to Irene, he was a quiet, serious man. He would work in the fields and sometimes he would lift his head and look out over the landscape as though organizing it according to whatever principles he was developing in his head.

He raised three daughters and bided his time. When his hair had started to grey, he took a small sheaf of paper from the rough wooden desk where he worked. He walked up to the house belonging to Don Christophe, who owned all of the land locally. It was Sunday morning and the priest was at Don Christophe's house. He was received courteously. A glass of wine was poured for him. He spent the morning explaining how the farming practices could be reorganized, how irrigation could be developed to make the land more productive and how the tenants could be given security of tenure in return for vastly increased productivity. The two other men listened to him gravely. They suggested places where his plan could be improved, suggested other crops such as tobacco which could be introduced.

When he got home, he told his wife in detail what had happened. She expected him to be elated, but he shook his head. He looked exhausted. He fell asleep sitting in his chair. Next day, he went back to work as normal. Two nights later, they came for him. Four men. If they had just killed him, that would have been enough, Irene said. But they had mutilated him before his death. He was found tied to a tree the followiing morning. A wire around his neck had bound him to the tree and had almost severed his neck.

After the funeral, the girls' mother had taken them to the city. She sewed clothes until her fingers were bent and crabbed and her eyes were ruined. The oldest daughter became a prostitute. The youngest had always been sickly and died of a chest infection. Irene had studied because that was what her father had done. And when a wave of political activism swept the island, she had joined the liberation movement.

I had some vague notion of the movement. I remembered that two activists had been executed for attempting to assassinate an American president – was it Lyndon Johnson?

There had been some fighting in the interior of the island. That was where the photograph of Irene in fatigues had come from. They thought that the peasants would rise up and fight the bosses, the plantation owners, the big corporations. I learned a hard lesson, Irene said. Most of the time people prefer the certainty of slavery over the risks of freedom. Their support ebbed away. One day, Irene burned her uniform. She was afraid to return to the city where her political affiliations were known, so she returned to her old village. She rebuilt the house where she had been brought up and started to till the land. She worked her fingers to the bone on the land and came home every evening to fall exhausted into bed. Until the evening she came home and Don Christophe's eldest son was sitting on the bench beside her door.

He had been a captain in the army, he told her, and he knew all about her involvement. He said he could have her arrested. He said he could have her mother and sister arrested. He told her that he would keep quiet, but that there was a price for his silence.

He came to her house two or three nights a week for a month. Irene thought about her father and how he had died. But then she thought about her mother and what prison would do to her. In the end, she could take no more. One night, she waited until the man had fallen asleep, then she took her rifle from where she had hidden it in the rafters. She placed the barrel between his eyes, then wakened him with her foot. She waited until his eyes were open and horrified realization had dawned in them, then she pulled the trigger.

She ransacked his pockets and took his money. She left that night for the coast. She took the first boat that she could find going to America. She had met Jesus's father on the boat.

'And now,' she said, 'the Christophe family have found me.'

She indicated the man on the floor. 'This is the youngest brother. The man with the rifle is, I think, a cousin.'

'After all this time?' I said.

'It is the place I come from,' she said. 'There is a history of vendetta. They have been looking for me ever since then and now they have found me. I think they found Jesus first. That was why they tried to kill him. But now they know I am still alive. They will kill Jesus if they can because he is my son. But it is me they want.'

She looked down at the dead man on the floor. There was real sorrow in her eyes.

'He was the best of them. A friendly child. Imagine. He had servants, housemaids, people to lift and carry him all his life.'

I said nothing. I had trouble reconciling the shabby, archaic figure on the floor with the privileged life she described. Jesus managed to look both hard and lost at the same time. It was a dangerous combination. I could see Liam looking at Irene. He looked troubled, as if he sensed that something had been held back. Jesus tapped his gun on his knee.

There was a knock at the door, a quick double-tap. Jesus opened the door immediately. A small Puerto Rican with a luxuriant moustache came in. He was carrying a doctor's bag and he knelt beside the dead man without looking at any of us, as if by not looking at us we weren't there to witness what he was doing. After a cursory examination, he disappeared into the next room with Jesus. He came out after five minutes and practically ran across the room to the door. Jesus came out. He had papers in his hand.

'Death certificate for my Uncle Carlos,' he said laconically. 'Tragically died of a coronary infarction while on holiday and being attended by Doctor Santos. Body to be shipped back to Puerto Rico.' He turned to Irene. He took her face in his hands, turned it towards him and kissed her on the forehead.

'I want you to stay at my place for now. If these men want vendetta, then they will get it.'

I looked at my watch and nodded to Liam. It was time to go. On the way down the stairs, we met two men dressed in black suits. They were carrying a battered black metal coffin up the stairs.

There was more bad news.

I rang the hospital in London to bring Paolo up to date. A nurse answered the phone. She asked me if I was a relative. I said that I was his brother, knowing that I wouldn't get information otherwise. After a few moments, a doctor came to the phone. I was feeling very uneasy.

'Mr Casagrande is very ill,' the doctor said. 'He suffered a cerebral haemorrhage several days ago. I can only describe his condition as grave. He is currently comatose and there are no signs of any progress in his condition.'

I replaced the receiver with a feeling of deep foreboding. It seemed that what I was doing was all right as long as I had the moral authority of Alva's father to validate each step. Now that was no longer there, I felt very much alone.

Seven

Liam had brought his car, a battered Lincoln town car. I knew when he started it up, however, that the engine wasn't standard. Liam had a liking for fast cars. He dropped me off around the corner from Eddie's place. There was a black BMW 7 series sitting outside Eddie's door. Eddie had told me that Xabarra liked to drive his own car. I wondered why he would risk leaving the car unattended in that neighbourhood. I was to find out later that there was no risk to the car. No risk at all. As I reached the door, I was aware of Liam pulling in behind me. He would wait and watch for signs of trouble. I rang the doorbell and was escorted down by the Scotsman. For some reason he reminded me of the two undertakers we had seen at Jesus's place. The thought didn't reassure me. He showed me into the gallery. The first thing I saw was the Mapplethorpe. The second thing I saw was Xabarra standing off to one side. I scanned the shadows and cursed inwardly. There was no sign of Alva.

Eddie bustled up behind me.

'Jack,' he said, greeting me warmly, 'allow me to introduce you to Richard Xabarra.'

Xabarra turned and smiled. He shook my hand warmly. For some reason, I hadn't expected this. He was smiling broadly as if he was genuinely pleased to meet me.

'Mr Valentine,' he said, 'I have to say this is a beautiful piece, stunning. I'm grateful you brought it to my attention.'

I muttered something. The charm was genuine. He had the knack of the great charmers, of making you feel the warmth of his attention on you and you alone. You forgot about that strange face, the high cheekbones.

He stepped back and looked at the photograph again. He laughed.

'You know,' he said, 'they were right in a way to try to ban public funding for Mapplethorpe. There is something quite unwholesome about it, isn't there?'

I found myself agreeing with him. He hunkered down, almost comically, in front of the photograph, examining the textures that the photographer had achieved. Eddie stood behind me. It was a strange scene in Eddie's bunker beneath the pavement. The strange, high-cheekboned man and the pale-skinned Eddie, like two strange underground creatures.

'I hear you haven't decided whether to sell privately or go to auction,' he said.

I nodded dumbly. Eddie had obviously been working a little scheme of his own, trying to push the price up.

'Well then,' he said, 'if you like, we can discuss it over dinner at my house. I have some artwork out there that might interest you.'

My heart leaped. Alva would in all likelihood be there. But at the same time I couldn't shake a cold feeling. Xabarra turned and walked towards the door. Before Eddie could react, he was in the corridor. Eddie raced after him. I took my time. I heard Eddie's voice calling Xabarra as he walked swiftly along the corridor.

I took this as a technique employed by Xabarra to deal with the world, make things happen quickly and unexpectedly, keeping the world off-balance.

At the door, Xabarra stood over Eddie as he fiddled with the locks. We emerged on to the pavement and got into the BMW. I made a point of avoiding eye-contact with Liam. Xabarra drove fast and expertly. I knew Liam would be behind us, and I had to resist the temptation to look over my shoulder. He told me he kept a house in the Hamptons as well as one in Manhattan and that it was the Hamptons one we were headed towards. One of the city gallerys was showing work by Damien Hirst and we argued about Brit Art, the value of it. He said that he knew he should value it, but that some part of him rejected it as fake. This led on to an argument about conceptual art in general. Before I knew it, I had forgotten about Liam and we were swinging through the gates of a large mansion. Xabarra grinned in a self-deprecating manner.

'I know it's a bit Gatsby,' he said, 'but that is the thing about new money. It has a certain gauche charm. You get the sense of somebody who can't quite control themselves.'

In fact, there was nothing Gatsby about the house. It was a long, low, flat-roofed building like a modern Californian beach house, but blended into the mature gardens so that it was hard to tell where garden ended and house began. The walls were pale stone and silvery weathered timber. The hidden lighting was subtle, but not subtle enough to leave any shadows where an intruder might approach the house unseen. I noticed the high wall and half-expected the gates to swing shut behind us with an ominous clang. They didn't. They stayed open, but I saw the little cameras on either side of the gate.

We swept to a halt in front of the house. I half-expected flunkeys to fling open doors, but I had to open my own door. Gravel crunched under our feet as we walked towards the door and into a large hallway paved with rough limestone. It was very quiet. The absence of other people was starting to become quite pronounced. There was a photograph of a dustbowl family in the hallway. It seemed incongruous. The composition and accident of lighting were beautiful but the pale, desperate faces fixed the camera with a sombre stare. A terrible melancholy photograph of people long dead and not one I would have chosen to hang in my house.

'Anonymous,' Xabarra said, obviously pleased with it. 'I bought it in an antique shop. Thirty dollars. The fact that the man took such satisfaction in the image told me something about him. I wondered if he could see the despair. Or worse, if he could see it, if he found some perverse pleasure in the way these people had been undone.

'Come on,' he said smiling. I followed him through a large, stainless-steel door and found a gleaming industrial kitchen behind it. Again, there were no servants. Xabarra took off his jacket.

'You like lobster?' he said. 'One moment.'

He opened a side door off the kitchen. I looked through. There was a vast room with the same limestone floor. The furniture was sparse but not sparse enough to be minimalist. The wall about the fireplace was dominated by a massive stone frieze of what I took to be a Mayan woman. She was naked, kneeling, her face almost obliterated by the centuries. Directly in front of it, Alva was sitting on a rug. Her legs were curled under her. She was reading and her long hair hid her face. She looked beautiful and elegant and one of a piece with all the other beautiful things in that house. Xabarra called her name softly and she lifted her head and fixed him with a gentle, quizzical look. He smiled.

'Alva, we have a guest. Perhaps you could help us in the kitchen.'

She put down her book and Xabarra held the door for her. I waited for recognition to dawn in her eyes, but it was clear that she did not remember me. Her handshake was light and cool. Her smile of welcome seemed genuine but there was a distance about her. She seemed very far away. She asked me if I had come far, told me how she liked New York in the autumn. Her conversation, like her manner, had a certain remoteness to it. She asked me if I would like a drink. I asked for a whiskey. She went back into the other room and returned with a bottle of Paddy. I sipped my whiskey and watched as she prepared a salad and set the table.

Xabarra went into a store-room and returned with three lobsters. He plunged them into boiling water and I heard the tiny shriek of steam escaping from their shells. It seemed an act of deliberate cruelty, though I had done it myself many times, and I noted the way that Alva looked up, the calm expression momentarily replaced by a small frown.

I had eaten many meals in many strange places but something about that evening made it the strangest of all. Xabarra was cultured, humorous, but above all totally unreadable. I had no sense that I was being probed, yet I seemed to reveal more and more of myself as the evening went on. For his part, he told me that he was from near Oaxaca in Central Mexico. His parents were Zapotecs. He said there were millions of Zapotecs in that region, living in poverty and speaking a language that had never even been transcribed.

'When I was young,' he said, 'I asked my father why we never sang songs in Zapotec. He said there were no songs in Zapotec. When I asked him why, he looked at me and said, "What is there to sing about?"'

Throughout the meal, Alva sat quietly, only joining in when we talked about photography. She obviously knew what she was talking about and I saw Xabarra talking to her with the look of the master watching a pupil perform. She was incurious about anything apart from that. The evening seemed brittle and glittering with the cracking of lobster shells, the Tokaj in fine crystal glasses. I felt that I was walking a tightrope, but I didn't know why. My persona as art enthusiast and minor dealer stood up to scrutiny as far as it went and no direct questions were asked. At the end of the meal, Xabarra asked me how much I wanted for the photograph.

'I'm authorized to ask three hundred thousand dollars for it.'

He raised his eyebrows.

'I'm surprised. I had the impression that you were the principal.'

'I'm afraid the principal wishes to remain anonymous,' I said.

'There is something curious about this,' he said. 'I only know three or four men in Europe who would be interested in a work like that, and none of them would sell it for any reason. So I am wondering why it is available now, if there is something that I should be aware of?'

'I can assure you,' I said, injecting a little frost into my voice, 'that the provenance of the picture is beyond reproach.'

In fact, I knew that he wasn't accusing me of shady dealing, but his antennae were telling him that there was something out of the ordinary about the whole thing. He bowed his head slightly and smiled.

'Of course, of course,' he said airily. 'I didn't mean to imply any impropriety. It's just that, as you may understand, Jack, when a group of men are collectors, there is a kind of telepathy between them regarding the objects of their desire, and there is a puzzling lack of that telepathy with this work. I suppose I should be glad that you are not making us bid against each other. I accept your price. Will you take a cheque now?'

'That would be fine,' I said, hoping that it would provide an opportunity to talk to Alva on my own. Xabarra patted his pockets and a frown crossed his face.

'Excuse me, Jack,' he said, 'I seem to have left my chequebook upstairs.' He moved swiftly to the door, glanced at Alva, who was making coffee at the far end of the kitchen, then was gone. I got up and moved casually down the kitchen. Alva was still standing with her back to me. Now that I had my moment, words seemed to desert me. Standing behind her, I could see the nape of her neck. It made her seem vulnerable, more girlish than the poised woman I had seen earlier. When she spoke, she kept her back to me so that I could barely hear her, or believe what I had heard.

'How is Paolo, Jack?'

'Paolo?' I repeated stupidly.

'Yes.'

'You knew me all along?'

There must have been something dubious in my voice, a suggestion that she could not have maintained such a sustained deception. For the first time, she turned to face me. There was something else in her eyes now. I felt that I was the one being tested, that my quality was being measured.

'It wasn't that hard to hide it, Jack. People in my position learn habits of concealment. You didn't answer. Quickly please, Jack. He will be back in a minute.'

I hesitated, remembering my promise to Paolo.

'He's good,' I lied.

'Then why didn't he come?'

'What do you mean?'

'Why didn't he come to rescue me? That's why you're here, isn't it?'

The corner of her mouth curled up a little when she said the word 'rescue', a small, cynical gesture. My first thought was that this situation was a lot more complicated than I had thought. My second thought was that Xabarra had poisoned more than her blood. But when I looked at her, she was smiling again. A distant smile, but the distant smile of someone recollecting a pleasant memory.

'It is good to see you, though, Jack.'

'I didn't think you would remember.'

'Of course I remember. I had just lost my mother. I remember going to bed at night and listening to you and Paolo talking downstairs. I remember thinking that things were all right because you were there. But now . . . I argued with him very badly before I left. I probably don't deserve to be rescued.'

She must have seen the look on my face.

'Don't look at me like that, Jack.' There was a tone of authority in her voice. 'This is not a case of a spoiled little girl running off to make a point in a childish argument. Paolo and I have serious differences.'

75

It was the moment when I should have forgotten what Paolo had said and told her what had happened to him. But I didn't have the chance. She shoved the coffee tray into my hands and pushed me towards the table. When Xabarra came back in, I was half-way across the floor. He looked quickly between us. There was something eager and unsettling about his glance, as if he was hungry for signs of something untoward. Then he handed me a envelope and held out his hand. I shook it and put the envelope in my pocket.

'Now, Jack, a brandy.' The brandy was Mexican, not as fiery as French brandy, but beautifully smooth. As we drank it, he told me about land he had bought in Mexico, close to the Pacific, an area of deep ravines and bare desert.

'In fact,' he said, 'it was originally sub-tropical forest and we are in the process of restoring it. It is an area of some five square miles, so it is a big task.'

As he talked about his project, he became animated, almost excited in a schoolboyish way. He was intimate with the flora and fauna of the region, and although it seemed alien and harsh to me as he talked about cacti and lizards, I recognized the same feel that I had for the part of Scotland I lived in. As he talked, Alva put her hand over his and looked at him with what seemed like genuine fondness. More complications, I thought grimly. As Xabarra laughed out loud with enthusiasm for the project, I forced my mind back to the cripple he had left in a hospital bed in London, Paolo's face twisted in pain and loss. More than ever, I wished I had told Alva. Now it looked as if I wasn't going to have a chance. The telephone in the kitchen started to ring. Xabarra went to it. After a brief, murmured conversation, he turned to me.

'I am afraid there is something I have to attend to, Jack. Will you excuse me?'

'Of course,' I said.

'Alva normally goes to bed at this time.'

Obediently, the girl came over to him and kissed him lightly on the lips. She kissed me on the cheek.

'It was good to meet you, Jack,' she said. 'Perhaps we can have you out again.'

She glanced at Xabarra as she said this, but he didn't react. I watched her leave with a sinking feeling. It would be hard to get close to her again. Xabarra's manner had changed. He was businesslike now.

'I won't be able to drive you home,' he said, 'and it's hard to get a cab from here.'

He brought me down a corridor which led off the kitchen and into a vast garage. There were all the things you would expect in a rich man's garage – expensive cars, boats – but with the exception that Xabarra's collection were all design classics: there was an E-type Jag, a Ducati 916 superbike, even a Ford RS2000 with gleaming paintwork.

'I didn't know you were interested,' Xabarra said, seeing me looking them over. 'I have a weakness for classic European cars.' He touched the paintwork of the RS2000 lightly. I wondered what Liam would have made of it. I knew that he had done some rallying when he was younger.

'Sometimes I come down here and work on them,' Xabarra said, 'just to polish them. New cars don't have their depth of paintwork, the tones.'

We walked past rows of shining retro cars until we reached the front of the garage where there were more prosaic vehicles – several Jeeps and SUVs. He threw me the keys to one of the Jeeps.

'You can park the Jeep in any car park and give the keys to Eddie tomorrow, if you don't mind,' Xabarra said. He stepped forward and shook my hand.

'I'm always curious about people who collect Mapplethorpe,' he said softly. 'There is always something unsavoury about them, a hint of corruption if you like. You say you are not the collector, but I wonder. You have that hint of corruption about you, did you know that? Something that is not quite wholesome and gets worse as you get older.'

In the dim lights of the garage, his skin seemed yellow and his gaze took on a burning intensity. I felt as if I was being judged by an ancient primitive raptor. Uncomfortably, I muttered something and slid behind the wheel of the Jeep. I hit the ignition and drove off without looking back. I didn't want to see those eyes again. I didn't want that kind of judgement being made of me. It was too like the judgements I made of myself in the long nights.

The garage was ramped to the outdoors. Once you came out, you had to make a right turn and follow the driveway which seemed to go up to the front of the house them loop around back towards the gates. The property was bigger than I thought. I passed a stand of oak trees, giving way to lawns which ran down to a river. The gardens had that natural look which is only achieved by painstaking planning and labour. On the other side of the driveway there was a long low building which looked like a covered swimming-pool. I thought there might have been a gym attached as well. There were lights on over the pool area and I could see the water reflected on the ceiling. There were two cars and a van outside the pool. I drove past, but the building was hidden by a row of dogwoods. I swung round the corner and passed a rose garden, and then I was at the gate.

I swung through the gate with a sense of relief which left me feeling slightly ashamed. I had succeeded in extricating myself, but I hadn't got any further in the task of bringing Alva home to her father. What was more, Deirdre was right. She was, seemingly, a self-possessed young woman and I had no right to come barging into her life like some half-baked Galahad. I was brooding on my failure as I got to the end of the road and turned right towards the city. Normally I drive fairly fast, but this time I was distracted and depressed and I was driving slowly, trying to work out what I would say to the others when I got back, what I would say to Paolo on the phone. Otherwise I might have missed it. As it was, I had forgotten that Liam had been on our tail. But as I drove past a secluded park, I saw a car parked under the trees. It looked familiar. I backed up. It was Liam's Lincoln town car. It was half-slewed across the pavement and the doors lay open.

Eight

I resisted the impulse to jump out of the Jeep. I drove past the Lincoln slowly and carefully. It's a kind of restraint you learn in the way of keeping yourself alive, particularly when the reflexes aren't as good as they once were. There was no sign of anyone near it. I parked the Jeep around the corner and walked along the pavement, trying to look like an innocent citizen out for a late constitutional. As I did so, I felt the first cold drops of rain on my head. When I got to the car, I dropped the pretence. I started to examine it. The interior was empty, but there was blood on the seats. The steering-wheel was broken and part of the dash had been kicked in. It was amazing how much damage a desperate man could do. I checked the exterior. The Lincoln had been expertly tail-ended and driven off the road into the railings. I cursed myself inwardly. My assumption that Xabarra had been travelling without security had been wrong. His security had been with him all right, following at a discreet distance. They had picked up Liam as he tailed Xabarra, hit him hard and expertly and now they had him.

I forced myself to think. The rain had started to hammer down on the roof of the Lincoln. I remembered the van and the cars at Xabarra's swimming-pool. I hadn't seen any sign of damage on the van, but it was the right size to have driven the heavy town car off the road. My mind was working now. It seemed to be working the way it used to, coldly, calculating the odds. I knew what I was going to do. I was going to pull Liam out of that building. It always struck me as odd that I had always wanted to do good for the world in a vague way, but then found that my true talents lay in semi-mercenary covert operations, drained of anything that might be called morality.

I realized I had no weapon. I checked the interior of the car and found nothing. I popped the catch for the engine compartment. I checked under the insulation on the underside of the bonnet. It was a favourite hiding place and I struck lucky. The weapon I pulled out was a custom Glock and there were only two of them in the world. Liam and I had got them in the same place – a gunsmith's in what was then known as South-west Africa. I felt under the bonnet again and found a couple of ammunition pouches. The rain was thunderous and I was soaked through. It suited my purposes, though. I ran back to the Jeep and swung it into the road, gunning it towards the Xabarra estate. If Xabarra was the kind of man I thought him to be, then time wasn't on Liam's side.

I drove carefully along the wall of the Xabarra estate, trying to match what I had seen inside to the blank exterior wall. I turned the corner of the wall and drove until I had reached what I reckoned on being the most secluded part of the estate. Tall pine branches reached over the top of the wall, casting the wall into shadow. I reckoned that the rose garden was to the right. I could see a wire running along the top of the wall. An electric fence would have been a little bit vulgar in such surroundings, but I was reasonably sure it fed into some kind of touch-sensitive alarm. The camera, too, pointed along the top of the wall.

People trust walls in a way that is not necessarily justified. For every impenetrable stone wall, there are a hundred that are made simply from blocks. In fact, most exterior garden walls don't even have a cavity with two rows of blocks. On several occasions in Bosnia, I had seen a sniper carefully work out where his target was in a room and simply place his bullet in a spot on the wall.

The high-velocity round went through concrete like paper. The hit might not be in the head or heart, but with the kind of weapons those men were using, it didn't have to be.

The rain was still drumming off the roof of the Jeep, huge drops hitting the road and splashing upwards. It suited me. I engaged the four-wheel drive and put the front bumper of the Jeep against the wall. I started rocking the big vehicle against the wall, switching quickly from drive to reverse and back again, almost using the front of the Jeep like a hammer, tapping at the wall, loosening the mortar underneath the render, until I started to feel a little give in the wall. I wound down the window and looked out. As far as I could see, the wall was bowed five to six feet either side of the impact site, with the parapet remaining intact. I gave it a few more taps. The sound of the rain was deafening. Unless someone was standing directly behind the wall, they wouldn't hear the noise. The wall was looking battered now, with pieces of render knocked off and the blocks behind exposed. I reversed back six feet and hit the wall with one hard blow. The wall shuddered. I did the same thing again, hoping to knock through the wall while leaving the parapet intact. It worked. With a crash of concrete landing on the front of the Jeep, I was through. I ducked as a block starred the windscreen in front of me. I threw the Jeep into reverse. With a wrenching sound, I pulled it out and reversed it under the trees. There was a hole in the wall about eight feet long and four feet tall. I checked the Glock, knocked off the safety catch and slipped through.

Under the trees on the other side, it was much quieter, the sound of the rain muffled by the pine needles. Even so, I crept forward, moving quickly. There was no guarantee that I hadn't been spotted or that there wasn't some kind of surveillance at work in the garden. I reckoned I had a sixty per cent chance of having evaded detection. They might have body-heat detectors, movement sensors, but my experience was that complex electronic systems need teams of highly qualified people to operate them round the clock. It is difficult enough for an army to keep high-tech spookery up and running, harder by far for an individual. The one thing I was worried about was dogs, although I hadn't seen any sign of them when I was at the house. Still, I ran through the trees, determined to hold on to whatever element of surprise I had.

I reached the edge of the trees. I could see the lights of the swimming-pool complex on the other side of the lawns and the lights of the house beyond that. Behind the swimming-pool, I could see a boiler house. I put my head down and ran for it, my feet slipping in the wet and muddy grass, my breath coming in great gasps, almost blinded by the rain which streamed down my face. If there was anyone looking, I would be seen. I threw myself down in the shelter of the boiler house and waited for the shout of discovery, the flat report of shots. They didn't come. I picked myself up cautiously and tried the door of the boiler house. It was open. The room beyond the door was dimly lit. A big diesel boiler hummed in the corner, heating the water for the pool. Someone had been working on the building. The sheeting had been removed from the roof and there was heavy-duty cabling and electricians' tools on the floor. I looked for the maintenance passage that would take me under the pool. Once again, the floor of the passage was littered with debris and heavy cabling lay alongside, probably for a temporary supply for pumps and lights. I crept along the passage, the Glock ready in my hand. If I was lucky, there would be a manhole cover that would take me up into the pool area, enabling me to take them by surprise.

Underneath the pool, it seemed a strange, dank world, water under your feet, pumps humming, the drip of water. In places, the water was ankle-deep and the lights flickered eerily. There were obviously serious structural problems in the pool building. I found this a reassuring thought. Xabarra was a dark and dangerous man, but he was as vulnerable to bad contractors as the rest of us.

After a minute of two of clambering through builders' mess, I was under the pool. I could see the draining mechanism to my left but it took a minute or two to find what I was looking for, which was basically a steel pipe with a ladder bolted to it leading up to the pool floor level.

The access shaft was at the end of the passage. It was a nightmare of torn ducting, water pipes and cable. It took me several minutes to get through it, trying to stay away from bits of wiring that looked live. But as I got to the top, I could hear the sound of voices. First of all, the strange, over-inflected voice that I had heard on the phone, then two or three other men, all with what sounded like New Jersey accents. And then I heard a long, low moan which chilled me. The voice was Liam's, but whatever they had done had rendered it almost unrecognizable. In response to the moan, I heard the unmistakable sound of a boot against flesh. Liam gasped, then I heard a low stream of invective from him. I couldn't make out the Irish words, but at least, I thought grimly, he was still capable of defiance. The resistance earned him another few kicks. I got myself wedged in under the manhole cover and tried to work out the locations of the men. I realized they were still very close to the actual cover. The pool must have been overflowing. A steady stream of water was running through the manhole cover down over my neck and shoulders, which made it difficult to hear what was going on, but as far as I could make out, the man with the formal voice who was addressed by the others as Saul was planning to bring Liam up to the main house. I put my shoulder gently against the manhole cover and tried to shift it. I needed to know where each of them were standing. The cover wouldn't move. Cursing, I tried again, with a little more force. I heard Liam moan again and the sound of something being dragged across the pool tiling, Saul's voice receding.

I thought quickly. It would take me too long to get back to the boiler house. The hole in the wall couldn't stay undiscovered for long. I tried the manhole cover again, with no luck. I realized that the stream of water was concealing a small hole intended for a key to lift the cover. I put my eye to it. I saw one polished black shoe and a section of trouser cuff. The reason I couldn't lift the cover was that someone was standing on it. I could hear two voices. They were talking quite softly, which probably meant that they were standing close together. I had to move them, and there was no time for subtley. As fast as I could, I shinned down the ladder, taking skin from my hands and tearing my shirt on a jagged piece of pipe. At the bottom, I found what I was looking for: a wooden pallet standing on dry ground. I stood on it, then pulled a piece of the heavy cabling towards me. I couldn't be sure if it was live, but I thought I could feel the power in my hands, the lethal buzz of a high-voltage power line. Two sections of the pipe were joined with a heavy socket arrangement. There were two large clips on either side of the socket. Making sure that my hands were dry, I slowly unclipped one and then the other. I pulled the two halves apart. There were heavy copper couplngs in each. I weighed them up, then laid one carefully on the ground and threw the other end into the stream of water running down from the manhole. Nothing happened.

I picked up the other half, feeling I was wasting my time. It looked dead. Almost casually, I tossed it towards the water. Time seemed to pause. Then there was a loud bang, a blue flash. I felt the pallet being tugged out from under me and I spilled on to the floor. The air filled with acrid smoke and a harsh metallic smell and debris crashed on to the floor.

I got to my feet cautiously. Whitish ash was drifting gently down from the ceiling. I started up the ladder. It felt warm to my touch. The chaos in the shaft was even worse. It was dark, but some light was getting into the shaft from above. When I got close to the top, I saw that the manhole cover had been blown off. I emerged cautiously into the half-light. There was a sickening smell of burnt flesh. One man lay beside the open shaft. He was

85

wearing a suit, but his face was blackened and it was impossible to tell what age he was or what he looked like. As I examined him, a small orange thread of flame licked along his lapel and then went out again. I looked around for the other man, but couldn't see him for a minute. Then I saw a shape floating face-down in the pool at least ten yards away. I started to wonder what voltage had been flowing through the junction that I had unclipped. I wondered again when I saw that the metal manhole cover was embedded in the wall.

I opened the door of the pool. One of the cars that had been there was gone. I headed for the house at a run. In other circumstances I would have spared a thought for the two dead men I had left in the pool, but my mind was running cold and clear with a kind of deadly elation, the kind of unreflecting sharpness you need in circumstances of maximum danger. I would think about the two men afterwards. Perhaps I would find myself filled with remorse. Perhaps I would be better saving my remorse for somebody who needed it.

Coming up behind the house, I realized just how large it was. And suddenly the architecture started to acquire a mazy, unreliable quality that I hadn't noticed before. I ran along the back of it, looking for a door, but seemed to be presented with blank surfaces at every turn. I was running so hard through the blinding rain that I didn't see I was approaching the sunken entrance to the underground garage. I went over the edge and hit the concrete ramp hard. I was dragging one leg behind me when I got up, a feeling of loose cartilage in the knee.

The silence of the garage almost stopped me in my tracks. I felt like some uncouth barbarian, dripping and bloodied, in the warm hum of temperature-controlled environmental heating. More than ever, it seemed a shrine to a certain kind of twentieth-century motoring, the edgy, pure kind. There was a smell of fine lubricants and chrome polish. I had reached the door when I hesitated. I gave myself five minutes in the garage. By the time I left, my fingers were sore and cut and I was sweating. With the Glock in my hand, I belted up the corridor that led towards the kitchen. It was empty. The wine glasses from earlier on were sitting on the sink. It had only been an hour. I opened the door that led on to the big room where Alva had been earlier. It was empty. Again I became aware of the size of the house. They could be anywhere. I looked down. Blood from some cut or other was tracked across the limestone floor. The fire in the big fireplace was very welcoming. The stone-faced Mayan woman above the fire looked as if she had seen it all before. I suddenly felt very tired, the challenge in front of me suddenly felt very daunting, far beyond what I was capable of. I knew that I wouldn't go back. It wasn't a matter of courage or pride, but of existence. If I turned back, then I turned back on everything. It was too late in my life to recover. If I made an honest account of my life, I hadn't much apart from people like Liam. People who inhabited their lives fully.

As this flashed through my mind, I thought I heard my name spoken. Then I heard it again. I looked up. There was a gallery running around the room about twenty feet from the ground. Alva was kneeling on it, calling my name through the balustrade. She was wearing jeans and a T-shirt and had her hair scraped back in a ponytail. She looked like an ordinary young woman and that, above all, gave me heart, the very normality of the way she looked. I was starting to realize the way things worked around Xabarra, the way you got sucked into the dead heart of things, the way it worked on your own mind. I looked up at her with a stupid expression on my face, as if I had been visited with salvation from above.

'Come up,' she said in an urgent whisper, 'come on up here.'

I believe I smiled.

When I got to her, Alva eyed me suspiciously, as though she had made up her mind to trust me, and then had started to

87

doubt her judgement. I started to hit her with urgent phrases, letting the professionalism take over, reassuring her.

'Where is Liam?'

'Your friend?' she said hesitantly, as if she had seen him and did not like what had been done to him.

'Yes, Alva,' I said, 'and I know he is hurt but he is the strongest man I ever met. If he is still alive, I'm taking him out of here.'

'He didn't look so tough to me.'

Again there was that cynical turn to the corner of the mouth, making her seem momentarily ugly. I started to say something, then stopped myself. What did she know about Liam or what he had done? She was still a teenager after all, I reminded myself.

'Come on,' I said urgently. 'We've got to find him before they do any more damage.'

She ran down a small staircase and pointed towards a door leading off the west side of the big room.

'Down there,' she said, 'go to the end of the corridor. It's the big room at the end. You'll have to go on your own.'

'Why?'

'I won't go there,' she said.

She wrapped her arms around herself and frowned. There was something worrying about that frown. It was like a little girl's frown when she doesn't get her own way. I took her by the shoulders and turned her until she was looking directly at me.

'I'm going to ask you to do something, Alva,' I said firmly, 'and I want you to do what I tell you. I want you to sit here and wait for me to come back. Will you do that?'

With a conscious effort of will, I saw her shake herself free of the little-girl persona.

'Why, Jack?'

'You're coming with me when I get Liam.'

She looked at me. Suddenly my words seemed ridiculous, paternalistic to the point of parody. I saw this reflected in her eyes and for the first time I think I realized that Alva had left Italy with Xabarra because she had wanted to.

'Do you have an escape plan?' she asked. I told her quickly what I had planned. She nodded.

'It might work' she said. 'Go and get your friend. You won't hurt him, though, will you?'

I realized it was Xabarra she was talking about. I didn't answer. As I went through the little door, I turned and saw her watching me and realized that I didn't have the slightest idea of what was going through her head.

The door led into a small passage which led downwards and round, with steps at intervals. I realized that I had been spending a lot of my time underground lately. I had never particularly liked being underground. I was reminded of the Victorians, the way there was a fad for connecting a coffin to a bell on the surface in case the corpse wasn't really dead. Something about this corridor made me wish there was a bellpull I could ring so that somebody would come and rescue me.

Xabarra had been thorough when he built this little diversion for himself. At the end of the corridor was one closed door and one open one. I went through the open one. It led into a small gallery which in turn overlooked what was essentially a large cell. Xabarra was in the cell with the man called Saul. There was very little furniture in it. Some electrical equipment in the corner and a few kitchen chairs. It seemed large and warm and pleasantly lit. It was the kind of room you wanted to warn people against. The kind of room that you took the first steps towards when you started chipping away at individual liberties, at things like free speech and the rights of suspects, the messy paraphernalia of justice. There was no confusion in rooms like this. Everything was very stark. Especially for the man at the centre of the room whose whole existence had been reduced to pain. The torture they were using on Liam was centuries old and was almost laughable in its simplicity, although those who have been subjected to it have attested that the pain is indescribable. They were inflicting the torture known as bastinado on him, whereby the victim is suspended upside-down and the soles of the feet are beaten with a flexible rod. The man known as Saul was holding a length of plastic sewer rod in his hand and Xabarra was standing with his back to the wall, rubbing his chin like a terrible connoisseur of pain.

Something in me snapped at the sight of Liam hanging upside-down, barefoot, his face contorted in agony. Deirdre Mellows would have called it macho in me, that I cared as much about the humiliation that was being inflicted on my friend as the pain. A roar of anger in a voice I didn't quite recognize burst from my mouth and I spun towards the door. As I reached the door, several things happened very quickly. I heard Alva's voice distorted and amplified by the corridor, shouting, 'Jack, look out!' As she did so, I instinctively dived towards the ground and felt rather than heard bullets stitching the air over my head. As I hit the floor, a second burst hit the doorframe, sending splinters flying into the air, with one large shard ripping into my cheek just below my eye. I managed to bring the Glock up and fire an unaimed burst as I half-rose to my feet. The man who came through the door had obviously been running full tilt when my bullets hit him in the chest and killed him. The momentum kept him going and the weight of his body slammed me across the room, arterial blood drenching me almost instantly. I emptied the Glock through the open doorway to discourage anyone from following him and glanced to my left in time to see Liam swinging his body through the air. He had obviously taken a few swings to build up momentum and now he turned the weight of his body towards Xabarra and Saul, who were standing with their backs to him, trying to work out what was going on. Liam had his hands tied behind his back, which meant he had no weapons. I'd forgotten about the Glasgow kiss. With the full force of his body weight behind him,

Liam propelled himself forwards and headbutted Xabarra in the back of the skull with terrible force.

Saul looked at his boss, dazed on the ground, then looked at Liam. You could see the fear in his face. Liam's features were streaked with blood, but he shook his head and howled in triumph, a terrible, broken, exultant sound that sent Saul scampering towards his stunned boss. I started towards the door again. This time I came face to face with another member of the household, a tall, thin man who said something in Spanish as he tried to bring his gun to bear. I grabbed his gun hand and he grabbed mine and we struggled like that for a while. He tried to knee me and I sank my teeth into his gun hand, but he wouldn't let go. I couldn't bring my own gun into play, so I let him force it downwards until it was pointing towards the ground. A bit of fine tuning and it was pointing at his foot. I shot him through the top of his foot. He yelled as much in surprise as pain and let go. I clubbed him on the back of the head twice with my gun hand and he went down. I remembered when I started in this business that I had the idea that you could knock someone out with ease and they would recover from it with equal ease. Then, on a routine operation which got rough, a young colleague got hit over the head with a rifle butt. As far as I know, he is still a paraplegic with the mental capacity of a five-year-old. The man groaned once and slumped into unconsciousness. I didn't wait around to see if he was still breathing. I looked up and I could see Alva silhouetted in the doorway at the end of the corridor. There was a stillness about her that I could not interpret.

I burst into the cell, but Xabarra and Saul were gone, drag marks on the floor leading towards another small door that I hadn't seen. I had no doubt that reinforcements would arrive any minute. Liam was breathing steadily and only glanced at me. I could see he was engaged in husbanding his resources. He knew we needed to get out of that place, and he knew I couldn't carry him far.

Xabarra and Saul were nothing if not efficient. A well-oiled pulley lowered Liam to the ground. The shackles on his ankles and wrists snapped off. It occurred to me that this grotesque thing had been designed for use on a regular basis. Liam got to his feet. Or rather he tried to get to his feet but he groaned in pain and sank to the ground again. He forced himself up again and managed to take his weight on his damaged feet, but he was standing like a new-born foal, unsteady and uncertain and capable of a few halting steps at most. I handed him the gun and slung him over my shoulders in a fireman's lift. I felt the weakness in my own legs almost immediately and realized I should make some ground straight away. I wasn't going to be able to carry him for long.

Like that, we staggered down the corridor. I set my target as the middle of the corridor and then I aimed for the end. I used to believe that mental discipline could enable you to do almost anything. But as I got older, I realized that that theory belonged with the one that says positive thinking can cure you of cancer. Sometimes the machine just can't take it and that is all there is to it. We reached the end of the corridor and fell in a tangled heap on the limestone floor, smearing more blood on to the stone. Slowly we got each other to our feet. I became conscious of Alva watching us. Liam looked up at her, staring at her with that strange, appraising look he shared with his sister, the one that gave you the uncomfortable feeling that your very genetic material was being appraised. He looked away from her.

'You'll never get it out,' he said.

'Sorry?' she said, sounding confused.

'The blood, on the floor. Limestone's porous, you see. The stain'll never come out. The good floor is ruined.'

She stared at him in disbelief. At that moment Liam looked more like a walking corpse than a man. As I looked at him, I realized that a lot of the blood on the floor was dripping from the place on his left hand where his fingernails used to be.

'It's a lovely floor though,' he said, by way of an appreciative afterthought.

'You'd better go,' she said, trying to regain whatever equilibrium was left in the conversation. I decided on a gamble.

'We can't,' I said. 'Liam can't walk and I can't carry him.' She didn't seem to question the fact that he couldn't walk. I wondered how much she knew of what went on in that cell. I didn't want to think about it. I had once known a policeman, a decent man, who was a superintendent in Castlereagh Barracks, where torture was practised on a regular basis. I reasoned that there was no way he could not have known about it, and it shadowed our relationship. If I had been brave about it, I would have asked him straight out. But I couldn't bear the thought of seeing the lie in his eyes, or worse again, hearing the justification in his voice.

'You want me to help you?'

'If you don't, we'll both end up back in there,' I said, looking back at the corrridor. Dread seemed to seep into the room through the open door.

'It's all one to me what you do,' Liam said, 'but this is a wild bad house for a lassie like you to be in.'

'I'll help you as far as the garage,' she said after a moment's thought. 'But we have to go now. Before he comes.'

She allowed Liam to put his arm over her shoulder and he put his other arm around my shoulders. After a few steps we realized that for Liam to put his feet on the floor was the equivalent, in terms of pain, of sticking your hand in a furnace. After that, we carried him. Alva took her share of the weight and she did not complain.

'What's in the garage?' Liam said as we entered the corridor between the kitchen and the garage.

'A surprise,' I said.

We almost didn't make it. As we reached the end of the corridor, Alva was labouring. Liam stopped us.

93

'There's only one way to do this,' he said. He dropped to his knees and began to crawl forward. There was logic in what he was doing, keeping the damaged and screaming nerve-endings in his feet from contact with the floor, but I couldn't bear to watch him. Alva must have felt the same. She darted forward before I could move and put her arm around her shoulder, gently coaxing him upright again. There were tears in her eyes. Together, we got him into the garage.

'Look over there, Liam,' I said. 'There's our ticket out of here.'

'Jesus Mary and Joseph, am I dreaming?' he said. 'A bloody RS2000 in full rally spec. Car must be nearly thirty years old. Jesus, Jack, I used to rally one of these.' He took an unconscious step forwards and winced with pain.

'Is she going?' he asked.

'I hot-wired her earlier,' I said, 'and there's juice in the battery. I reckon she'll go. She'd better.' I heard a shout in Spanish from the direction of the kitchen. The hunt was on.

'Get in,' I said urgently. He managed to lever himself into the driver's seat. I turned to Alva.

'I don't know what to say to you,' I said, talking fast. 'I'm supposed to get you out of here, but we could all get killed in that car. If I leave you here, and Xabarra knows that you helped me . . .'

'He wouldn't harm me,' she said. 'Haven't you got it yet, Jack? He loves me.'

I was lost for words. Any moment now, the pursuit would arrive and it would all be over. But Liam knew what to do. He leaned out of the window of the RS2000 for all the world like somebody on his way to a country disco in 1976.

'You want to see what an Irishman can do in a rally car, Miss?' He gave her what he fondly imagined was a winning smile, but which in fact was more a bloody leer. She smiled.

'I might,' she said. 'I might just give it a try.' She swung into the bucket seat and I slid across the two of them into the space where the back seats used to be, now more or less occupied by a roll bar. I glanced through the back windscreen. Three or four men had charged into the garage and were looking around wildly. I watched in disbelief as Alva settled herself primly in the passenger seat and looked to Liam expectantly. He fiddled with the ignition wires. Nothing happened. A shout went up from one of the men and almost immediately a bullet shattered the wing mirror. As Liam worked at the wires, a Mini Cooper S beside us took a full magazine, rocking on its chassis. I realized what was wrong. Liam's damaged hand couldn't hold the wires properly. I dived over the front seats and connected the wires for him and the engine burst into life. There was real beauty in that sound. I knew that rally cars now went far faster and had engine-management systems and telemetry and all sorts of things. But this was a pure engine note, greedy for fast tarmac and slippery forest tracks, and Liam didn't waste any time. The rear of the car fishtailed as he floored the accelerator. The adrenalin was flowing now, although he winced and gritted his teeth as his foot hit the pedal when he double-declutched. The engine pitch rose to an almost unbearable level in the enclosed space of the garage and the men who had come in hesitated for a moment at the strange, archaic-looking automobile, painted bright yellow, that was suddenly in their midst.

One of them took a glancing blow from the wing of the car that threw him into the concrete wall. The rest of them dived for cover. Liam hit the accelerator.

There was only a narrow passage between the parked cars, a doglegged narrow passage that you would be nervous of taking at more than fifteen miles an hour. Liam went through the gaps at close to sixty, using the handbrake to drift the compact car sideways towards the exit ramp. He threw the gear lever into third as we hit the ramp and accelerated. As we hit the top of the ramp, I remembered that I wasn't strapped in. The impact smashed my head against the roof of the car. On the way down, the roll bar caught the base of my spine. Dazed, I didn't realize that we were airborne. We hit the ground with another bonejarring impact. I thought I was seeing stars until I realized that the sumpguard had hit the ground, leaving a blazing trail of sparks behind us. Liam went for a gear and missed it. He tried again and missed again. The engine note dropped. He turned to Alva. I realized that it was his injured left hand again.

'Can you work a stick shift?' he shouted over the engine noise. She nodded. 'Can you change a gear each time I call it, fast, without mistakes?'

'I come from Turin,' she shouted, as though this was sufficent to prove her virtuosity.

'Two!' Liam shouted. Alva clicked the gear lever into place. The car leaped forward. We sped past the swimming-pool, the complex now dark and empty. We passed the rose garden and my spirits rose, only to sink again when we turned the corner towards the gate. Two SUVs were pulled across the entrance and there were armed men behind each of them. Liam threw the car sideways, battling with the wheel, the manœuvre made more difficult since he couldn't use the handbrake. The rear wheels span, struggling for purchase as the car slid towards the barricade. I heard a bullet strike the bodywork somewhere and then the tyres bit and the car leaped forward.

'Two, three, four!' Liam yelled in quick succession, Alva snicking the gear into place each time. I knew that the thoroughbred gearbox would be unforgiving. One wrong gear would strip the box, leaving us helpess. But that wasn't the immediate problem. The men who had been in the garage had been busy. They had blocked the driveway with a small truck. An SUV was coming up the drive fast behind us. There was no way out. At least I thought there was no way out. Then I saw Liam eying the swimming-pool's glass wall.

'For Christ's sake, Liam,' I moaned, hiding my face in my hands.

'Three!' Liam shouted, and I heard the snick as Alva dropped the gearstick into third. The engine screamed. I kept my head in my hands. I didn't see the glass wall of the swimming-pool approaching at close to seventy miles an hour. I didn't see the lawn mower half-hidden in the grass that clipped the Escort's front wheels ten yards short of the wall. Then I looked up.

It is a cliché of car crashes and accidents in general that everything moves in slow motion. I've found the slow-motion part doesn't start until you realize that the accident becomes inevitable. I felt that I was able to sit back and watch with detached interest as the out-of-control Escort hit the glass wall and giant shards of glass twisted and turned in the air, the small pieces drumming down on the bodywork of the car like a deadly hail. I saw the edge of the pool and heard Liam cursing as he struggled with the wheel. I saw Alva's face, pale in the lightless interior of the car and heard the small noise that she made, then I saw Liam take his hands from the wheel, reach one hand to the ceiling to hit the emergency fuel kill switch, and then cross his hands calmly on his chest the way you're supposed to in case a wildly spinning wheel breaks your arms.

And then the car was in the air over the pool and we waited. There was a crash. I bounced upwards. I heard brakes screeching, then another heavy impact on one side of the car and a lesser impact on the other, and finally silence as the fuel-starved engine cut out. We sat there in the darkness.

'There's no water in this pool,' Liam said, with a faint air of disapproval, as though he had fully expected to be sinking through ten feet of water, and felt that somebody had let the side down.

He was right. We were in the deep end of the pool, having slid down the gradually shelving shallow end. I reckoned that when I blew the power source I must have triggered the sluice and allowed the water to run out of the pool. It seemed very quiet in the car. The hot engine block ticked. Alva wound down the window. I could hear a man walking over a pile of broken glass, trying to move cautiously. A voice called out softly in Spanish. Another voice answered. Liam hit the fuel cutoff again, turning it on. He turned the starter. The noise seemed incredibly loud in the empty pool. But nothing happened. He turned the ignition off and waited. I knew he was waiting for the fuel to be pumped down to the engine, and that there was nothing else to be done, but I stlll felt like screaming at him. I couldn't understand why our pursuers weren't on to us, why they hadn't reacted to the engine noise. Liam turned the key and the starter whined again. I peered up nervously towards the lip of the pool above my head. If it was me, I would stand on the poolside and fire down through the roof of the car. But they weren't me and that wasn't what they did.

Instead, they came walking down the pool from the shallow end in a row, like gunslingers, carrying their weapons loosely. I realized that they had no way of knowing that the car was still working, that sooner or later, if we didn't flood it, the engine would start. Liam tried the starter again. I could visualize the fuel pump pushing the amber fluid through the fuel lines. In my mind's eye I could see the blue flash leaping the contacts of the spark plug. I mentally tried to put fuel and spark together. Then I stopped thinking and loaded up the Glock. The men stopped and stood in a semicircle, facing the car, then started to bring their guns level.

Liam said afterwards that if they hadn't been so worried about the choreography of it, they would have had us, if they hadn't heard some overblown film soundtrack playing in their heads as they strode down the slope towards us. They had us at their mercy, he said, and they should have killed us.

Instead, the engine caught and as it did so I leaned over Alva's shoulder and stuck my left hand holding the Glock through the open window and opened fire. They could still have had us, if they hadn't suddenly become very aware of the fact that they had no cover. One of them looked back over his shoulder, dropped his gun and started to run. Another tried to scale the sheer, slippery wall of the pool. I directed my fire at the three remaining men. The engine misfired and then caught again. The noise in the enclosed area was deafening. Then Liam slipped the clutch, the car once again stepping out sideways as he tried to feed the power evenly to the wheels. The rubber squealed on the pool tiles, then caught. We leaped forwards, the exhaust crackling, the wheel twitching as Liam fought to keep the power under control on the slick tiles, the car dancing in a way which unnerved the three remaining gunmen to such an extent that they dived for cover, one of them diving the wrong way, so that we felt a bump and heard a shriek as the car went over his legs.

If Liam felt any concern for him, it didn't show on his face. The car hit the top of the pool where it sloped gradually up to ground level and he handbraked it level with the remaining glass wall of the pool. I didn't shut my eyes this time and a quick glance at Alva was enough to tell her to drop a gear. This time we hit the glass hard and true and we were half-way across the adjoining lawn before the first shards started to hit the ground. I saw a few ineffectual muzzle flashes behind us and then we were back on the driveway, where it looped around the back of the swimming-pool. Liam slowed.

'Is there a back exit to this place?'

'Locked,' Alva said.

'I know how we're going to get out,' I said. I levered myself up to get a good look at the terrain in front of us. Half-way between the swimming-pool and the gate, I saw the rose garden and the copse of trees beside it.

'See the roses?' I said. 'There's a gap between the rose garden and the trees. At the very end there is a hole in the wall maybe big enough to take a small car if you hit it in exactly the right place.'

'Maybe big enough?' Liam repeated after me. I shrugged. We

were running out of options. Liam looked at me for a moment, then nodded to Alva. She dropped the car into first gear and snicked it into second as we hit the grass at sixty-five and accelerating hard.

When I look back on that night, I seem to see the last bit in slow motion. The rose garden was still covered in late blooms, huge and pink as they loomed out of the night. Liam put the Escort into the gap between the outer rose hedge and the trees. What I remembered was the smell of wet earth and roses as the speeding car stripped the blooms from the hedge. It is a smell I will carry to my grave. Liam remembered something different. As the car crashed through the hedging, he said, it seemed to carry a cloud of pink rose petals with it, the air of the car's passing pushing it in front of us, a storm of roses. If Alva remembered any such image, she did not share it with us.

I started to tell Liam about the hole I had knocked in the wall. But I had overestimated the distance between the rose garden and the wall. And I hadn't realized that we would exit ten yards away from the hole in the wall. I heard Liam curse as he reached for the handbrake to try and slide the car sideways. It was an exuberant curse, the kind of curse you heard from Liam when he was on the edge, bearing down on a solid wall at seventy miles an hour in a lightweight rally car. Then, in milliseconds, the tone of his voice changed as his injured hand refused purchase on the well-sprung rally driver's handbrake. He spun the wheel wildly without slowing the forward momentum, then, quick as thought, I saw Alva haul the lever upwards. Liam whooped as the car did a one hundred and eighty degree spin, turning to face the way we had come, the rear wheels still turning flat out and fighting to slow the momentum, the engine at peak revs, the slide slowing to fifty, to forty until it seemed we were moving in slow motion and then we reached the point of equilibrium and there was the faintest of metallic noises that I somehow sensed over the crescendo of the engine, as the rear bumper of the RS2000 touched the wall with the lightest of touches. Liam heard it too and he turned to me with the old grin on his face, defiance and joy mixed in there. Then Alva snicked the gear lever into second and we leaped forward again, back into what was left of the roses.

'There's a hole in the wall about ten yards up,' I shouted over the din. Liam nodded. He only had to look at Alva for her to apply the handbrake.

This time we emerged in the right place, at half the speed. Liam didn't hesitate. The RS2000 shot neatly through the hole in the wall and slewed sideways on to the road. Alva slipped smoothly through the gears into fifth. Suddenly we were on a paved road with road signage slipping past, going far too fast with an injured man at the wheel, but free. I saw Alva look back towards the house. Relief, defiance and regret seemed to flicker across her face. Then an emotion which seemed like fear. Not fear of Xabarra, I thought. Then I saw her hand slip down beside her to clasp the small bag she had brought with her. Not fear of Xabarra, I thought, not any kind of physical fear, but perhaps a psychic one. William Burroughs maintained that heroin altered the molecular structure of the body and people thought it a writer's fancy, although science is now beginning to suggest he might have had a point.

Alva lifted the bag and held it in her lap, her hands working nervously at the surface of it. Then two things happened. The car suddenly slowed and veered towards the side of the road. I looked anxiously at Liam.

'I'm sorry,' he said apologetically, 'I don't think I can drive any more.'

Berating myself for my inattention, I climbed out through Alva's side and we helped him to slide over into the passenger seat. The driver's footwell was slick with blood and I could see that Liam was lightheaded to the point of unconsciousness. I was about to get into the driver's seat when Alva stopped me.

'I can drive,' she said, tentatively. She put the bag carefully between the seats and took the wheel. As I got back in again, the second thing happened. My cellphone started to ring. I looked at it. I thought I recognized the code that preceded the caller's number. It was a Virginia code. I thought I had better take the call. When that number came up, most people did. I pressed the answer button.

'Hello, John,' I said.

'Hello, Jack.' John Stone's voice was grave, urbane. I waited for what he had to say.

'I hear you're on the East Coast,' he said.

'News travels fast,' I said, regretting the glibness as soon as the words left my mouth.

'Not fast enough,' Stone said. 'It might have been an idea to call me before you embarked on your current course of action, Jack.' I felt cold. Firstly I wondered how Stone knew what was going on. Secondly I wondered why he was concerned.

'I didn't know you would be interested, John.'

'I wish I wasn't.' His gravelly laughter didn't have a lot of humour in it. 'I would like to talk to you.'

'When?'

' What are you doing for breakfast?'

I looked at my watch. In five hours' time, it would be morning.

'I'll be ready to eat,' I said.

'You always are.' There was a little more warmth in his laughter now. 'Meet me on the corner of St Mark's and First Avenue,' he said. 'I know a place.'

'Trouble?' Liam said, after I had hung up.

'John Stone,' I said. He arched an eyebrow. He had met Stone before, and knew what was involved. But what interested me was Alva's reaction. Her head half-turned as though she recognized the name, then she turned back to the road with what seemed to me like a studied casualness. I sighed, wishing I had foisted a less complicated young woman on myself. I saw Liam's eyes close. It was an instinct I had seen in people before, the body enforcing shutdown in the face of trauma. Most people fought it, fear and adrenalin forcing alertness on them, but Liam abandoned himself to it, letting sleep take over. I could feel my own eyes closing as Alva smoothly floored the accelerator, driving fast and expertly. It was the first time I had seen her relaxed, unselfconscious in the most profound way, flicking the thoroughbred car through the growing traffic with ease. I felt my own eyes start to close over.

Nine

When I first met John Stone, I took him for an amiable diplomat, a man working out his last years towards retirement in a politically sensitive but comfortable posting at the US embassy in Dublin. After a few years, and particularly after the Sirius affair in which I had involved Liam and Deirdre, I knew that there was a lot more to Stone. You thought of Richelieu or Mazarin, the original *éminence grise*. A subtle and dangerous man with a vast understanding of power and the uses of power. He considered himself a patriot, while being aware that infinite corruption was one of the consequences of patriotism. 'Look at Christianity, Islam, Communism,' he said to me once. 'Isn't it odd how many people have been slaughtered in the name of abstractions?' 'How about capitalism?' I had asked him. The comment earned me a withering look and a growled aside to the effect that capitalism wasn't an abstraction.

He had told me about serving in Vietnam as an intelligence officer. How he had directed fire on to defenceless villages. He went back to Vietnam every year, and had become a student of that society and its Confucian values. It was less a penance, I thought, than an exercise in forcing himself to contemplate the terrible consequences of his own actions and still be able to justify what he had done. Each year I saw him, I thought that the justification became harder and harder.

I was standing on the corner of St Mark's Place and First

Avenue with rain whipping across my face. I felt edgy and badly slept. Jesus had called his doctor for Liam. He had tended to him with the same impassiveness that he had shown when he signed the death certificate for the dead Puerto Rican. He reported no bones broken in the feet, but severe lacerations and torn tendons in his left hand. He had given him some painkillers and told him to stay in bed for two weeks. Jesus had given Alva a room. She disappeared into it with her bag and when she emerged half an hour later she seemed abstracted, only peripherally aware of the people around her. Jesus watched her with a hooded look I couldn't read.

I could remember telling Jesus that I would move Alva in the morning. Then I remember sitting down on the sofa, and nothing after that, except for Paul gently putting a blanket over me at some stage during the night.

I saw Stone coming down the street. Even bundled up in an overcoat and hat, he had a certain authority about him. What I could see of his face looked a little more tired, and there seemed to be more grey in the little hair that I could see, but his eyes swept the street restlessly, missing nothing. His handshake was firm.

'Let's get some breakfast,' he said.

'Suits me,' I said. We walked down the street, the wind and sleet making it difficult to talk. A man passed us going the other way. He was wearing jeans and a New York Dolls T-shirt. He waved at me and grinned and I recognized Billy E. He seemed oblivious to the cold.

'A vet,' Stone grunted, as we passed him.

'How do you know?' I said.

'The tattoos,' Stone said. I was surprised. Mentally I revised Billy E's age upwards.

Somewhere between Tenth and Eleventh, Stone ducked into a doorway. We found ourselves in the sort of old-fashioned diner that I thought had disappeared from the city. The windows were fogged and there was a smell of damp overcoats. We got seats at the counter and ordered bacon, homefries, eggs over easy. It was the perfect foil to the day outside. Stone obviously felt the same way about it.

'Place has been the same since I was a student,' he said, as he mopped up the last of his egg with a slice of toast. 'I thought you'd like it.'

Thoughts of condemned men and last meals went through my head, but I didn't say anything. Stone ordered another refill of coffee and sighed.

'There are a lot of people, important people, very annoyed with you, Jack. In fact, I'm a little vexed myself.'

'May I ask why?'

'I'm surprised you have to ask.'

I didn't say anything. A car bomb in London, at least two dead Puerto Ricans, who knows how many dead Mexicans, and a very angry and powerful man who had had his house violated and his girlfriend snatched from under his nose.

'Looked at in a certain light . . .' I admitted.

'I wonder if that is why you are still alive?' Stone said, as if he was turning over my past and future prospects in his mind. It was a kind of assay that left me with a cold feeling.

'A certain lack of what? Call it gravitas. Enables you to stay ahead of situations, not get bogged down. The world is full of checks and balances, but certain people behave as if they aren't there. Take your friend Liam. Seen from a certain point of view, he is a former IRA man who is running around Manhattan with a gun in his hand as if it were the backstreets of Belfast in 1970. Imagine what certain people could do to the peace process with that bit of information. Can you see your friend in cuffs paraded in front of the cameras? How many of his former colleagues would be damning him for a fool?'

'I have a feeling this conversation isn't about Liam,' I said.

'What do you think you are doing, Jack?' he said, turning on me

106

with sudden vehemence. 'What in the name of God do you think you are doing?' His hand struck the top of the counter and we got a few curious looks. Stone lowered his voice. 'Do you know who this man is, this Xabarra? Do you think he will leave you alone after this? Or do you think he deserves to have his tail pulled, that he is the big bad drugs dealer? Tell me this. Where does most of the world's heroin supply come from?'

'The Pakistan–Afghan border, around Jalalabad,' I said.

'That's right,' he said, 'and you would agree with me that it is a particularly unstable part of the world at the moment, with many vital interests colliding there.'

'Demanding stability,' I said. I thought I knew where the conversation was going. Xabarra was a big player in the heroin scene, perhaps *the* big player. Destabilizing him could destabilize the whole region. It was one of the balances that Stone talked about. Assuming that you couldn't wipe out the heroin trade, for instance, did you allow, even encourage, one big player who could be watched and controlled to a certain extent, or did you take them out and allow the trade to fragment in violence and chaos? Sometimes it simply became a matter of resources. If the big player was removed, you had to start building up your intelligence resources from scratch.

'There are vast interests involved here, Jack.'

'There is obviously more than heroin involved.'

'Heroin,' he snorted. 'Heroin has hardly anything to do with it. Just form a picture of the region in your mind, and think about oil.'

'Oil? The former Soviet Republics?'

'Correct. Little countries floating on a sea of oil. The problem is getting it out.'

'It has to be a pipeline.'

'A pipeline which has to go through Afghanistan. Which has to be stable for that to happen.'

'So it's about money.'

'God save us from a former student socialist. Use your head, Jack. Look at the way this country keeps getting dragged into involvements in the Middle East.'

Sometimes it didn't take a whole lot of dragging, I thought, but I didn't say anything.

'It is our dependence on Middle Eastern oil that leads us into those entanglements. Think about an alternative supply. That would add greatly to global stability.' His eyes flashed. 'A pipeline through Afghanistan is a prize worth having, a prize worth a lot of sacrifice.'

I had the uncomfortable feeling that I might be part of that sacrifice, and I said so. Stone gave me a long searching look.

'If Xabarra were a different man, you would already be dead by now. I would have been called to meetings in small offices in Washington. I would have been told in tones of deep regret that there was an impediment to progress in the Xabarra sphere. Everything would be talked about in euphemisms. Your name wouldn't be mentioned. The fact that you were going to be killed wouldn't be mentioned. I would express my sorrow.'

I knew that what he was saying was true. I looked out at the rain beating against the window, anonymous figures moving through it, and wondered if you could walk out of the door and join those anonymous figures and somehow melt into them, never to be found. But I knew it wasn't possible. If they wanted you, they would find you.

'Fortunately for you, Jack, there is a confluence of interests here.'

'You said something about Xabarra being a different man.'

'Yes I did. Xabarra is of course ambitious. That goes without saying. He is also vastly wealthy. Of course when you get to a certain stage, then power becomes the thing that you want. Money in itself is meaningless. So Mr Xabarra is empire-building. He is developing his own heroin-growing operation right on our doorstep.'

'Where?'

'Let us say in various mountainous areas stretching across Central and Southern America. Let us say that the governments involved are friendly, and would not take any direct action from the United States lightly. Let us also say that Xabarra is powerful to the point of being untouchable in these areas.'

'It has to be Mexico,' I said.

'It is irrelevant to this discussion in any case, Jack. Tell me this. Do you know how much the average opium grower earns?'

'Not an awful lot, I would imagine.'

'About three hundred dollars a year. That is enough to feed and clothe his family. It is a good subsistence wage. And it is that wage that Xabarra threatens.'

'You could just give the farmers three hundred dollars a year.'

'You can't just pump cash into an area. It distorts everything, wipes out the local economic structures quicker than war or famine. Ask any aid worker.'

'So,' I said, knowing what he was going to say, and feeling an odd, sick feeling in my stomach.

'So you are going to kill Xabarra for us.'

'Sorry, John,' I said, 'I don't do assassinations.' I meant it. I had killed men, but only in the context of an operation, or in self-defence. Being hired to kill someone was a different matter.

'I don't think you really understand. Do you think Xabarra is going to let you live after what you did last night? Either you kill him and do it soon, or he will kill you, and probably everyone you care for as well.'

We looked at each other. Someone came into the diner and cold air poured in from the street. I knew what he was saying was true. I didn't ask him how he knew about the previous night.

'Call it self-defence,' Stone said softly, not looking at me.

'Or murder,' I said.

'You've seen him,' Stone said, 'you know what he is like. You know what he likes to do to people.'

'I can't decide now,' I said.

'You have to,' Stone said. He leaned closer to me as if to say something that he didn't want anyone else to hear. With one swift, almost savage movement, his right hand pushed through the opening of my jacket, pulled the Glock from my inside pocket and stuck the barrel in my stomach, his hand still hidden by the jacket. I was taken aback by the speed and virtuosity of the move. The hand holding the gun to my gut was hard and professional. No one else in the diner had noticed a thing. The gun barrel pressed hard into my gut, then the pressure relaxed and I felt the weight of the gun slipping back into my pocket again.

'Just a reminder,' Stone said. 'If you don't take this job, then death will be everywhere and it will be swift and sudden, if you're lucky.'

I'd seen the kind of move that Stone had used on me, or something similar, before. A despairing martial arts instructor who had been trying to teach me some basics of the art had introduced me to his own master. He was a small, wizened Japanese man with sparkling blue eyes and we spent the afternoons when I was supposed to be learning my trade in conversation about East and West and aspects of Eastern thought that took his fancy. Then one day he disappeared on me. I mean, he physically disappeared. One moment he was sitting in an armchair across from me and the next moment he had vanished into thin air. I was almost in physical shock. It was as if he had slipped through some crack in time. I don't know how long I sat there staring until I became aware of the old man's cracked and wheezy laughter. I found him behind a sofa at the far end of a large room, laughing so much that he couldn't get up. When I eventually got him into a chair and he had stopped laughing, he explained to me what he had done.

He said that our attention span is much shorter than we think, and that in his view of it, our brain was continually withdrawing conscious attention in order to sort through and analyse what was being perceived. It was merely a case of taking advantage of one of those interludes to slip away. It sounded simple, I said. The simple things take the longest to learn, he said. Then I said that his laughter wasn't very Confucian. No, he said, he just couldn't help himself when he saw my face.

Stone had used something of the same technique, on me and on the rest of the people in the diner. Every time I thought I had come to grips with who he was, I met somebody else.

'Have you decided Jack?' he said. I nodded dumbly. He was right.

'I can give you money, but no other assistance,' he said briskly. 'This is maximum deniability.'

I could have asked him for covert assistance, but I knew it didn't work that way. If a government agency gets involved in an issue like this, it has a way of hallmarking the operation, no matter how oblique the involvement, and anyone in the trade has an instinct for those hallmarks. My involvement would be a different matter.

'You know the way people think of you now?' Stone said, as if reading my thoughts. 'They think of you as a rogue agent.'

'Somerville?' I said. Somerville was my old boss in MRU. Still nominally my employer, but there was no love lost between us.

'Partly,' Stone said, 'but partly the slightly . . . cavalier aspect to the previous operation.'

He pronounced the words as thought they had a bad taste, which was a bit rich considering he had been up to his neck in it. The suspicion entered my mind that Stone might have had more than a little to do with my rogue-agent status. It would have suited him to have someone like me outside the fence. I was the covert equivalent of a clean gun. Unused, untraceable and ultimately disposable. It was a bleak thought. A thought I wanted time to mull over. I forced myself to focus.

111

'There is one thing you could do for me.'

'What do you want me to do?'

I told him about the Puerto Ricans. 'I want them taken out of circulation,' I said.

'That's easy.' Stone's tone implied that he thought the matter trivial.

'I'm not much good to you with a hole in me,' I said, 'no matter who puts it there. I'm sure you could lift them under some immigration pretext. Anything to keep them out of the way for the time being.'

He considered it for a moment.

'Fair enough,' he said.

'If they are lifted, I want access to them,' I said. 'Maybe I can sort something out.'

Stone shrugged in a gesture which implied that if I wanted to waste my time sorting out someone else's ancient feuds, then it was none of his business.

We stood on the pavement outside the diner. It was bleak and cold.

'One more thing,' I said. 'How untouchable is Xabarra?'

'Very. Even in New York, don't expect the authorities to lift a finger to help you.'

'Is that what happened in London? With the car bomb? It was almost as if it hadn't happened.'

Stone gave me a steady look.

'Do you really think,' he said, 'that Xabarra would set an operation like that in train merely to get rid of an awkward father? But I'll tell you one thing. I had to exert a lot of influence to keep the whole thing low-key. A lot of influence. So don't let me down on this one, Jack.'

He turned and walked away. You never knew anybody in this business, I thought, but I thought I had known Paolo. Now I wasn't so sure.

There was more trouble in store when I got back to Jesus's place. Jesus was standing in the kitchen. When he saw me, he made a dumbshow of frowning at me and miming cutting his throat. When I looked in the bedroom where I had left Liam, I saw Deirdre redoing the bandages on his injured hand. She had enough experience as an aid worker to do it well. She was calm and solicitous but when she looked up and saw me, her expression changed. Her face went pale with anger. Two spots of colour burned high up on her cheeks. She motioned to me to wait, then finished off the bandages with deft movements. Liam looked over her. When she spoke, her voice was low and controlled.

'Did you see the state of his feet?' she said. 'Did you see what they did to him? It's one thing getting yourself into these situations, but you have no business dragging Liam in after you. Do you not see what is going on? Do you not see the day for tearing round the world like a lost romantic saving damsels in distress is over?'

I had known she was angry but I hadn't been prepared for the withering scorn in her voice.

'When Liam left Ireland and came here, he realized he had nothing. His past was a string of bad memories and lost causes. But he knew he had a few years left to build something for himself.'

I started to say something but she didn't give me a chance.

'Look at him now, Jack. It's not what happened to his body, although God knows it has taken enough abuse. His head's as full of war and death as it ever was. I wish to God you'd never come to New York. The truth is, Jack, that you have nothing either. You're empty and you're trying to make him as empty as you are.'

She turned abruptly and left the room. I tried to convince myself that she did it so that I wouldn't see the tears in her eyes. It's something, I suppose, if somebody who loved you sheds tears of regret for what you have become. I walked towards the window. As I did so, the Glock banged softly against my chest like a tawdry metallic heartbeat.

113

I was sitting on the front step when Paul came out. He shivered with the cold, but sat down next to me anyway.

'I thought she was hard on you,' he said.

'You heard it?'

He grinned.

'The neighbourhood heard it,' he said.

'Trouble is,' I said, 'she was right.'

'Maybe,' he said, 'and maybe not.' He smiled again. 'Look at it this way. I can't really see Liam settling down to a long and productive life as a building contractor, can you?'

I had to admit that he was right. I thought it was unlikely myself.

'I take a very determinist view of the world,' he said, 'it must be the Mayflower blood running in my veins. You're put on the earth with a certain amount of talent and ability and there's a certain amount of things you are supposed to do, and it's hubris to think you can second-guess fate.'

'The parable of the talents?' I said.

'Something like that. You and Liam are too suited to the things you do for it to be any other way, it's as simple as that.'

'And when other people get dragged into our crusades, then it isn't our fault, is that it?'

'I didn't say that. I didn't say that at all. But I will say something about Deirdre. She was reacting to seeing how badly Liam was hurt and thinking about what might have happened to you. She cares for both of you and the way she sees it, she can't bear to see you hurting yourselves. Maybe that is her talent.'

I was shocked when Liam showed me his feet. They had swollen to over twice their normal size. The doctor had left painkillers for him, but they made him groggy and he was reluctant to take them. His face was drawn with pain.

He had asked Alva to fetch Paul and Jesus, and we all sat around the bed. But it was me he spoke to first.

'The way I look at it, Jack, is that Xabarra is going to come after you sooner rather than later, and we're a danger to anyone harbouring us in the meantime. I reckon I've got a little business with Xabarra anyhow, but I'm not sure that Jesus and his mother and Paul should be involved.'

I could see that Jesus looked anxious and I knew he was thinking that he had enough troubles of his own.

'I agree,' I said. 'I've got an apartment to go to and Liam will be safe in Queens. The problem is what Alva wants to do.'

I looked at Alva. I couldn't read what she was thinking. If she had turned round and said she wanted to go back out to the Hamptons, then I wouldn't have been surprised, but she merely met my gaze.

'What do you think I should do, Jack?'

I sighed inwardly. I thought about Paolo's stricture about not telling Alva and how much it had cost him to deliver the message, but she was away from Xabarra now, and knowledge of her father's condition might be enough to sway her towards returning to Europe.

I took a deep breath and told her what had happened, starting with the day that Paolo had arrived at my house in Scotland. When I had finished, she looked blank, but her nails were dug into her palms.

'Richard would not have done that,' she said faintly. 'I need some time.' She got up and went into her room, stumbling slightly as she went. We waited for half an hour but she didn't come out.

'I've got things to do,' Jesus said. 'I guess you staying here another night won't hurt.'

I was grateful and I said so. I didn't like the idea of having to shift Liam. Jesus left, but was back within a few hours. Paul went down the street and returned with shrimp which he cooked in honey and orange. We had them with a bottle of good white burgundy. After that, we all felt a little more optimistic. I was able to give Jesus some good news when Stone rang my cellphone.

'That request you made,' he said, 'it has been fulfilled. You can see the subjects tomorrow, if you wish.'

I told Jesus that the Puerto Ricans were under lock and key, and that we would be able to talk to them tomorrow. We went to bed at eleven and I lay awake for a while, listening to the noise from the street outside, and decided to grant myself absolution from remorse for one evening before slipping into a dreamless sleep.

Ten

They came that night. Afterwards, Jesus told me that he had posted runners on the street to give warning, but they came across the roof-tops, fast and silent, almost a score of men in balaclavas and Kevlar body armour and semi-automatic weapons, testimony to Xabarra's power that he could put together a large squad with twenty-four hours' notice. They snapped the lock on the roof-top door with bolt cutters, but not before one of them had plugged a laptop into Jesus, sophisticated alarm system and disabled it. They must have had the building under surveillance because they seemed to know exactly where they were going. Their master wished to recover his possession above all else, and they went straight to Alva's room.

It was Paul who saw them. By sheer chance he had gone to the bathroom and had seen the movement on the landing above him. A man was carrying Alva up the stairs. She was naked and appeared to be unconscious and she was slung roughly over his shoulder. He realized that there were other men on their way down, hidden in the angle of the stairs. He went in and woke Jesus and Jesus came out shooting. That was what woke me, the gunfire and the crack–thud of a stun grenade. My room was on the floor below Jesus, and as I emerged with my gun in my hand, Jesus and Paul came tumbling down the stairs. The detonation of the stun grenade had ignited the wood of the stairs above us. I could see the first tongue of flame licking at the banisters. I shouted to Jesus, but he couldn't hear and I realized the grenade had temporarily deafened him, so I grabbed Paul by the shoulder and pushed him into Liam's room. Liam was trying to stand, but it was obvious his feet wouldn't carry him. We got his arms around his shoulders and burst out on to the landing. As though this was a signal, a hail of fire came down the stairs and we heard booted feet running. Jesus pointed down.

On the way down the stairs, I had to let go of Liam and start firing upwards with Jesus. Paul and Liam struggled down the stairs in front of us. The stairwell was filling with cordite smoke and our faces were already dark with gunoil, smoke and grease. And above it all were ominous threads of smoke and a distant crackling noise.

'The basement!' Jesus shouted. Paul cried out as a heavy-calibre round slammed into the woodwork beside him and splinters peppered the side of his face. Jesus was firing straight upwards, trying to pierce the stairs, but the heavy old timber seemed too thick. Another stun grenade tumbled down the stairs. I found myself calculating as if I had all the time in the world. A five-second fuse. One second to arm and throw it, another second in the air, another second falling down the stairs. In one swift movement, Liam caught the grenade with his good hand and threw it upwards. I kept up the count. He had a second to spare. The grenade went off and I heard an angry shout in Spanish. Paul had a gun in his hand now and was firing inexpertly upwards. I slung Liam on to my back in a piggy-back and stuck my Glock in his hand, before realizing that he had his own pistol. I started to back down the stairs and Liam opened up with both guns at the same time, almost deafening me and scorching both of my ears with muzzle flash. A big man appeared on the top landing. I don't think he meant to step out. One barrel of the stuttering automatic pistol hit him in the chest. The rounds didn't pierce the Kevlar armour, but the force of the hit threw him against the wall and pinned him there.

Then Liam lined up the second barrel on him. The man looked down, watching in horrified fascination as the bullets stitched upwards from the middle of his stomach towards his unprotected face. It seemed to take a long time. Just before the bullets reached the top of the body armour, he wrenched his eyes away from them and I found myself looking directly into his eyes, an expression in them as if to ask, how had it come to this? Then his face exploded in a mess of blood and bone, and another man knelt beside him, half in cover, and started to fire careful, aimed shots.

And still we went down. It seemed a long way, although in reality we had only covered four floors. As we reached the ground floor, the second team came through the back of the building. One of them cannoned into Jesus, knocking him over. Before the man could recover, Jesus had grabbed a fire extinguisher from the wall and swung it at his head. He went down and I saw blood and skin on the extinguisher before Jesus banged it off the ground and threw it at the men coming through the door. The corridor filled with noise and CO_2, blinding the attackers as they charged us. Once again, Jesus pushed us down until we were going full tilt down the narrow stairs which led to the basement. I hoped he knew what he was doing. We burst through the basement door and he swung it and locked it behind us. It was a heavy, steel-lined fire door and it might hold them for a while. Jesus dived in behind the big old boiler and started frantically hauling asbestos sheeting from where it was stacked behind it. I looked around. I seemed to keep finding myself in the hidden utilitarian places of this city. I didn't know then how much worse it was going to get. I examined the side of Paul's face quickly. He had pulled out most of the splinters. There was one big one left. I would have been inclined to leave it, as it was close to the aorta, but then in that case I would have been inclined to immobilize him and get him straight to hospital, and that wasn't an option here. The splinter might get dislodged or shoved deeper in, so I told Paul to hold still and yanked it out. There was a gush of blood, but if it had been the aorta I would have been drenched in blood and Paul would have been dead before he hit the floor.

I heard a running body hit the steel door outside. The handle turned once, then twice. I had expected them to hammer at it, but all that happened was the handle turning. There was something a little creepy and ominous about it. There seemed to be absolute quiet outside the door. Meanwhile, Jesus had revealed a large opening in the wall behind the boiler.

'Come on!' he said.

'Wait a moment,' I said. I grabbed a few planks and some jute sacking that was lying on the floor. Jesus shoved Paul into the blackness behind the boiler.

'Jack, fucking come on!' he shouted again. I shoved the wood and sacking into the hole and heard it clattering as it fell. It seemed a long way down. I tried to ease Liam into the gap but Jesus put his hand on top of Liam's head and shoved him uncere-moniously into the hole. I was half-way into it myself when the door exploded inwards, accompanied by a heavy chattering noise that sounded like an insane industrial process. I recognized it as a general-purpose machine-gun, although I'd never heard it in any-thing like this confined space before. The heavy metal door span wildly across the room and crashed into the opposite wall. I couldn't believe they had such a heavy weapon with them. It opened up again. Jesus didn't wait for me to get into the hole. He dived in on top of me and we fell into the darkness.

I must have hit something metallic when I went down. I felt a tremendous impact on the side of my head, then I hit concrete with a bone-crushing impact. I lay there without moving for a moment, trying to see if I had done myself any damage. I put my hand to my head and felt it wet with blood, but that seemed to be all. I opened my eyes then and felt a sudden wave of almost uncontrollable panic. My first thought was that I had somehow damaged the optical centre of my brain and blinded myself. I heard Jesus speak each of our names in turn and I forced myself to answer.

'Nobody move until I find a torch.' I realized then that we were in darkness, a darkness so absolute that it seemed an actual presence, something enormous and feral.

'Where are we?' Liam said. If the darkness worried him, you couldn't hear it in his voice.

'Old subway tunnel,' Jesus said. 'It's been closed for years. Runs right under the river.'

A torch came on in the darkness and I saw that we were in the middle of a tangle of equipment, welding gear, bits of rail and generators and old rail bogies.

'This a storage area,' Jesus said. 'There's more light when you go out on to the main track.' As my eyes got used to the dim light cast by the torch, I could see cardboard boxes stacked in one corner. Beside that were several steel boxes.

'Time to get some firepower,' Jesus said. He opened several of the boxes and I could see enough weaponry to keep a small army going. I looked at Jesus. His oily face creased in a grin.

'The consignment was going cheap,' he said. 'I can't resist a bargain.' I looked at the markings on the boxes. Some kind of Cyrillic script. The stuff obviously came from the other side of what they used to call the Iron Curtain, and some of the weapons were unfamiliar to me. I picked out a machine pistol and filled my pockets with ammunition clips for it. There was a light sheen of oil on the weapon, but the barrel seemed clean. Liam picked out some kind of stubby machine-gun with a huge magazine, and Paul took what looked like a Kalashnikov copy.

'The only shooting I ever did was at clay pigeons,' he said apologetically. We heard voices in the shaft above us, followed by a burst of fire. Bullets richocheted around the storage area.

'Let's go,' Jesus said.

'Wait,' I said. 'Can you hold them for a few minutes?'

'OK,' Jesus said, 'if I have to.' He fired a few shots back up the shaft. I started to lash the two planks of wood together, with the sacking in between. Liam saw what I was doing and pulled himself over with his hands to help.

'Hurry up,' Jesus said urgently, 'before they drop another one of those grenades on us.'

Within a few minutes we had a crude sleigh that we could drag Liam on. It was quiet up above.

'Maybe they've given up,' I said.

'Xabarra isn't going to give up on you,' Jesus said grimly. We got Liam on to the sleigh. On an impulse I shoved a flare gun and some cartridges into my pocket. We moved out of the storage area and I found myself standing in a subway tunnel. Some light seemed to be coming from around the curve.

'There is still some emergency lighting left intact,' Paul explained, 'it stays on all the time.' It seemed odd that this strange twilight kingdom existed underneath the city streets.

'It's a deep tunnel,' Paul said. 'Has to be to get under the river.'

'How far do we have to go?' I asked Jesus.

'About two miles,' he said.

'What?'

'There is no way out between here and the river. We've got to go right under the river and come out the other side.'

I looked at Liam. If we were able to run, we might be able to outpace the men behind us, but there was no way we could go faster than walking pace with the sleigh. I heard voices in the shaft we had slid down. They were coming fast. I took one arm of the sleigh and Paul took the other and we started forward, Liam, grim-faced, cradling the machine pistol, Jesus walking backwards up the track, watching behind us. The sleigh bumped over the uneven ground, threatening to spill Liam, and I could feel the strain of hauling it in my shoulders already.

'We're going to get to a point where you're going to have to leave me,' Liam said quietly. 'When we get to it, I don't want to hear any argument.'

I didn't say anything. If it came to it, then I would stay with Liam, hoping that the other two would go on. I looked anxiously over my shoulder. The long curve of the tunnel kept us hidden from the pursuit, but it also meant that we had no way of telling how far behind us they were. I felt a definite downward gradient in the tunnel, probably the start of its descent under the river. It made it easier to pull the sledge but I realized that the other side would be even more difficult. We would be dragging the sledge uphill, and would probably be at the limit of our endurance. I looked over at Paul. He looked tense and strained and I reckoned that he had been brought up a long way from urban streetfighting. In contrast, Jesus moved quickly on the balls of his feet, a picture of concentration and determination. The curve of the tunnel was flattening out. We would be able to see them soon. I quickened my pace. Liam squinted along the barrel of his gun, aiming into the shadows, waiting for the first man to appear. I listened for voices, but I couldn't hear any. Their discipline worried me. These weren't the casual gunmen we had seen at Xabarra's house. These men were professionals. I could see Paul trying out his cellphone.

'No signal,' he said, 'we're too far underground.' No one said anything, but we were all aware of the sense of isolation that descended with his words. Suddenly a shot rang out and a piece of the tunnel brickwork exploded into dust beside Paul. They were closer than we thought. One of them had used the shadows where the tunnel wall met the ground to get close to us. Liam saw him first and opened fire and the rest of us followed suit. But as I opened up, I saw him turn and slip silently away into the shadows. I had the sudden, worrying feeling that these men knew exactly where the tunnel led, and that they could afford to be patient, knowing that we couldn't escape until the other side. I had an even more worrying thought. If they knew about the tunnel, then they must also know where it came out. We might be fleeing from one danger into even more deadly peril. I looked down at Liam. He was reloading his gun in an unconcerned manner, but I reckoned he must have figured out the spot we were in. I looked up at the ceiling. It must have been six o'clock in the morning. Up above, people were beginning to stir, early traffic was starting to move. I wondered if I would ever see it again. I put my head down and trudged on.

There was less light than there had been when we started. Water seeped through the ceiling in many places, shorting the bulbs of the emergency lights, so that we were moving in a very dim glimmer, with an emergency light only every hundred yards or so. It gave me an idea. Despite Jesus's protestations, I made him take the other handle of the sleigh. I dropped into the shadows. Two could play at the shadow game.

I waited until they were almost on top of me, two of them moving close together. As they got close to me, I could hear them whispering to each other. I moved further into the shadows and waited. It was a trick I had learned as a child. In the flats complex where I was reared, some of the older children were hostile to the smaller ones in a way that I can only think of now as psychopathic. If you were out after dark, you were in need of protection of some kind, a tough father or an older brother. I had neither, so I enlisted the shadows. I became used to spotting the places where you could hide, almost in plain view as long as there was some shadow. I found that you could hide in a patch of shadow in a dim light. The trick was to make yourself small and not to move: even the slightest movement would attract attention. That was the easy part. The hard part was making sure that your face was turned away from the pursuit. If you were looking at them, they would see you. I was never sure whether it was the same, almost psychic ability that makes you feel someone's eyes on you in a crowd, or simply that we are programmed to spot and respond to the actual physical shape of a face. Whichever it was, it took all of a child's strength and courage to turn your head away when you were squashed into the angle of a wall only feet from the feet of someone who would be happy to kick you half to death for the pleasure of hearing you squeal. It was a trick which required an almost zen-like degree of concentration, both focused and unfocused at the same time, and I used it now, pressed into the side of a pile of old sleepers propped against the edge of the tunnel. As the two men went past, I felt one of their boots brush the sleeve of my jacket.

I risked a quick look backwards. As far as I could see, there was another man ten yards behind them, and then a whole group. I let the single man approach until he was almost five yards away and then I shot him once in the chest.

It was one of those things that happen in the covert business and in warfare, one of the things I had seen happen to other people, and then had seen the look in their eyes as they realized what had happened. Often I had seen them die with that same look in their eyes. Not regret at dying or anger at their enemies, but an almost bemused look that all their experience and training had let them down on something so simple. I could sense a feeling that was almost resignation wash over me as I realized that the men had all been wearing Kevlar body armour. The chest shot would have hurt about as much as getting hit hard in the chest with half a brick, but it wouldn't stop the man coming to kill me now that I had shown my hand. I dived to the ground about the same time as my opponent did. I heard him give a hoarse shout to the others behind him and I sensed rather than saw them hit the deck and start crawling forwards. I tried to move backwards but my way was blocked by some old sleepers that had been piled there. To get past them, I would have to climb over them and expose myself. My bright idea had left me trapped between the main body of the pursuers and the two leading men, who had got about fifteen yards ahead of me. I thought what I would do in their position. Get down on my belly and crawl forwards, keeping under cover, try to psych out my prey, pushing forwards until the impulse of the trapped man to get up, to get off his belly, was too strong and he exposed himself.

That's what experience had taught me to do. In practice, I would probably have done what the two men actually did. Spooked by the darkness of the tunnel into letting their instincts overwhelm their training, they came rushing back to see what the firing was about. As they did so, one of their own men started to fire. He did not make the mistake that I had made. His shots were aimed low, for the legs. The lead man groaned and fell. The other man dived over the sleepers and hit the ground beside me, screaming something to the others in Spanish as he did so. At first, he wasn't aware of me. He lifted his head anxiously from the ground and looked towards the other men. As I moved to bring my gun to bear on him, he turned and saw me. With surprising speed, his hand shot out and knocked my gun hand aside. I dropped the gun and reached for his throat with both hands before he had a chance to shout to the others. I dug my fingers into the arteries on either side of his neck. It should have cut off the blood supply to his brain. I had seen it done, but I never had much of a knack for such things. He hit me hard on the head and I reeled for a second. His other hand was feeling for a pocket in his combats. I didn't know what was in there, but I was pretty sure it would spell sudden death for me. He twisted sideways. He was strong. Much stronger than me. I was already tired and cold and I could feel the beginnings of a fatal weariness with this fight, a kind of resignation gripping me. He twisted again and I fell across one of his legs, losing my grip on his throat. He kicked and a boot caught me full in the face. I grabbed at him desperately, not really knowing what I was doing, but an instinct telling me that the one

126

thing I had to do was to stop his hand emerging from his pocket. I realized that the reason he had twisted was to get proper access to the pocket. I grabbed for the hand under the fabric. It was wrapped around something cold and hard, the butt of a small gun, or more likely the haft of a knife. I held on for grim death while his other hand clawed for my eyes. In trying to get away, my own free hand touched his belt. I felt the hard metallic surface of a stun grenade. I wrenched it free without much idea of what I was going to do with it. I was vaguely aware of the others calling to him in Spanish. His arm was strong and sinewy and I knew I couldn't keep it in his pocket for long.

One-handed, I tried desperately to lift the cover off the grenade. In the old war comics, men pulled the grenade pin with their teeth, but a real grenade has a cover and a stiff pin. I wrestled the cover off it but I couldn't shift the pin one-handed. With one late, writhing twist, he threw me off him and I landed at his feet. He was sitting down now, facing me, but there was an evil grin on his face and a short stabbing knife with an ugly, serrated blade in his hand. I knew it was a belly knife. You stabbed and pulled upwards and the serrations tore flesh and organs. I had both hands free. I pulled the grenade pin and slipped it inside the elasticated cuff of his combat trousers, shoving it as far up as I could. He looked at me in disbelief, then jumped desperately to his feet, but the grenade caught in the fabric and would not move. He dropped the knife and tore desperately at the trousers. It was almost comical. I grabbed my gun and, using the standing man as cover, I rolled over the top of the pile of sleepers. As I landed on the other side on my back, I looked up and saw that he had the grenade in his hand now. He made to draw his arm back to throw it away, then realized it would bring the grenade past his head. He made to throw it underarm, then realized it would bring the grenade close to his belly. We both knew that the grenade would explode before he did either. It was a stun grenade but it could still kill and maim.

Sometimes, when I shut my eyes at night, I see what he did then. I don't know if it was the right thing or not. I don't know if I would have had the courage to do it. He knew he didn't have time to throw the device, so he simply straightened his arm, still holding it, and turned his head away. I rolled away and did not see it go off, but over the shattering noise of the grenade exploding in the enclosed space, I think I heard him scream as his arm was severed.

No one fired after me as I ran back towards the others. I knew it would be personal now. The night seemed to have changed around me and to be full of a cold madness. It would be becoming light in the streets above, but around me the darkness seemed to thicken.

Eleven

When I got back to the others, neither Liam nor Jesus said anything. Paul looked at me. Then I saw him settle himself, feeling for the strap of the weapon over his shoulder for reassurance. The downwards angle of the tunnel had become more pronounced. At the same time, it had become colder and there seemed to be more water on the floor of the tunnel.

'They have two injured,' I said. 'They'll have to stabilize them. It'll take a little time.'

'How mad are they?' Liam asked mildly.

'Very,' I said.

'That's a pity,' he said.

I followed his eyes towards where I had lashed the sleigh together. The lashings had started to come loose. They wouldn't last another hundred yards.

'Right, this is what we do,' Jesus said.

A few minutes later, I was going down the tunnel at a dead run, or as near to a dead run as I could manage, with Liam on my back. When I couldn't go any further, Paul took over. He managed almost two hundred yards before handing over to Jesus. The running was difficult and becoming more so as the track deteriorated. We were trying to step from sleeper to sleeper with each foot either side of the central electric rail. The problem was that sometimes the sleepers were missing. We could almost feel the pursuit now, deadly and intent, determined to finish us. Jesus fell heavily with Liam on top of him and cried out in pain. There was a foot of freezing water in the channel which held the electric rail and both men's clothes were soaked through when they managed to get up.

'You're going to have to leave me,' Liam said.

I could see that Jesus was weighing up the options.

'If we keep this up, we're all dead men,' Jesus said. 'The only way to go is for us to go on and round up some people up top, come back for you.'

We all knew it was a forlorn hope. It might take hours to get up to the top and get heavily armed help. Anyone who was left behind had little hope of surviving.

'Come and see this,' Paul said to me quietly.

He was standing by the obstacle that had blocked Jesus and Liam's way. I examined it, a faint hope growing. It seemed like a rail version of what we used to call a bogie when we were young, a home-made cart for racing down hills. Someone had taken an old rail bogie and mounted a crude wooden body on top of it. Kids, by the look of the graffiti. I looked at the wheels. The two front ones had come off the rail. Either the kids hadn't the strength to get the thing back on the track, or some subway employee had come along and disturbed them. Whatever had happened, the bogie was there with a good half-mile downhill slope in front of it and we had the strength of desperate men. Just then a burst of automatic fire struck the ceiling above us, showering us in brick dust.

'Liam, cover us!'

He rolled to one side of the tunnel, where he could draw fire to himself, and emptied a magazine down the track. He was met with a fusillade of fire. Paul was saying something to me but I couldn't hear him. The noise in the tunnel was deafening, but I should have been able to hear something. I put my hand to my left ear and felt blood coming from it. The effects of the stun grenade. I turned my right ear to him and heard him say something about a lever, but Jesus was already trying to haul a a half-sleeper off the ground by himself. Together, we managed to get it under the wheel of the bogie and lever it back on to the track. Pieces of stone and brick ricocheted off the metal of the wheels. I turned and saw that Liam had almost disappeared inside a choking cloud of brick dust thrown up by bullets striking the tunnel walls around him. I motioned to the others and we all turned and started to fire towards the pursuers. Their firing slackened momentarily and Liam came rolling out of the dust, coughing and spluttering. Without any ceremony, we grabbed him and tipped him into the bogie. Then we put our shoulders to it, feeling very vulnerable with our backs turned. The bogie wouldn't move. We strained until I could feel the veins standing out my forehead, but there was no joy. I grabbed a heavy piece of pipe and started to hammer at each wheel. They would be seized by rust, I realized. Being hammered would help free them as long as the bearings weren't gone.

'Push!' I yelled. 'Push, for Christ's sake!'

It seemed to go on for ever. Liam had all our guns now, firing each in turn until the magazines were empty. We had lifted plenty of ammunition, but there wasn't time for him to reload. I hammered at the wheels like a miner condemned to toil in some hellish shaft. Jesus and Paul strained every muscle, intent on shifting the cart, until it seemed that even the gunfire was forgotten and their whole universe centred on the bogie. And at last it began to move, the wheels turning with a harsh, unlovely shriek of metal against metal that sounded almost symphonic to us. I took over from the exhausted Paul, who had to be helped into the body of the bogie. Together, Jesus and I laboured, slowly building up momentum. I heard a careful, aimed shot over my head, then another, I looked over my shoulder and thought I saw a man rear up in the darkness before dropping his gun and falling out of sight. I looked up and saw Paul lining up another shot, and there

was a fierce joy in his eyes, a killing joy that would have frightened me if I had not seen it so often before, and felt it myself more
times than I cared to admit.

The bogie was still moving slowly but the gunfire was becoming
too intense for us to stay out. Jesus swung easily on to the bogie,
but I had to be hauled on, my legs too weak to scramble up. The
bogie rolled forwards at walking pace, then began to build up
momentum, swaying from side to side alarmingly as it did so.
Liam kept blazing into the darkness.

'Any brakes on this thing?' Jesus yelled.

I looked. There weren't any. Liam had to stop firing to hold on.
The thing made a terrible noise as it careered down the track, dry
bearings shrieking, the wooden body groaning and banging. I
started to wonder about the track as the bogie went faster and
faster. I had noticed sections of rail missing further up the track. I
looked over the side but was blinded by the fine spray of water
thrown up by the wheels. There was no firing from the rear now.
The bogie swayed so far to the side that it struck a steel support in
the tunnel wall and showered us in sparks. In the blue light of the
sparks, I saw Jesus and Paul staring fixedly ahead. Only Liam
seemed relaxed. He seemed to be staring off in the distance. The
bogie was moving with such speed now that the wheels leaped
clear of the track each time it struck some small imperfection in the
rail. Once it went up on two wheels and I thought we were dead. It
seemed to stay on two wheels for a long time before righting itself.
I could hear Liam laughing over the shriek of tortured metal. Next
time, I thought grimly, we'll be over. And still the wheels picked
up speed. I felt a strange shuddering sensation from the wheels, as
if something was dragging at them. I looked back but there was
only darkness. Then the shuddering increased to a dragging and
then the bogie slewed sideways suddenly and I felt myself flying
through the air as it tipped me off. I steeled myself for the impact
of iron rail against skin and bone, but it didn't happen. Instead, I

hit cold water so hard, it winded me and I half-bounced before hitting the water again and finding myself suddenly deaf, blind and choking as cold, oily water forced itself into my nose. I felt sudden panic invading me and I made myself calm down. I allowed myself to float upwards. My head burst free of the water and my feet touched the bottom. As I looked, Jesus broke the surface and I saw Liam holding to the side of the tunnel. The water was about five feet deep and it had acted as a brake on the bogie before it tilted. Beside us, level with my hand, was what appeared to be a station platform, a deserted station with no signage to indicate what its name might have been or where we were.

'Where's Paul?' Jesus said.

It was the only time I had ever found real fear in his voice.

'Where the fuck is Paul?'

He looked around wildly.

It took us almost five minutes to find him. Jesus dived and dived again into the freezing, filthy water, but it was Liam who found him, lying face down in the shadows of the deserted platform. A smear of blood showed where he had been thrown on to the platform and had skidded across it until his head hit the wall. He was breathing slowly and evenly, but a head injury was always worrying. His arm was twisted under him at an unnatural angle. We did our best to make him comfortable. Jesus stared down at him, seemingly lost.

'You're going to have to go up and get help, Jesus,' Liam said. 'There's no other way.'

'I'm not leaving him here,' Jesus said. 'You go, Jack.'

'Liam's right,' I said. 'For a start, I'm not in great shape.' It was true. I was blue with cold and shaking. I knew my energy levels were dangerously low.

'Jack doesn't know anybody up there,' Liam said urgently, 'and I can't walk. We can't carry Paul out. You have to go, Jesus. If you don't, then we're all going to die down here.'

I found what weapons we had left in the wooden body of the bogie, which had broken free and drifted loose. Liam found Paul's rifle, its barrel full of water. There was still half a clip of ammunition. It might fire damp. Or it might blow up in someone's face. We had the two Glocks with maybe a magazine each. It wouldn't hold them off for long. Jesus's face was grave.

'What is this place anyway?' Liam asked.

'Old pumping station,' Jesus said. 'Kept the tunnel dry. You're right underneath the middle of the river.' I looked at the ceiling and thought of the millions of tons of water flowing over our heads. I didn't like the feeling that it gave me.

'Go, Jesus,' Liam said, urgently. 'We don't have time.'

Jesus knelt beside Paul. He put the palm of his hand gently against his cheek and left it there for a moment. Then he stood up.

'It'll take me an hour, perhaps more, to get to the other side,' he said. 'Maybe more to round up some people . . . I just don't know . . .' His voice trailed off as the hopelessness of what faced us became clear.

'You do what you have to do, and we'll do what we have to,' Liam said. 'We'll be here when you get back, so get going now.'

Jesus nodded slowly, then without another word he slipped into the water. It came up to the middle of his chest, but as he waded forwards, it got deeper. The last I saw of him, it was up to his shoulders and then he was gone, slipping into the darkness.

'We should move Paul,' Liam said. 'He's in the line of fire here.'

I dragged him back into what seemed to be the pump room and placed him behind one of the big pumps. Liam hobbled in behind me. The machinery was in bad shape, rusted and broken. Water seeped through the joints of pipes. When I touched the head of a bolt, it crumbled in my hand.

'Let me have a look in here,' Liam said thoughtfully. 'You'd better get out and keep watch for them.'

I went back out to the platform and lined up some empty oil barrels to create the illusion of a barrier. Then I sat down, bone-tired and frozen. I gave the pursuit half an hour before they would reach us, maybe less.

As I sat, my thoughts drifted to Paolo and to what Stone had said. Was it possible that there was more to it than what Paolo had told me? My heart said that Paolo would not betray the trust between us. My head told me not to be stupid. In my business, loyalty was a commodity like any other, to be traded at will, if the price was right. My thoughts drifted back to the time I had met Paolo, many years ago, in a small town in Central Spain.

Twelve

I'd gone to Cuenca to see the collection of contemporary Spanish art in the hanging houses there. Cuenca was a pretty town with an old medieval quarter clinging to a big crag. There was a cathedral with a square in front of it and a mayoral palace to one side. As it happened, it was fiesta time. I stayed there for a week, drinking beer and eating pinchos – delicious kebabs skewered and cooked on barbecues at the side of the square. In the evening, they ran young bulls through the square, with men hanging on to a rope around the bull's neck to slow it down in the open space. Young men ran up to the bull and tried to hit it on the nose and get away without being gored. Most got away with it, but one slipped and was gored in the groin before the older men could haul the bull off him. I don't know what happened, but I suspect, by the amount of blood in the dust, the femoral artery had been severed. All through the night, young men played without rhythm on goatskin drums. As the week went on, the drums got louder and more insistent, they drank more and took more chances with the bulls. There was a sense of something primitive in the air, something to do with family and vengeance and spilled blood.

At the start of the week, I thought the dusty reds and ochres and dust textures of the paintings were cool and modern. By the end of the week, I saw that they shared the fierce primitivism of that society.

I met Paolo a few times that week. A young Italian man, polite but a little remote. Once or twice, I saw him engaged in intense conversations with some of the Spanish students.

The atmosphere continued to build. Early in the morning, exhausted drummers would pass around flagons of wine and keep on drumming in a kind of frenzy. The crowds at the bull runs grew larger, and the Guardia Civil started to appear in numbers for the first time. General Franco was dead, but you had the impression that nobody had told the hard-faced men in the three-cornered hats. Cuenca had been loyal to Franco. Change was in the air and the old order would be swept away, but there was no such certainty at the time. Nevertheless, you looked into those men's eyes and you saw suspicion and an undefined bitterness, particularly when they looked at the young students who thronged the town as the weekend approached. I saw Paolo more often, moving through the crowd. Sometimes he nodded to me.

In retrospect, it seemed inevitable that something would happen on the final night of the fiesta. There was a sense of frenzy about the place. The men handling the bulls almost let them run amok through the square. The sound of the drums was intense and insistent. People spoke loudly and there were passionate arguments on the steps of the cathedral. At one stage, I looked down at my feet and saw wine running in the gutters. The day was hot as well, the sun hung in the sky, burnished, merciless and alien. The evening brought no relief and I walked up the hill beside the cathedral to the small apartment I had borrowed to shower and change. It was dark when I came down to the square again, and there was a sense of expectation, the place packed with young people. It was as hot as it had been during the day and a pale and sickly moon hung in the sky. As I watched, a march seemed to appear from nowhere, perhaps seven or eight hundred young men and women, all wearing a distinctive red bandana knotted at their throats. To the cheers of the others, they gathered under the window of the mayor's palace. I don't know if the mayor was home or not, but I suspect the symbolism was more important than anything else.

One young man at the very front started a chant. I suspect there was something socialist in it, but it seemed harmless enough. The rest of the red bandanas took it up, and then the rest of the crowd, punching the air as they chanted. I looked around the square and saw Paolo leaning against a wall with his hands in his pockets and a cigarette in his mouth. There was something almost paternal about the way he was standing, as if he had been responsible for the whole thing. Later, I found out that he was at least partially responsible.

I turned back to the crowd. It was good-humoured enough, despite the passion of the shouting. One girl, sitting on her boyfriend's shoulders, flashed her breasts at the crowd and they roared approval.

When I think about it, she had probably copied the gesture from the film of Woodstock, for they were nothing if not innocent, these young people who thought that good will and a little chanting was enough to make cruel authority disappear. I could tell them now that it never disappears, merely reappears under another guise. But I couldn't have told them then. I didn't know it myself.

After that, things happened very quickly. I remember looking over and thinking to myself that there seemed to be a lot of Guardia Civil mingling with the crowd. I could see a few others throwing nervous glances towards them. And then the Guardia drew their batons.

They felt in no danger from the crowd. They didn't lay about them, trying to hit as many people as possible. They each picked one person and pursued them through the crowd, beating them to a bloody pulp before picking out the next victim. The crowd turned and ran, but the exits off the square were too small to take more than two or three people at a time, so the crowd simply swirled about in the square.

You think that if you keep your head in such a situation, then you should be able to find a way out, or at least stay away from trouble, but it doesn't work like that. You have no control over your own movements. People scream and curse and you scream and curse with them. The crowd seethes one way and you must go with it. There are currents in the mass of people, channels, and you are driven through them. It was enough for one Guardia Civil to charge at one end of the square to have a hundred people crushed and fainting at the other end. For what seemed like hours, I was pushed from one end of the square to the other, although in all probability it was only minutes. Then, suddenly, I spilled out into a quiet corner of the square as the crowd surged away. I saw the girl who had bared her breasts lying on the ground. There was a mask of blood where her face had been. Her hair was matted and she was moaning softy. One of the black-uniformed policemen was standing over her and as I watched he drove the point of his baton into her mouth and I heard teeth break. I could feel nausea rising in my gorge.

'*Puta*,' he spat at her. Whore. And he raised the baton to strike her again. As he did so, Paolo stepped from nowhere and plucked the baton from his grasp. Snarling, the policemen reached for the pistol at his belt. He got the clasp unfastened, but Paolo leaned over and rapped him smartly on the knuckles with the baton. The man yelped and held his fingers. Paolo pulled the gun from the man's belt and opened the chamber with the air of a man who knew what he was doing. He emptied the bullets on to the ground, kicked them away and put the gun back in the man's belt. I moved forward to pick up the girl. She was trying to cry through her broken mouth. As I got her to her feet, the crowd surged again and we were separated from Paolo. I struggled to get her arm around my shoulder in the crush, and it was a few seconds before I looked up. I didn't like what I saw. Two of the Guardia Civil's colleagues were bearing down on Paolo. Paolo saw the wolfish grin on the first man's face and turned. It was too late to get the baton up to defend himself, but Paolo had one last trick. As the first man aimed a vicious kick at his back, Paolo swung the baton backwards and caught his kneecap. The man howled and went down, and then the other two were on Paolo, smashing him to his knees with the baton.

It took half an hour to get the girl out of the square. I handed her over to some of the red bandanas. With her teeth capped and some careful stitching, her beauty would be restored but she would never be innocent again.

I didn't have much hope of doing anything for Paolo, but I went back to the square again anyway. The place was deserted except for an apartment building in the corner which had a knot of Guardia Civil around the entrance. I approached it, feigning the innocent tourist. One of them growled something and swung a baton at me. I heard groans from inside the building and a half-stifled cry. I circled around the back of it. Afterwards, I learned that they had taken the ones they deemed the ringleaders into the ground-floor office of the building for special treatment. I stood on a box in the alley beside the building and looked in. The window was dirty, but I thought I heard Paolo among the others. As I watched, two of the policemen came in and dragged a poor, half-dead youth out of the room. I heard the thud of their batons against his head and torso. I badly wanted to get them out of there, but the window was barred and the door was impossible. Then I had an idea.

I went around the corner. A smell of blood, sweat and dung filled my nostrils. There was what must have been a store-room around the corner which had been used as a byre for the bulls during the fiesta. There was no one watching it. I crept closer. I had been reared in a city and knew nothing about animals. I peered in through the window at the bulls. They milled around, looking angry and mean-spirited. I undid the lock on the door and opened it.

Nothing happened. The animals looked at the open door and snorted and pawed the ground, but they made no move towards it. I put my head around the door but they still didn't move. I picked up a rock and threw it at them.

Most of the Guardia Civil who stood at the entrance of the apartment block were middle-aged men, some of them carrying weight, but they moved quickly enough when they saw the bulls coming round the corner. The bulls were only half-grown, but they had the mistrustful look in their eyes of full-grown bulls and their skittish little hooves danced on the cobbled street. There was no one with a rope around their neck this time and they knew it. Two of them trotted past the doorway, appearing to ignore the two men who had stood their ground. Then just as quickly they turned, both of them. One of the men at the door reached for his pistol, but it was too late. The bull put his head down and gored his thigh. The animal lifted his head and the man was lifted with it, dangling almost upside-down from the animal's horn and screaming piteously. The other bull trotted right into the foyer of the building. I slipped in after him. Men fled from the animal in panic. One or two with cooler heads reached for weapons. That wouldn't do. I saw what I wanted to the left of the door. An old-fashioned fuse box. I jumped on to the back of a chair, swung the fuse box open and started flicking switches. Suddenly the whole building was in darkness. I jumped down and was knocked straight over by the hindquaters of the bull, its lithe body trembling with power, rage and fear. It bellowed loudly and I dived for the door of the office where the captives were being held. They were sure of themselves and hadn't bothered to lock it.

'Get out!' I yelled. 'Everybody out!'

There was a pistol shot in the foyer. Someone aiming for the bull, I thought. But I had no sense of anyone in the room moving. They were beaten and cowed. It was time to go. Any minute now, they would switch the lights on. I heard the skitter of hooves on the tiles and a man's cry of pain. Then I felt hands clutching my shirt. I recognized Paolo's voice.

'I can't walk too good,' he said. 'Help me.'

I got my arms around him and we moved into the hall like that. Once again, I felt the hindquarters of the bull brush against me. I could feel Paolo shaking and thought he was in shock, but then I realized that he was laughing. Outside in the dim light, the gored man lay on his side, moaning, and bulls rambled around the square as if they were in green pasture. Somehow I found myself smiling as well, as we slipped around the corner, full of youth and laughter and the conviction of our own immortality.

It had all happened a long time ago and now Paolo was in hospital, crippled and in a coma, and I was in a shadowy tunnel with a crowd of assassins after me. Paolo and I had enjoyed many years of friendship since then. But there was a dark current running through this affair that I didn't understand.

A cold shiver ran through me. A rat scuttled through the darkness and I felt its yellow eyes on me from the shadows.

Liam called me softly. I went through into the pump room. He had found tools somewhere and these were scattered across the floor, but it was Paul that he was concerned about. His breathing was shallow and rapid and there was a cold sheen of sweat on his skin.

'It doesn't look good,' I said.

'We need to get him to a hospital,' Liam said.

'Not much chance of that until Jesus gets back,' I said. If Jesus gets back, I thought to myself, hoping that he would get to the tunnel entrance on the other side before the Mexicans got there.

I helped Liam back on to the platform. There was little cover. The barrels I had lined up were of cosmetic use. A bullet would pass straight through them. We decided to take cover in the doorway to the pump room, to give us a line of retreat. We didn't ask each other where we were going to go after the pump room. I started to ask Liam what he had been doing in the pump room, but he held up one hand to silence me. I didn't question this. I couldn't hear anything, but I knew that Liam was intuitive about things like this. I peered into the darkness. There was a single emergency light between us and the tunnel. All you could see was darkness beyond the light. But this meant that all they could see was darkness as well.

I moved my feet and metal clanked behind me. I cursed my stupidity in helping them to pinpoint our position, but I checked the contents of the cans as well. Then I lifted both of them, hoping I had time. I scuttled to the edge of the platform and left both cans lying over the edge of the concrete, emptying into the water, and got back into position. Minutes passed. The noise I had made meant that they knew we were here, but they weren't trying to attack us. The cold had long overcome the adrenalin of the first alert. I couldn't feel my feet and I had to clench my jaw to stop my teeth chattering. Liam was perfectly still and motionless. But as I watched, I saw his expression change. He turned to me, his face a mask of alarm, and motioned me to the ground. As my face hit the ground, the tunnel seemed to explode in fire and noise. Somehow they had got a spotlight into the tunnel and they were using it to guide fire from the general-purpose machine-gun.

Massive chunks of masonry flew from the walls. Heavy bullets churned up the concrete of the platform as if it were wet clay and sent the barrels flying and ringing like bells as they ricocheted off the tunnel walls. The light was blinding. The sustained machine-gun fire stopped and resumed in short bursts. It occurred to me that they could only have brought a very small amount of ammunition for the big gun into the tunnel. But they were making up for it with small-arms fire now. I kept my head pressed to the floor. I could feel every strike of the heavy, metal-jacketed bullets against the platform. Then suddenly the light went out. Liam didn't fire and neither did I. We had to save our ammunition for single, close-quarter shots. Under the noise of gunfire, I could hear men wading through the water, half-running and splashing as they went. I took the flare gun that I had lifted earlier from my inside pocket. I fitted a flare into it, stood and fired at the place where I had emptied the two cans into the water.

For a moment, nothing happened and I loaded up another flare. Suddenly the entire surface of the water seemed on fire. A man rose from it, screaming, his body a cloak of fire. One of the cans I had poured into the water was petrol, but the other was heavy diesel oil. Between the two, the surface of the water was covered with a kind of napalm, the heavy oil making the volatile petrol adhere to skin and clothes, the petrol igniting the slow-burning oil. Yet there was one thing that I hadn't anticipated. There was a current in the water which had carried the burning fluids down the tunnel. Five or six men had got between us and the flames and they were coming forward, firing as they came, and now another two were clambering on to the platform from where they had concealed themselves in its lee. We were both firing now, single, aimed shots, but they were coming at us from three directions and we didn't have the ammunition for any sustained fire. Suddenly I heard Liam shouting. When I looked to him, he slid his gun across the concrete to me and disappeared into the pump room on his hands and knees. Suddenly I felt very isolated on the platform. I fired at black shapes that moved in front of the flames but I didn't seem to hit anyone. Then I felt a great weight fall on me from above. One of them must have somehow climbed the piping along the roof. I was lucky in that he hit the ground awkwardly and I saw the knife in his hand spill away, but then he was on me, kicking and clawing, and I fought back, forgetting about the others momentarily. He had his hands around my throat and I could feel the darkness starting to descend, but my hand cast around for a weapon and I found the butt of the flare gun. With all my strength,

144

I pushed the man away and as he staggered backwards I brought the flare pistol to bear and fired. The flare caught him under the breastbone and exploded. He screamed in agony and the man who had appeared beside him clutched at his face as red-hot embers struck him. I looked down at myself and realized I was covered wth the fiercely burning detritus of the flare. Almost sobbing, I tried to put them out but they would not come away and it was Liam, tottering and in agony, who rolled me in the water, then dragged me into the pump room.

As I lay on the ground, too weak to move, I heard cries in Spanish outside. We had no gun any more, and no hope. I lay back on the ground. As I did so, I heard a low rumbling sound in the distance. I turned my head and saw Liam turning one of the great wheels connected to the sluice pipes. The metal creaked and groaned, but the wheel turned and the sound grew and now there was uncertainty in the voices of the men outside the door.

'Up here, Jack,' I heard Liam say. 'Help me with Paul.'

Between us, we got him on top of one of the huge pumps, but he was limp and his skin felt cold. Then the rumble increased to a roar and there was another change in the men's voices outside.

I had listened once to a tape that Liam had been given. It had been recorded in the thirties on Tory Island, off the coast of Donegal. A navy ship, the *Wasp*, had been sent to recover uncollected taxes from the natives, and she had been wrecked in a storm with the loss of all two hundred and twenty men. The old man on the tape had been one of the island lightkeepers and he recounted how he had said to his companions on hearing what he thought were seabirds outside, 'Them birds is making a fair noise tonight', but the other man had replied, 'Tend to the light, them is not birds, them is the screamage of men.'

The screamage of men. I had not known what he meant by the odd, archaic phrasing until I heard Xabarra's men being swept away that night by the waters that Liam had released through the old sluice. And I would have been swept away as well, along with Paul, if Liam had not held on to us on top of the old pump.

It was an hour before the water receded, but we had no energy to get down from our perch on top of the machinery. Jesus found us there when he waded down the tunnel with Billy E and Tonto and two other men, all carrying assault rifles, Billy E moving through the dank tunnel with a practised wariness which some-how suggested an ease with a combat situation that he did not show elsewhere.

It was Tonto who examined Paul and had to tell Jesus that he was dead. A depressed cranial fracture, he said, probably some form of haemorrhage on the brain. Jesus looked blank, his eyes empty. I remembered the way he had touched Paul's face before he left. He did it again now, but the skin was cold to his touch.

It was a long walk out. Tonto and Billy E half-dragged, half-carried Liam. I stumbled through the water, half in a dream. Jesus carried Paul and would let no one else help him. In the end, we emerged on to the street through an iron service door which seemed to be at the rear of an abandoned station on the far side of the river. The sky was blue and cold and the skyscrapers around us seemed more unreal than the dark realm we had just left.

Thirteen

I waited in the room for almost half an hour until they brought the man in. It was one of those rooms you see on television with a single bulb and a battered and chipped table. There was one window high up in the wall and a one-way window in the other wall. A detective with acne scars on his face had met us at the front desk and brought me into the precinct.

'I don't know who you are,' he said, 'but apparently I got to let you see this guy.'

He didn't look happy about it, or about me, and he balked when I asked for Deirdre to come into the interrogation with me. She knew Spanish, but more importantly she had the intuition and judgement that she shared with her brother.

'Nobody said nothing to me about bringing any woman into this.'

In the end, he relented and let her watch from behind the one-way glass. They led the old man in after ten minutes. He shuffled in, looking older than I had expected, and more melancholy. I thought he would be reluctant to talk, that he would refuse to incriminate himself, but he admitted readily that he had come here to take revenge for his brother.

'Then I thought I could die content,' he said, 'but instead I lose another brother.'

His eyes were so sorrowful that I could hardly bear to look at him. Underneath the shabby suit he wore, I could see the proud bearing of a minor landowner, the provincial haughtiness.

'When will it end?' I asked.

'When they both die,' he said, 'the slut and her son.'

'The son has nothing to do with it,' I said.

'But if I hurt him, I hurt her,' he explained. 'First he dies and then she suffers. And then she also dies.' He seemed proud of his scheme.

I argued with him. I told him that he would die in jail if he persisted, but nothing would move him. I talked to him for over an hour. I learned that the police had found them easily, staying in a cheap hotel in a Puerto Rican area. I learned that there were four of them now, and that they were being held in Rikers Island. The man in front of me had tried to kill me, but something in me resisted the thought of the humiliations and worse that could be visited on an old man in a place like Rikers Island. But there didn't seem to be anything that I could do. I signalled towards the window that I was finished. When I looked back as I left, I could see the old man sitting staring off into space with a faint smile on his face.

When I went into the observation room, I found Deirdre and the cop with their heads together, talking like old friends. It didn't surprise me. Deirdre had a way of making friends with people in authority when she needed something.

'Detective Rodgers doesn't mind if I have a word with Señor Hernandez,' she said.

I opened my mouth to say something and closed it again. There was always a chance that Deirdre could get something out of the old man.

'I can't stay,' I said.

'That's all right,' she said. 'I can manage.'

'What are you going to ask him?'

'You don't see it, do you?' She looked amused.

'See what?'

'Never mind, Jack. We can talk later. I'm going to talk some history with an old man.'

148

Jesus was staying in my apartment on Christopher Street. His own place was a mess. The fire that had started on the staircase had been extinguished by the sprinkler system, but the water damage was immense, before you started looking at the bullet holes, bloodstains and smashed windows. In addition, the police were convinced that some sort of drug war had broken out and were looking for Jesus. I had no idea what had happened to the men who were in the tunnel. There had been no reports of any bodies found. When we had emerged into the small park we had passed some homeless people but if any of them had any thoughts about our strange cortège, they kept it to themselves.

Liam and I had brought Paul's body to the casualty unit of the De La Salle Hospital and had slipped away when the emergency people had descended on him. Billy E and Tonto had to stop Jesus from coming with us. Paul had a serious head injury and his clothing was covered with firearms residue. If Jesus was connected with his death, he was in serious trouble, but few people could have identified Liam or me.

I didn't know how to talk to Jesus. He had withdrawn into himself. He was polite but distant. Irene came to see him. I could see she was worried. She came again the night after I left Deirdre at the precinct. I put on my coat and left them to talk. I had no idea what way his loss would take Jesus, and I wasn't sure if Irene could help him, but I knew that I was no use.

It was a cold, crisp night. I walked, without knowing where I was walking, through Washington Square park and turned on to Broadway, a wind blowing down the old street that numbed my face, though I welcomed it, as if the freshness of the wind could bring some clarity to my thoughts. I couldn't get rid of the image of Alva being carried unconscious from Jesus's house. I wondered where she was now. I wondered if Xabarra would let her live. I thought about Paul as well, the way he had slipped from our lives, the terrible, undramatic way he had died. If Deirdre had been with me, she would have asked me if it was better to die in a dramatic way, if it would have made any difference to Paul. I realized how often I used her as a sounding board in my head, and how increasingly she was right and I was wrong. Dead is just dead and it doesn't matter if you see glory or ignominy in the manner in which death takes you.

I turned for home, but when I reached Washington Square park again, I found I couldn't face anyone. I sat on one of the seats where men played chess in the morning.

Stone found me there, I don't know how. He sat beside me.

'Appropriate enough place for us, I suppose, Jack,' he said, 'the chess players' seat.'

'I'm not really in the mood, John,' I said.

'I understand. No one likes to see young lives ruined. Or taken away for that matter. He was from a very good family, you know, young Paul.'

'Not good enough to keep him alive,' I said.

'No,' he said, with a soft laugh, 'and not a very good family in the moral, as opposed to the social or financial, sense either. Notorious strikebreakers and scab employers in the twenties, big investors in rotten cheap-labour regimes like Burma now. Your friend Paul rebelled. They weren't too keen on the fact that he was a homosexual either. And they were appalled by his choice of boyfriend.'

'Doesn't really matter now, does it?'

'No, I suppose it doesn't.'

'What about Alva?'

Stone chuckled.

'I have to give you this, Jack, you have Xabarra rattled. The means were a bit excessive, I grant you, but he isn't a happy man.'

'Alva, John.'

'She's with him. Unharmed, as far as I can see.'

I had the uneasy feeling that you wouldn't be able to see the harm that Xabarra might do.

'He won't let her go twice.'

'Not if he is still around, no, I can't see it.'

'So we're back to the same place.'

'We're back to the same place.'

'There's been too much killing, John.'

'I think your friend Jesus might think that there hasn't been enough killing. A very vengeful part of the world he comes from, it seems. Here, take this.'

He pressed an envelope into my hand.

'What is it?'

'Money. Plane tickets. Some basic information on Xabarra's Mexican holdings.'

'Why do I need this?'

'If you decide to go after Alva, and Xabarra, you'll need them. I told you that he was rattled. Xabarra has gone to Mexico and he has taken the girl with him.'

Jesus was sleeping when I got back to the apartment. Deirdre and Irene were sitting in the kitchen. Irene's eyes were red.

'How is Jesus?' I asked.

'Irene got him to take a sleeping tablet.' Deirdre stood up. 'I should go.' She turned to me. 'Would you walk with me?'

'Of course.'

We didn't speak for a long time as we walked towards her apartment on Fifth Street. In the end, Deirdre broke the silence.

'You really didn't see it, did you?'

'With the Puerto Ricans? No. Is there something I should see?'

'What did Irene tell you about Jesus's father?'

'She said she met him on the boat to the States.'

'That wasn't true. The man she killed in Puerto Rica, the brother . . .'

'Christ. Jesus's father?'

'She admitted it to me tonight.'

'Jesus doesn't know?'

151

'Of course not. And how can she tell him now?'

'What about the others – the old man?'

'He was a little shocked when I told him he had been trying to kill his own nephew. He pretended he didn't believe me at first. But he knew the moment I suggested it to him, I could see it in his eyes, he knew it was true.'

'How did it happen?'

'He was one of the ones went after her father. She knew he was vain so she led him on a bit. To get him on his own. But things got out of hand. She had a gun hidden in the hut she brought him to. But he got to her before she could get to the gun. When he'd finished with her, she crawled in her own blood to the place she had hidden the gun. He was laughing at her, she says, when she shot him.'

'But she was pregnant.'

'Yes.'

'And she kept the baby.'

Deirdre glanced at me quickly, then turned away, biting her lower lip. I put my hand on her shoulder.

'I'm sorry. That was stupid.'

I had put Deirdre in danger and she had been shot. The injury had left her unable to have children.

'It's all right,' she said.

'So Irene raised Jesus and invented a lover on the boat to be his father.'

'Yes.'

'What did you say to her?'

'I told her to leave it that way.' She turned to me. 'What would you have done?'

I thought about it.

'What did Señor Hernandez say?'

'He said that everything was changed and that he was confused. That he would have to consult with his family.'

152

'If they go home, I would leave things the way they are. If there is a chance of them contacting Jesus and of him learning the truth, then Irene has to tell him.'

'Just as cold as that? Take the expedient way out?'

'I didn't create the situation, Deirdre. I think he has a right to know who his father is, but he's not in good shape and I wouldn't want to be the one to pull the rug out from under him. Or Irene for that matter. Would he forgive her? She was raped after all. The crime was against her.'

'But that's not the way the world works, is it, Jack? She is the victim, but she has to take responsibility for the crime.'

'That's about it,' I said.

Then she took my hand. We walked on in silence. When we got to her apartment, she opened the door.

'Hungry?' she said. The apartment was cluttered with flea-market stuff, some good paintings, odd pieces of furniture. A classic Dior suit was draped over a mirror. A Philip Treacy hat hung on the corner of a Victorian wardrobe.

'I tried to go minimalist,' she said, 'but it's not really in me.'

She had made a bouillabaisse that morning, she said. As she warmed it, I sat at the kitchen counter and watched her. She was wearing a tailored Chanel skirt and a silk blouse. More formal than I remembered her. I could see the fine hairs on her arms catching the light, the weight of her breast against the silk. Her hair was pinned up and I found myself wanting to touch the back of her neck. I reminded myself that I had no rights here, that the prerogative of a shared past had been erased the day I took her into danger and got her shot.

'How is it really,' I said, 'working in an office? I can't imagine you doing it.'

'It probably does more good than dashing about Africa or somewhere, trying to get a lorryload of food in,' she said. 'In the end, policy saves more lives than food parcels.'

'But still,' I said.

'But still,' she said, 'I don't think I'm made for it. I'm going to hit somebody one of these days. There are so many bureaucrats, people who just can't see that they are dealing in human lives.'

She put the bouillabaisse on the table. We ate it with chunks of fresh bread and a Montrachet. As I wiped the bowl with a piece of bread, I looked up to see her smiling at me.

'What?' I said, with my mouth full.

'Makes a girl feel good,' she said, 'a man who enjoys his food.' She made espresso. I thought of a meal a long time ago in an old cottage in Edentubber, then afterwards with the rain beating against the window beside us. I put the thought out of my mind, depriving myself of it as a penance. We sat on her battered sofa with the coffee.

'I don't feel like talking,' she said. 'Do you mind if we don't talk?' She turned on the television and found a rerun of *The Quiet Man*. The kind of film that, despite all the stage Irishry, has never lost its authority. We watched it in companionable silence. I got a kick in the shins for being able to quote most of Barry Fitzgerald's lines.

It was something we had never really shared, a sense of domesticity, easy and unsensational. In the end, I got up to go, yawning She came over to me and took my hands. Her eyes searched my face. I had no idea what she was looking for. I held my breath. And then her lips touched mine. I touched her hesitantly, but she pulled me closer. I could feel her flesh under the silk of her blouse, her urgency and the authority of what she was demanding. I did not hesitate or question, or ask for any more second chances. I touched her breasts, then remembered what had happened. She felt the hesitation and she took my hand and placed it on the scar below her breast where the bullet had entered and been deflected downwards from her ribs. It seemed part of a strange betrothal, this torn flesh both condemning me and freeing me from blame.

And then her hands fell away and she lay back on the sofa, her face half-shadowed and her body open to me.

Later, we stood at the window together and watched the rain and the traffic and people hurrying past under umbrellas, the rug from the sofa wrapped around our shoulders.

'I thought that was it,' I said. 'You said some things to me and they were all true.'

'I claim rights of inconsistency,' she said. Then, more sadly, 'I can't keep my hand out of the flame, Jack. Neither of us can. Or Liam for that matter.'

'I'm going to Mexico,' I said.

'And Liam?'

'I haven't asked him.'

'He'll say yes.'

'Probably.'

'I've never seen Mexico,' she said.

'Neither have I,' I said. 'I always wanted to see Frida Kahlo's house.'

'The place she had with that bastard Diego.'

' Yes. Would you like to see it as well?'

'Yes,' she said in a muffled voice. 'Yes I would.' When I looked down at her, her eyes were wet with tears and she would not look at me.

PART II

Fourteen

The 747 climbed steadily out of Newark and banked right so that we passed over the city before cloud obscured our view of it. We had stayed on in New York for Paul's funeral. It had been a miserable affair, with Jesus unable to attend the ceremony, which was held in a private chapel on the family's estate in upstate New York. They could not keep him from the interment, but Liam scanned the crowd and reported hard-eyed men in plain clothes. Cops or ex-cops working as security men, spelling bad news for Jesus. We watched the funeral from the hill above the cemetery. Liam and I stood together. Deirdre linked arms with Jesus and held him as the coffin went into the ground and he faltered and almost fell.

Later that night, I went back to the cemetery with Liam and Jesus. Under cover of darkness, Jesus went into the cemetery to say whatever words he could find at his lover's grave. We watched the dark approaches to the cemetery, though it was the darkness at our backs that made us feel uneasy.

I had been in two minds about bringing Jesus with us. He had withdrawn into himself, barely answering when you spoke to him. I didn't want a passenger, particularly a passenger who was potentially unstable. On the other hand, he was an accomplished and resourceful streetfighter. On balance, I decided to take him.

So four of us flew to Mexico City. A few days' rest had left Liam able to walk again, although he had to use a stick to cover any distance. He seemed lighthearted as we boarded the plane. Jesus was distant, but he talked to Deirdre for long stretches at a time and I left them to it. When we were airborne and the great light-filled masses of New York, adrift in a sea of blackness, had fallen behind us, I joined Liam and we examined the information that Stone had given us. It seemed that Xabarra had two main residences in Mexico. A villa in a town called Patzcuaro, to the west of Mexico City, and a house near the city of Oaxaca.

'Extensive holdings in the south, stretching into Guatemala,' Liam read from Stone's notes.

'If he's planning to start growing opium, that's where he'll do it,' I said. 'It's pretty lawless up there, well out of harm's way.'

Food arrived and we put the notes aside. While I ate, Liam thumbed through a Lonely Planet guide. He stopped at one page and I could feel him reading intently.

'What date is it today?' he asked.

'Thirtieth of October,' I said.

'I think Xabarra wanted us to follow him to Mexico,' Liam said quietly.

'Why?'

'Because the start of November is a special day in Mexico.'

'Is it?'

'The night of the fist of November is called All Souls' Night where I come from. Then the second of November is All Saints' Day. My parents had this tradition on All Souls' Night. They would put chairs around the fire in a semi-circle and bank up the fire before they went to bed. You see, All Souls' Night is the night that the dead come back, and the chairs were for all the people belonging to us who were dead.'

'It's a bit eerie, Liam.'

'Not really. It would have been traditional for people to call in the evening and sit around the fire talking. Many's the night the sound of voices from the fireside downstairs lulled me to sleep. It was a reassuring sound, and the thought of all our family gathering round the fire one night of the year was a comforting idea to us. The Mexicans have different traditions, but the thinking is the same.'

'What did you call it again?'

'All Souls' Night.'

'What do they call it in Mexico?'

'The Day of the Dead.'

It was just before dawn when we reached Mexico City and Deirdre was dozing beside me. I woke her to see the ring of peaks around the city which made it seem, from this altitude, like some fabled place, and towering above them all the snow-capped volcano of Popocatepetl.Then it was the steep, ear-popping descent into the airport and then, after the chaos of the baggage hall, we emerged, pale and blinking, into the early morning sunshine of Mexico City.

Liam scanned and refused a few cabs, then we got into one driven by a small, broad man with a sardonic look on his face, the expression enhanced by what looked suspiciously like a knife scar at the corner of his mouth which lifted that side of his face into a permanent grin. When we got into a cab, I saw a photograph of a pretty, worn-looking wife and a teenage boy and girl, scrubbed to within an inch of their lives and smiling at the camera. Deirdre complimented him on his family and the grin broadened with genuine pleasure. I half-regretted getting off to a good start with him, as he spent the rest of the journey looking back towards us instead of looking at the road.

His taxi was a green Volkswagen Beetle, of which there seemed to be tens of thousands in Mexico City. As we sped through the traffic, I remembered the chief design feature of the Beetle which set it apart from other cars, the fact that the engine was in the back of the car, not the front. The worst thing about this, I thought gloomily as we squeezed through a tiny gap at seventy miles an hour, was that there was no engine mass to protect you in the event of a frontal collision.

None of the rest of them seemed to mind. Deirdre talked non-stop in Spanish to the driver, but Liam made them switch to English so that we could all understand. The driver told us that people called him Sonny, and that he had been an ex-cop who had been invalided out of the service. The same attack that had left him with a scar on his face had also severed a tendon in his leg so that he walked with a limp. Liam gave him fifty dollars and asked him to find us a comfortable hotel off the beaten track. We were waiting in traffic at the time, and Sonny turned and looked us up and down with a look which made it clear that he knew exactly what kind of men we were. Then he started to laugh as he pocketed the money and put the car into gear.

'What's funny?' Deirdre wanted to know.

'I'm thinking to myself,' he said, 'that life has been too quiet for too long.'

He found us a quiet hotel with a cool, tiled interior around a central glassed-over courtyard. I was glad of it. I was tired, and the teeming city outside had fatigued me even more. No one knew how many people lived in Mexico City, but thirty million was a conservative guess. Sonny went in and emerged having booked two single rooms and a double. I looked at Deirdre, but she kept her eyes on the ground. Liam shrugged, as if he had long ago given up trying to interpret what was going on between his sister and me.

Before I could work out what had happened, Liam and Deirdre had disappeared with Sonny and Jesus had walked off, saying something about wanting to find a church. I didn't try to follow. I went upstairs and lay down. Deirdre woke me just before noon. She had been shopping, with Sonny as her guide. She handed me a bag.

'We're going for lunch,' she said. 'I got you some clothes.'

I opened the bag. There was a Dries Van Noten shirt and a pair of black Armani jeans in it.

'You can pay me back later,' she said. 'Try them on.'

At least I felt human. Jesus met us in the lobby of the hotel. Liam was waiting outside in Sonny's taxi. He took us to Sanborns, near the Zocalo. The beautiful mosaic walls made the place feel cool. Outside, the midday sun beat down on us.

'Just because you're on a mission of terrible vengeance or whatever,' Deirdre said, 'it doesn't mean you can't dress properly for lunch.'

The lunch was good and expensive. Gambas with aioli, white tuna steaks, salsa with everything if you wanted. It struck me that it was the kind of place you might see Xabarra if he was in town. But I didn't think he was in town.

'Where do we start looking?' Jesus said. I noted the eagerness in his voice. Jesus was keen to look into Xabarra's eyes and ask some searching questions on the theme of life and death.

'Patzcuaro,' Liam said, 'I found out that it is a central place for celebrating the Day of the Dead. Why else would he have a villa there?'

'Fair enough.' I said.

'Sonny's going to come with us. He's got a friend with a pilot's licence'

I gave Liam a look.

'He's all right,' Liam said. 'We need somebody with local knowledge and the fact that he's a former cop can't hurt either. He gets five hundred dollars a day.'

'Does he know . . .?'

'He knows we're not here to look at Inca remains, but I told him to take us to wherever we want to go, then cut loose and find somewhere to stay. We can call him when we need him. That way, he isn't implicated any more than he has to be.'

'Things have a way of going wrong.'

'I think he knows that, but he appreciates that we're trying to keep him out. To tell the truth, I think he's itching for some action.'

'That's what I would be afraid of.'

After lunch, we walked through the city down to the Zocalo, the vast central square. There seemed to be some kind of permanent protest going on in the square, with a small tent village set up. There were young people with Hispanic features going from tent to tent, but as far as I could see, most were native people in traditional costumes.

'*Indigenas,*' Jesus said, 'Indigenous people. They're demanding land rights, recognition of their language.'

I should have welcomed the sun on my hair and the heat after all the time I had spent in the dark and dank places of New York, but I couldn't shake the feeling I had been left with after hearing Liam's story. I wondered, if it came to it, who would be sitting around my fire on All Souls' Night. I tried to pursue a reassuring image of parents and uncles, a gathering of humour and memory. But another image kept returning to me. Of a gathering of ghouls, of all those whose deaths I had had a hand in over the years, men with blood-soaked clothes, grinning skulls, men with half their faces blown away, mouths twisted in deathly snarls. Suddenly I felt cold. Deirdre took me by the arm.

'Are you OK?' she said.

'Just a strange thought,' I said.

'Your skin feels cold,' she said, frowning.

'It's nothing,' I said, turning away. I didn't want to start believing in premonitions. That was the way the dead got you, with their shadows and their regrets.

Later that evening, we drove out to the airport and spoke to Sonny's friend who had the chopper. I exchanged looks with Liam when I saw the helicopter. It was an old Bell Huey, the kind you see in Vietnam movies and I hadn't been aware that there were any still in the air. The last time I had seen one was in South-west Africa, many years ago, and the men on board were trying to kill us.

The pilot was called Ricardo. He wore Ray-Ban Wayfarers which seemed to be welded to his head and a leather flying jacket, and I got the impression that he did a lot of little trips with people who didn't necessarily want others to know their business. The chopper was expensive, but money wasn't a problem. Inside the envelope I had been given, I had found a platinum Amex card with my name on it. It also had a perfect copy of my signature on the back. The people who did such work for John Stone were thorough. Ricardo disappeared into an office and returned with a chit for me to sign.

'We go tonight,' he said. 'No drugs, no guns.' He turned abruptly and walked back into the terminal building.

Liam sent Sonny back into town to collect things from the hotel.

'Weapons might be a problem,' he said to me. 'There's no problem picking up something in Mexico City, but I don't know about this Patzcuaro place.'

'Play it by ear,' I said. 'We don't know what might happen. I know that if we start putting bullets in prominent Mexican citizens this far from the border without a way home, then we're in big trouble.'

That afternoon, I took Deirdre to Frida Kahlo's house in the suburbs of the city. I thought it would be an act of voyeurism. The house itself was beautiful, its colours muted over the years but still part of her aesthetic. But you saw her bed as well, where she had spent so many years of her life. You saw the metal corsets that had held her tortured body together after she fell under the wheels of a tram and was impaled by its undercarriage. And you saw where she painted the strange, beautiful self-portraits, a woman nude, mutilated and adrift among the strange symbols that floated up from her people and their long history. Deirdre looked at a photograph of her, the jet-black hair, the high cheekbones, a face driven to a preternatural beauty by suffering.

'She was a handsome woman,' she said, and I knew what she meant by the phrase.

We took off at dusk. I didn't know whether Ricardo was qualified to fly a helicopter at night. I didn't know if it mattered. We sped through the warm night towards Patzcuaro, each of us alone with his or her thoughts, the only light in the cabin the glow of the dashboard lights on Ricardo's face. After two hours, he pointed downwards.

'Lake Patzcuaro,' he said.

We could see the outline of the lake with the lights of towns dotted around it, then a larger patch of light which we seemed to be flying towards. We lost altitude, crossed the lake and passed the shoreline barely thirty feet above the ground. We missed a powerline by inches. It didn't seem to concern Ricardo, but Sonny looked at me nervously and blessed himself.

We touched down outside an old, corrugated hangar. There was a battered yellow cab waiting for us. The Day of the Dead had not been prominent in Mexico City, but it was everywhere in Patzcuaro. Windows and doorways were dressed with arches of marigolds. Although it was only ten o'clock, a row of *indigenas* women slept in the archways of the mayor's palace. Others were selling marigolds on the street or cooking chickens on braziers made from oil drums. We checked into the hotel, Sonny beaming with pleasure as we did so. He said that he knew a local police chief and he had had guests ejected in order to fit us in. Deirdre was eager to get outside, so we left Jesus and Sonny to carry the bags in and Liam accompanied us into the crowded square.

There were stalls selling everything on the street – brightly coloured wraps, iguanas hung up by their ankles and glaring at passers-by through ancient eyes, stalls selling dried whitebait, pulque, the milky alcoholic drink, and dozens of other foods. In front of the Mayor's Palace, a mariachi band had struck up and the brassy music seemed to penetrate the whole town. Liam pointed out a stall with a wooden bus driven by a cheery skeletal driver. There were more skeletons at different stalls – skeleton cowboys, skeleton policemen, skeleton priests.

'Look, Jack,' Deirdre said in a quiet voice. She picked up a little cradle made from coloured candy. Inside it was a tiny skeleton baby. She stared at it and I dared not guess what she was thinking. I looked down at the stall. There were hundreds of the little cradles.

'*Por los ninos*,' the stallholder said, smiling. For the children. I smiled back at her. It was a way of dealing with death, by simultaneously embracing it and mocking it. I admired it, but the forms of death that I had known for so long would not be mocked. As we walked further down the street, I saw an old *indigenas* woman watching Liam. He was able to walk without a stick now, but he still limped. The woman beckoned to him.

'She wants you to go over to her,' Deirdre said.

Liam went to her. She motioned to him to take off his shoes. He took them off and she examined his feet carefully, feeling along the line of the bone, tracing the knuckle of each toe with her hand.

'Bastinado?' she said, looking up at Liam in enquiry.

He nodded.

She didn't seem surprised. She took a foot in each hand and said something else.

'She wants to know if you can feel the heat from her hands.'

Liam nodded. All his attention was on the old woman now.

She blessed herself and started to speak under her breath. I caught enough words to realize that she was praying in church Latin. When she finished, she blessed herself again and released his feet.

'She wants to know how they feel now?' Deirdre translated.

'Good,' Liam said. 'As good as new, in fact.'

167

The old lady waited for Deirdre to translate, then she shook her head and wagged her finger sternly.

'What is she saying?' Liam asked.

'She says they will never be as good as new,' Deirdre said, 'but that she has done what she can to help.'

We walked on down the street. A procession came towards us with another mariachi band leading it. They were carrying a statue of the Virgin bedecked in marigolds. Shy schoolchildren in traditional costumes followed. All the *mesquites*, those with Spanish blood in them, seemed to be enjoying themselves. It was hard to tell how the *indigenas* felt about it. After a while, I saw Deirdre yawning. We went back to the hotel. Firecrackers went off in the street. I was reminded of the night in Cuenca, the night I met Paolo, the sense of things building to a crescendo.

Jesus and Ricardo were sitting in the hotel bar.

'Where's Sonny?' I asked.

'Gone drinking,' Jesus said, with a shrug. I wasn't all that happy with this, but there wasn't much I could do about it. I sat down beside Ricardo.

'Where did you learn to fly?' I asked, then wondered if he would take it as an insult. He regarded me for a moment, then took off the big Ray-Bans. They were not an affectation as I had thought. The skin around his eyes was scarred and raw-looking. I looked down and realized that his hands were in a similar state.

'US Air Force,' he said, 'flying Green Giants. Then I took a job flying for an old company, you know, servicing the rigs. Until I got this.' He touched his eyes. 'One of my corneas was scarred. The federal air people wouldn't let me fly after that.'

'What happened?'

'Do you remember the Bravo 90 disaster?'

The name was familiar. I realized it was the big oil rig that caught fire in the Gulf of Mexico in the early eighties. He told us

168

how he had just landed some machinery and was flying back to the mainland when the rig went up.

'You wouldn't believe the flames,' he said. The drill bit was expelled from the well with such force that the air was full of pieces of drill pipe and the bit itself shot past his chopper as though a malicious will deep in the ground was intent on bringing him down. He reached the helipad through thick smoke and flames and managed to pick up seven men. He dropped them on the rig supply ship which was near by and went back, but this time he couldn't even see the helipad for the oily black smoke. He pulled back and hovered. Every so often, a figure would emerge from the smoke, tumbling to the sea underneath. Sometimes they were on fire. The burning men landed on the unignited crude that had spilled into the ocean. Sometimes the flames were enough to ignite a patch of oil. The buoyancy of the oil kept the dying men afloat, so that they were denied even the mercy of drowning.

He was running low on fuel when a sudden gust of wind carried the smoke away from the west side of the rig and he saw men standing on the roof of the accommodation block. There were flames all around them and he knew that there was no chance of them getting out by themselves. Then the smoke closed around them again. With a mental picture of the superstructure in his head to guide him, he took the chopper into the smoke. He got as far as the roof with relative ease, the helicopter bucking and swaying as the updraughts from the flames caught the rotors. He touched the skids to the roof of the accommodation block and men started to climb aboard. The capacity of the chopper was eight. There were fourteen men on the roof. Eleven of them got into the cabin. The other three clung to the skids. As they did, flame burst through the roof directly in front of him, the perspex being sprayed with hot tar, cracking and blistering almost immediately. He tried to shout back to tell the men to let go of the skids, that they would all die if they did not, but of course they didn't, and the helicopter could not rise.

169

The perspex cracked and flame licked through the canopy.

'What did you do?' Liam said.

Ricardo replied that he put the craft into a tight, hard turn, throwing the three men off into the flames, then he took off, shooting straight into the air, the interior of the helicopter rotten with the smell of burning plastics. He thought that smoke had got into his eyes, but in fact the flames had burned them and the flesh was swelling and closing rapidly. Through slits, he looked down and saw that the instrument panel was on fire and that the flames were licking at his hands but he dared not let go.

The helicopter had been sprayed with burning oil and watchers thought that a piece of the fire had detached itself and had started to fly towards them. One thing he remembered was that he could not breathe because the fire was sucking the oxygen out of the cabin. He dived towards the sea, but misjudged it. Two more men died because of that, knocked out by the impact and unable to scramble clear of the sinking aircraft. He woke up in the naval hospital along with the other survivors.

'You lost those men,' Deirdre said, 'but none of the rest would be alive if you hadn't gone in for them.'

'One of them was a few beds away from me in the hospital,' Ricardo said. 'His brother was one of the men I threw off the skids. When he saw that I was awake, he came over to my bed and looked down at me and spat in my face.'

Ricardo put the Ray-Bans back on again, joined his hands and looked at the floor, as if waiting for something, as if a sense of the fairness of things might come in through the door there and then and set him free of his memories.

We were at breakfast next morning when Sonny came down. He looked wretched. His eyes were red and there was a strong smell of tequila. He ordered coffee and slumped at the table. He held up one hand as though somebody was about to remonstrate with him, although no one had spoken.

'I know, I know, I should not have drunk so much. But I was on a mission.'

'What sort of mission?' Liam said. He was watching Sonny intently.

'A mission of finding something,' Sonny said.

Liam looked worried. I wasn't very happy myself. Sonny was an ex-policeman and people who are up to no good can smell a policeman, particularly a policeman who is asking questions.

'I made a discovery,' Sonny said, momentarily brightening.

'What was that?' Jesus said.

'I found out where your Mr Xabarra lives. I had to ask in many bars.' I lowered my eyes to hide my dismay. Liam looked away. Sonny talked on about a villa in the countryside outside the town.

'Better go up and pack,' I said to Deirdre. 'We'd better leave the hotel.'

'There's a concert tonight for his guests,' Sonny talked on, oblivious. 'They say Xabarra flew in a whole orchestra. The bishop will be there. It's in the cathedral of Saint Francis. It's the oldest church in the province.'

While Deirdre was packing, I went into the town and hired a Subaru Jeep. We drove out to the hangar and left our things there. I asked Ricardo to take us up so that we could have a look at Xabarra's house.

'Can you creep up on it?' I said. 'Stay at a distance?'

'Sure,' he said, 'whatever you want to do.' He studied a map for a while and then we took off.

The house was only a few minutes' flight from the town. Ricardo flew behind a small hill about half a mile from the house, then slowly brought us to the summit so that we could see over the top.

'They'll hear the engine,' Liam said.

Ricardo shrugged.

'It won't matter,' he said. 'Many wealthy people come here in helicopters for the Day of the Dead. They think the festival puts them in touch with the people.'

The villa was large and rambling. In New York, Xabarra had to be subtle about his defences. There were no such restrictions here. The house was surrounded by a high wall topped with razor wire. There were cameras everywhere and I noticed that the ground had been cleared for a full five hundred yards on the outside of the wall, so that there was no cover for anyone who might want to creep up on the house.

'No way in there,' Liam said.

'No,' I agreed. 'I think one of us is going to have to go to mass.' I had found out from Sonny that the concert actually took the form of a baroque mass.

'It'll have to be Deirdre,' Jesus said.

Liam and I looked at each other. We didn't like it, but Jesus was right. Xabarra knew Liam and me, and the chances were that he had seen photographs of Jesus.

'I don't mind,' Deirdre said. 'I didn't come along to see the sights.'

'All you'll have to do is see whether the girl is with him, and whether he has any bodyguard in the church with him.'

'Don't try to take the girl tonight,' Liam said.

'Why? Because the bishop's here?'

'No, because you'll be exposing him in front of his own people. I have a feeling that will matter more to him than anything. He will stop at nothing to catch up with you.'

'The girl probably won't be there,' I said. She's probably dead, I thought.

When we got back to the hangar, I sent Jesus into town to buy some sleeping bags, a gas stove and food. I had decided that the hangar was the best place for us to stay. If Sonny had been in town asking questions, then it was likely that Xabarra had heard there was a stranger enquiring after him.

172

'We should take a look at the church,' Liam said.

Deirdre said she would come too.

Sonny said he would stay with Ricardo, who wanted to do some work on the chopper. I think Sonny had belatedly realized his mistake and wanted to make amends.

The church was half an hour's drive on the other side of Patzcuaro. It was plain on the outside, a Spanish colonial cathedral, its exterior plasterwork stained and cracked, revealing the brickwork underneath. There were creepers growing up under its reddish tiles. Lizards basked on the low wall surrounding the church. The wood of the doors was sunbaked and cracked. There were no cars around, but we went in cautiously. We could see that the front of the church was rigged as if for a full orchestra. When our eyes got used to the gloom, we could see that the interior of the church seemed even more timeworn than the exterior. Huge damp stains ran down the walls and a liana had forced itself between the tiles and hung down into the body of the church. The stations of the cross hung in relief around the walls, faded almost to nothing, yet enough of them remained for you to make out the figures of the apostles and of Jesus and Mary, each of them painted with the broad faces and brown eyes of the indigenous people. Above the altar was a wooden Crucifixion, carved in the European style, its wood cracked and split, though the body of Christ was picked out and beautifully detailed, the strain of the face, its eyes closed, the anguish, compassion and authority etched upon it. I thought about the unknown hand that had carved it and what he would make of what had become of it. Deirdre pointed out that the arm had been broken at the elbow and that someone had painstakingly repaired the break with a hospital bandage and a wooden splint. It should have looked odd, yet it lent the carving a strange pathos.

Deirdre knelt to say a prayer and Liam lit a candle, both fitting and unselfconscious gestures which left me feeling uncouth. I

173

moved closer to the carved figure of Christ, thinking, I suppose, to work my way into a kind of spirituality through appreciating the art involved in it, an art which its maker probably supposed a gift from God. The more I tried to concentrate on it, the more a small insistent feeling of uneasiness grew in me. I started to feel edgy and uncomfortable. In the end, acting on an impulse which I couldn't explain, I took Deirdre by the elbow and hurried her towards the altar.

'Liam,' I hissed.

He came immediately. I motioned them behind the altar, towards the sacristy door. Praying that it wasn't locked, I tried it. The handle turned and we slipped through, just as the main church door opened. I left the sacristy door ajar and peered through the crack. I saw Richard Xabarra enter. The other man with him looked like a musician. He was talking animatedly about something to do with the concert. He didn't concern me, but the two men behind him whose eyes moved restlessly around the building did concern me. I wondered if they were looking for the owner of the hired Jeep that sat in full view in front of the church. I wondered if they had left someone outside. I silently closed the door and told Liam and Deirdre what I had seen. Liam slipped out the back door of the sacristy and came back to tell us that there were two cars beside ours, and two men leaning against them, smoking. Deirdre looked out of the sacristy door.

'If you go straight across the ground there,' she whispered, 'and over that little hill, you'll find the road. Meet me there.'

Before I had a chance to answer, she threw the sacristy door open and strode down the aisle towards the small group of men. The two guards looked wary. The musician looked irritated at the interruption. Xabarra did not have any expression at all.

'Hi,' Deirdre said, 'is this where the concert is tonight? I was looking for some information in the sacristy, but I couldn't see any.'

'There is a choral mass taking place here tonight, yes,' Xabarra said.

'It is a private event,' the musician said bluntly, 'by invitation only.' Deirdre turned to him, and I could see him quail a little.

'Where I come from,' she said, 'the house of God is open to everyone. An invitation is not required.'

A wintry smile flickered across Xabarra's face.

'I apologize,' he said, 'you are of course quite correct. Please forgive us our small snobberies, and kindly accept my . . . desire that you should attend as my guest.'

I could see Deirdre draw herself up to her full height before Xabarra started to laugh.

'I am sorry, I am sorry. It is not up to me to call you my guest in someone else's house,' he said, gesturing towards the altar and its splinted Christ, 'but if you would do me the honour of allowing us to share your company, I would be most pleased.'

Deirdre put out her hand.

'Deirdre Macken,' she said, using her mother's name.

'Richard Xabarra,' he said. 'You will sit with me tonight at the concert, if, of course you don't mind.'

Deirdre accepted with a smile. Xabarra watched her all the way to the door of the church. I wasn't sure if I liked the way he watched her.

We ran out of the back of the church and towards the top of the little hill. Liam's running was laboured, but he was able to keep up. Deirdre was waiting for us with the Jeep on the other side. We dived into the pick-up.

'I don't want you going to that mass,' Liam said.

I didn't say anything. I was inclined to agree with Liam, but I didn't think ordering Deirdre around was going to get me anywhere.

'I'm going, Liam,' she said quietly.

175

I recognized the voice. You didn't argue with it.

'Why?' Liam demanded.

'Because it's Bach,' she said. 'You know I love Bach.'

'I think he knows who you are,' Liam said.

'That's not possible,' she said.

'We're going to come as well,' I said. 'We can watch from outside. The graveyard will be full of people. Apparently the tradition is that people spend the night at the grave of their loved ones, drinking and eating. We can lose ourselves in the crowd.'

'You have no idea who this man is,' Liam said. 'You have no idea at all.'

'You're wrong,' Deirdre said.

But I wondered. There was no doubt that Xabarra possessed a dark charisma.

She arrived at the hangar at seven o'clock, wearing a black Versace dress.

'Sit down, sister,' Liam said, 'before Sonny here takes a heart attack.'

'I thought we were supposed to be discreet,' I grumbled.

Jesus laughed and slapped my shoulder.

'Don't be sour, Jack. Xabarra will be so occupied with Deirdre, we'll be able to steal the other girl and he won't even notice.'

'It's time to be serious,' Liam said, cutting through the banter. 'We're going into a very dangerous place here. A man like Xabarra on his own ground is not to be taken lightly. Deirdre is in more danger here than I think she realizes. And we're all in mortal danger if Xabarra realizes that we are here. Please keep that in mind.'

'Can I speak?'

It was Ricardo, coming towards us from the chopper, wiping his hands on a rag.

'Please,' Liam said.

'Nobody told me anything about terrible danger. Nobody

asked me if I wanted to look over my shoulder for the rest of my life to see if Xabarra is coming.'

'I have to apologize, Ricardo,' I said swiftly. 'This is my fault. I never meant for you to get close to danger. In fact, maybe it's better that you return to Mexico City now and forget that you ever saw this.'

Ricardo wiped his hands slowly on a rag.

'I don't know,' he said. 'On the one hand, the pay is good. On the other hand, no money is worth your life.' He thought for a moment. 'Double the money,' he said, 'and I'll stay.'

I made a show of hesitation but in fact I was delighted. The money belonged to John Stone, and I had a feeling we were going to need the helicopter. I agreed to Ricardo's fee with a curt nod.

'If you agree to be on twenty-four hour call,' I said.

He nodded.

'All right, we're settled then,' Liam said. 'Ricardo and Sonny stay here. I go with Jack and Jesus to the cemetery. Deirdre goes to the concert, and keeps her ears and her eyes open and doesn't do anything reckless.'

Sonny looked like a schoolboy who had been bounced from the school trip for bad behaviour.

'We'd better get going,' I said, looking at my watch.

Deirdre drove the pick-up and we sat in the back. When we got close to the church, we sat under a tarpaulin. We had armed ourselves with whatever we could find at the hangar. I had a big wrench, its handle wrapped in masking tape for grip. Liam had a short iron bar which he carried up his sleeve. Jesus was the only one with a proper weapon, a rusty machete he had found on the ground outside the hangar. He had spent an hour sharpening it, but I still didn't like the look of its jagged and rust-spotted blade.

The road was busy with families in old trucks and ancient, battered American cars, bound for the graveyard beside the church. Interspersed with this traffic was the occasional Mercedes and

Lincoln as the invited guests made their way to the concert. Looking out of the back of the truck, I saw the bishop being driven in a black Cadillac, looking the epitome of self-satisfied religious hierarchy through the ages. This area had once had a famous bishop, Vasco de Quiroga, who helped the *indigenas* become self-sufficient and protected them from the worst depredations of the Spanish conquerors. Unfortunately, such men crop up among the hierarchy only every few hundred years.

When we got to the spot where Deirdre had picked us up before, she slowed to a halt. There were many people on foot now, heading towards the graveyard, carrying food in baskets, beer, mescal and wreaths of orange marigolds, and it was easy for us to join them discreetly. There were plenty of European faces there as well, backpackers and travellers. I was older than them, but at least my white face wouldn't stand out too badly.

I got out and went round to the driver's door of the pick-up. Deirdre put her hand on my arm through the open window.

'Be careful,' I said, and I had the same strange feeling of foreboding that had assailed me in the church.

'Don't worry,' she said, smiling, 'I can always pray to the splinted Christ. He'll look after me.'

I realized that the Christ figure had moved her as well. I watched the back of the pick-up as she drove off, and hoped that the sense of intuition was false. Liam put his hand on my shoulder.

'You're wrong to blame yourself for getting Deirdre into situations like this, you know.' He knew I was thinking about the night that she was shot. 'Deirdre is mistress to no man,' he said. 'She picks her own battles and woe betide any man who gets in her way. Let's go join the pilgrims.'

And indeed the whole affair did have the feeling that a medieval pilgrimage might have had. There were the pious and the profane, the wealthy and the poor, the sober and the drunk, all propelled forwards into the shadow of the cathedral. Cooking fires had been lit already in the graveyard and the air was full of their smoke and the rich smells of food. Many of the graves were surrounded by candles in glass jars. As we entered the graveyard, the smell of food became stronger: frijoles, fish fried in butter and garlic, burritos, meat grilled with charcoal, chicken with the unsweetened chocolate sauce they call *mole*.

Liam laughed at me.

'Jack's hungry.'

'Jack's always hungry,' Jesus said.

'Come on,' I said. 'We'll try to get close to the cathedral, see if Xabarra has Alva with him.'

It was easy enough to move between the graves at first. People crouched around the headstones, the women cooking, the men talking to their neighbours and children playing everywhere. But it became harder to move as the graveyard started to fill up.

The sun was almost set by now and a crescent moon hung over the cathedral. We reached a small hill from where we could look down on the people arriving for the choral mass. It was obvious that the wealthy and fashionable of the province had been invited. There were at least three limousines flying the Mexican flag. As we watched, a tall, smiling man got out of one and waved to the onlookers as photographers crouched in front of him. There were a few cars with diplomatic plates as well. Xabarra was indeed a well-connected man.

Finally, Xabarra arrived in a black stretch Mercedes flanked by two police motorcycle outriders. I ignored the outriders and focused on the casually dressed men in the two pick-ups behind the limo. They swung out of the back of the pick-ups before they stopped and moved up to form an escort on either side of the limo, their eyes scrutinizing the crowd. Their features were Mexican, but the technique and the execution was pure CIA. I knew there were ex-operatives who ran schools in that sort of thing, but sometimes their connection with the organization wasn't so much in the past as it appeared to be. At any rate, Xabarra emerged from the limo like a potentate receiving homage from his subjects. It was clear who was at the centre of this event. I strained my eyes, trying to see if he had travelled alone. The door of the limo remained open and he seemed to be waiting for someone. Then Alva stepped out. It was difficult to get a clear view of her. She kept her head down as she got out and then she shook her hair out of her eyes and straightened, seeming unaware of the crowd, a kind of hauteur surrounding her that seemed almost unnatural in someone so young.

I felt Liam nudge my arm. He indicated the porch of the church. I saw Deirdre standing there. Saul was standing beside her, looking solicitous, smiling and talking to her. She looked tense and strained and my heart went out to her. I didn't think that she had anticipated an event of this magnitude. I was surprised myself. I had expected a provincial artistic event with a few local luminaries present, but there was an unmistakable air of a celebrity event about this. Xabarra and Alva made their way slowiy towards the cathedral door, Xabarra shaking hands as he went. I looked back at Deirdre. She was looking towards the limo. Then she stiffened suddenly, her eyes narrowed and she put her hand to her mouth in an involuntary gesture.

'Something's happened,' Liam said, as tense now as his sister.

Saul noticed the gesture and, as he turned to her, she regained her composure, making a fanning motion with her hand and smiling as though the heat had momentarily affected her.

'I want to get her out of there,' Liam said. He sounded ready to walk into the crowd and walk her out with him.

'Forget it, Liam,' I said, in as hard a voice as I could muster. 'You'll get her killed. Let it play out. She's safe as long as she is in the middle of that crowd.'

'For Christs sake, Jack,' Liam said, 'this is Deirdre.'

'And that is Richard Xabarra, Liam. It isn't worth the risk.'

As we watched, Xabarra saw Deirdre. He kissed her on both cheeks and introduced her to Alva. Even at a distance, there was a sense of two women sizing each other up. Xabarra placed Alva on his right side and Deirdre on his left. It was a blatantly possessive gesture. He led them through the door. Saul stepped in behind them, and spoke briefly to the bodyguards. Two of them took up positions at the door. As they passed through, I had a glimpse of the interior of the cathedral, transformed since our visit with vast arrangements of flowers framing the doorway and the nave thronged with the wealthy and the favoured. The old wooden altar was now covered in a white linen cloth and glittering gold candlesticks, and behind it were the ranks of the orchestra, their instruments raised as though this was in honour not of the risen Christ but of the man I had just watched enter. I wondered if they had covered up the splinted Christ. And then the great doors closed with a muffled crash and Liam turned to look at me as though we had allowed something of terrible consequence to take place in front of us.

Fifteen

I cannot think about that night without hearing Bach, and without feeling the music as counterpoint to pity and terror. But Bach was addressing the eternal mysteries, the things that pinion men to their destinies, whereas the trap we fell into was more prosaic.

We went back into the graveyard and found Jesus. The atmosphere had changed during the half-hour we had been gone. Men were drinking openly now. A pick-up drove past, going fast, two young men in the back waving Corona bottles and firing single shots in the air from antiquated rifles. Here and there, small family groups sat at their gravesides, talking with quiet gravity, but a frenzy was building among the young men. Apart from the many smoking fires and the candles at the graves, there was no light in the graveyard, and it was difficult to see where you were going.

Jesus was standing close to the gate of the graveyard. He looked edgy.

'Those guys of Xabarra's,' he said, 'there are a few of them looking around the graveyard. As well as that, take a look.'

He pointed towards the little hill we had used to approach the graveyard. In the faint moonlight, you could see two men with guns sitting on it. It might have been a coincidence. It was an obvious place to put security if you were trying to protect someone in the cathedral. However, someone trying to protect the cathedral would be looking outwards. The two men we could see were looking down on the graveyard. A pall of smoke from the cooking fires drifted over and obscured them again. Then I heard a voice shouting in Spanish in the darkness, a voice I recognized.

'Saul,' Liam said.

'What is he saying?' I asked.

'To spread out along the perimeter,' Jesus said quietly. 'We're trapped.'

'It's going to be hard to get out,' Liam said quietly.

'So I suppose we go inwards,' I said, 'towards the cathedral.'

'There are trees the other side of the cathedral,' Jesus said. 'We might have a chance if we can get there.'

'I'm not leaving without Deirdre,' Liam said,

'Neither am I,' I said. 'We make our way towards the cathedral. Jesus, you get around the other side, try and see where we can get through. I'll wait with Liam for the mass to end. We'll try to grab Deirdre when they come out.'

'What about Alva?' Jesus asked.

'Let's get Deirdre,' I said heavily. 'Let's just get Deirdre for now. Let's move.'

We started to pick our way carefully across the graveyard, trying to slip between the graves. We tried to fan out but found that we lost sight of each other in the darkness. The smoke stung your eyes as well. There was a smell of candle grease in the air. Occasionally there would be a shout of laughter or a scream in the darkness and, more frequently now, two or three shots together, the sound of men firing into the air. We had our weapons, such as they were, in our hands now, and they somehow seemed to mark us down as men of another time, darker and more bloody, and I had a sense that the very soil under our feet, drenched in blood and violent history, somehow responded to this. I saw how people turned away from us, or blessed themselves when they saw us. I looked at Jesus with the notched machete in his hand and the shadow of death recently cast over him and I thought how little I would like to meet him in this place as an enemy, the fires and guttering candles giving it something akin to a hellish atmosphere now.

We kept low, protected by the darkness yet turning at every shadow, ready to strike. I thought that some innocent could yet get in our way and be struck down. From about ten yards away, I heard an instruction barked in a crisp, military tone. I didn't need to know what it said. I could see the back of the cathedral now and the great stained-glass window, its blurred colours and towering saintly figures adding to the surreal feeling of the night, the sense of the hallucinogenic that had descended upon us.

A figure rose up in front of Jesus, and I saw him lash out, quick as a snake, with the machete. There was a muffled cry, the figure fell to the ground and Jesus stood over him, blood creeping over his hand and wrist from the blade, which was dark and wet. He seemed to be looking for something. I could feel the madness of the thing. I had a terrible vision of a woman or child lying there, but I heard Liam's voice.

'Can you find his gun?' he whispered.

'He dropped the fucker,' Jesus said, still looking.

'Keep moving,' I said, 'keep moving. Take the guns the next time.'

I looked up and saw an old *indigena* man watching us by the light of the candles on his grave. He was wearing a *huelpe* and seemed to be on his own, as if all his family had preceded him and he was the only one left to bear witness. He looked at us but there was indifference in his eyes, an indifference honed over the centuries to the violence of Europeans, their incomprehensible will to hurt.

I was close enough to the cathedral now to hear the swell of the music, the voices of men and women soft now, almost whispering their devotion, but you could sense the great pulse behind the sound. The smoke swirled around us. I seemed to lose sight of Jesus and Liam. I looked up and saw that I was standing in front of a mausoleum, the figure carved in front of it unmistakable in its

European features and eighteenth-century military dress, one of the men whose ancestors had subdued this country with sword and fire. Equally unmistakable was the motif of empty-eyed skulls carved on the corners of the mausoleum. I edged around the corner of the mausoleum building and almost walked straight into one of Xabarra's men. As he tried to bring his gun up, I lashed out with the wrench, catching his forearm. His gun fell to the ground, but, as I reached for it, he brought his foot down hard on my hand and I fell backwards. He called out and I gave up on the gun and backed away fast into the shadows. I kept backing until suddenly I was in a marshy stand of trees behind the church. Two shots were fired then, very close. I started to run, then thought twice about it and got on my hands and knees and started to crawl through the undergrowth. Firstly, because the noise is distinct from the noise of a person running through foliage and is more difficult to locate, which is why an animal moving unseen through bushes is so disconcerting. Secondly, because people firing blind tend to fire high.

I kept crawling, but there were no more shots. I should have stopped crawling and taken my bearings, but a kind of madness seemed to drive me on. Not fear exactly, but an uncontrollable impulse to flight. I kept slipping on the swampy ground. I was covered in stinking mud and when I put my hand to my face I could feel it hot and swollen with mosquito bites. But I kept going. Kept going until I found myself sliding head first down a muddy bank, the knotty liana roots tearing at my hands as I grabbed for something to stop the slide, and then I was in water a few feet deep, muddy water full of the rotting detritus of the trees, but I pressed myself close to the bank and listened for the pursuit. I heard nothing, but in my disorientation I pressed closer to the bank and waited. I waited there for a long time, my heart hammering in my chest, the blood pounding in my ears, until slowly the madness that had driven me through the trees began to fade.

I got hold of one of the roots and levered myself out of the water. I realized that I had completely lost my bearings. The trees cast a lightless canopy above my head. I listened, but all I could hear was the sound of cicadas in the trees. Then I heard the pulse of the music in the distance, voice upon voice rising in layers to a crescendo. I moved towards the music, letting it pull me in, the tones of redemption and glory. Suddenly, through the foliage, I could see the glow of the great church window and I knew where I was. I reached the edge of the trees and went down on my belly again and crept to the edge, but I could see no one. Wave upon wave of music burst on the night air as the mass reached its final stages. I realized that I needed to be at the front of the church. If Liam and Jesus had made it through, there might still be a chance of rescuing Deirdre, and yet the music seemed to hold me in place, swelling to its full majesty, then dying away in slow tones until at last it faded and was gone. As it did, I heard what sounded like tiny footprints on the leaves over my head. I looked up and felt a raindrop on my face.

Throwing caution to the wind, I ran around the side of the cathedral, keeping close to the wall. The first guests had started to leave the cathedral. I couldn't see Liam or Jesus. There seemed to be some kind of commotion going on at the gates of the cathedral. As far as I could see, a truck carrying fourteen or fifteen men with bottles in their hands was attempting to get through the gate. Xabarra's men were trying to stop them. I saw that most of the men on the truck were drunk, and some of them had guns. As I watched, the shouting got louder and a bottle smashed on the ground beside one of Xabarra's men. He pulled a gun from his belt and a shotgun was pointed at him from the truck. The man who seemed to be the leader of Xabarra's men motioned to him to put the gun away, with a nervous glance towards the door of the cathedral. His boss wouldn't thank him for starting a firefight. Then a man on the truck swung his boot hard and hit one of

Xabarra's men in the mouth. Another of the men on the ground grabbed the foot that had been swung and tried to bring its owner to the ground. In the meantime, the driver started to rev the engine of the truck loudly. The guests were streaming out now and some of them had started to look nervously towards the gate.

It was my moment to get in amongst them. I couldn't see Liam or Jesus, but I could see the startled faces that were turned towards me. When I looked down, I saw blood on my shirt, mixed with the mud. My face was swollen and my eyes felt puffy from the mosquito bites. About ten yards away, I saw Xabarra emerge from the cathedral. He was holding Deirdre by the elbow, smiling and talking to her. I pushed towards them, depositing stinking mud on expensive fabrics as I went. I didn't really know what I had in mind, apart from getting her away from Xabarra. Xabarra's men appeared, two of them pushing their way towards me with determined looks on their faces. My only hope was that they would leave Xabarra unattended so that Liam or Jesus could shepherd Deirdre to safety. But where were Liam and Jesus? The truck at the gate suddenly lurched forward, taking one of the gate pillars with it. A shot was fired, then another and another, and one of the men on the truck pitched forward on to the ground. A woman in the crowd shrieked and the men looked uneasy. The truck lurched towards us. The two men who had come after me turned at a barked command from Xabarra and started to push both Deirdre and Alva towards his limo, Xabarra following. Desperately, I tried to get through the crowd, but they were milling around now, panic spreading. The truck lurched to a halt, just short of them, and the men started to jump off, running back towards the man who had fallen. Liam and Jesus weren't among them.

I almost got to her. I would have got to her were it not for the rain that started to fall, only drops at first, but big fat drops, and within seconds it had turned to a torrential downpour, the massive drops hitting hard enough to hurt, reducing vision to a few metres and turning the confusion to near-panic. I saw Xabarra, his hair plastered to his head, shouting instructions, then I saw Liam and Jesus approaching Xabarra's limo from the other direction. I was almost close enough to Deirdre to touch her. She turned, her face streaming with rain, and saw me, shock on her face, then leaned towards me urgently, the man with her forcing her into the car. She shouted something at me, but the rain was too loud. I shook my head.

'I know what it is . . .' she shouted, 'I know what's going on here . . .'

But before she could say any more, the rain started to come down in great thunderous sheets that drowned all sound, and the man forced her into the car and it took off in a spray of mud and water, followed by the next car, its window still open as it swept past me so that I could see Xabarra shouting instructions to the driver. At the window of one limo, looking directly at me with a slight smile, I saw Alva. The two cars slewed across the yard in the mud and a bumper caught one of the men from the lorry, knocking him aside, but the car did not stop and I watched as they roared through the gate, one after the other, and were gone.

The cars might have gone, but the locals weren't finished with Xabarra's men. They were enraged by the shooting of one of their own. Xabarra's men all had automatic weapons in their hands now and they were retreating towards their vehicles in a disciplined fashion. The locals only had shotguns or ancient rifles and they stalked the better-armed men cautiously, waiting for one to slip in the mud. The guests scattered towards their cars. Jesus and Liam came across to me. They looked as if they had been in a fight. Jesus was badly cut on the side of his head and Liam's knuckles looked flayed.

'We missed her,' Liam said, 'we missed her.'

'They're not going very far tonight,' I said. 'Look at the weather.

No chopper is going to take off in weather like that. They've gone to the villa.'

Liam didn't answer. I could see he was thinking about what Xabarra had done to him, and wondering what was going to happen to his sister when he got her back to her villa.

'I'm sorry, Jack,' Jesus said quietly. 'Four of them came after us when we lost you. We had to fight clear. It was too late when we got away from them.'

'We need to get into some shelter,' I said.

'And you need something for that face,' Liam said. 'This is Mexico, not Kintyre. Cuts and bites go bad.'

We heard a shout from one of Xabarra's men. They had spotted us. Two of them made to break towards us, but the cordon of Mexicans around them forced them back.

'Let's get going while they're pinned back,' I said.

We ran for the Jeep. Jesus hotwired it in a matter of seconds and we got out of the parking ground easily enough. We rounded the first corner to find that a big Mercedes had slid sideways in the mud and blocked the road. There were fifteen or twenty cars piled up behind it and it made a barrier that wouldn't be moved until morning. To make matters worse, the two pick-ups full of body-guards came round the corner.

'Jesus Christ,' Liam said.

He looked around and I could see what he was thinking. The riverbed that ran under the road had been dry up until half an hour ago, but now it had filled with foaming brown water.

'I don't think, Liam . . .' I said, but I didn't get to finish the sentence as he spun the wheel around and plunged into the water.

The water was deeper than we expected. As the four-wheel drive plunged in, the water flowed over the bonnet and the wind-screen, then the vehicle righted itself. We could hear the sound of boulders banging against the chassis as the current rolled them down the riverbed. And I could feel how the water was lifting the

189

lighter rear of the vehicle, attempting to float it away. Liam spun the wheel from side to side, trying to find traction, the wheels biting and releasing as the power of the current pushed against the back door. I looked down at my feet and saw water spilling into the footwell. Liam cursed as the front end sank into a hole in the floor of the river and threw his face against the steering-wheel. The back end lifted off the ground and gave enough purchase to the spate to lift and turn the vehicle sideways so that the full force of water was flung against it and we were forced down the river sideways, the whole vehicle threatening to overturn. Liam said nothing, but kept the engine revs high. I was thrown forward and hit the windscreen so hard, I thought I had put my head through it. Suddenly the Jeep executed a dizzying 360-degree turn and came to an abrupt rest half on its side and facing upstream. I turned to Liam. He dropped the gear lever into first. The wheels turned, but nothing happened.

'Interesting,' he said.

'Look,' Jesus pointed.

Through the muddy spume thrown up by the water, we could see Xabarra's men dismounting and unslinging their guns.

'We must be caught somewhere,' Liam said.

'Christ almighty, Liam,' I snapped. 'Of course we're caught.'

'If we're stuck on the bottom, I could rip the driveshaft out of her,' Liam said in a musing tone. I saw one man raise an automatic pistol and saw him judder with the recoil as he fired. Some more of them seemed to be working their way down the riverbank.

'Try something, Liam!' I yelled.

'Fair enough,' he said, and started to rock the four-wheel drive, alternating between first and reverse. The chassis groaned and there was a tearing noise. Liam kept it up. The tearing noise got worse. A bullet slammed through the door pillar, sending a spurt of water over us. The four-wheel drive shifted sideways with a creak of metal, then there was a bang and we were loose, loose without much of the rear driver's-side body work and with the driver's door half-torn from its hinges. Water poured in on top of us as we swung out into the current again, Liam half-submerged and battling with the wheel.

'Over there!' I yelled.

A spit of sand jutted out into the current. It looked for a moment as if the current would carry us past it, the vehicle lifting and swinging slowly, but Liam found some traction somewhere, the front tyres bit on the sand and slowly we found our way back on to dry land. I looked back, but the gunmen were hidden by a bend in the river. The rain drummed on the roof. Liam got out and inspected the damage.

'She's drivable,' he said, climbing back in again. 'Let's go.' Another half an hour took us to the hangar. Ricardo and Sonny had put the helicopter in the hangar under cover and we drove in. I could see Sonny looking for the two women.

'Xabarra has both of them,' I said.

'That is not a good thing, Jack,' he said. 'Not a good thing at all.'

Sixteen

It rained all night and into the next morning. Liam didn't sleep. I dozed fitfully, and each time I woke I saw him standing at the door of the hangar. My face was an inflamed mask and I felt alternately feverish and cold. At one stage I woke shivering and looked up. Ricardo was standing over me, his face expressionless but solicitude in his stance as he threw another blanket over me.

When daylight came, the light was grey and dull. Liam waited impatiently until eight o'clock, then drove into Patzcuaro. He returned an hour later with binoculars and a pair of mobile phones.

'I'm going up to that hill overlooking the villa. I'll report on any movement. Ricardo, keep the chopper ready to go.'

Ricardo nodded.

'What sort of a man do we have here?' Sonny asked. 'What sort of man?'

'Along with a whole lot of other things, he's a collector,' I said. 'He collects photographs, torture techniques . . .'

' . . . and beautiful women,' Ricardo said.

'I hope not,' I said. 'I hope not. Some collectors will do anything to obtain a specimen, and they'll do anything to hold on to it. Even if it is stolen or acquired by fraud, they regard it as their legitimate property once it is in their hands.'

Sonny left to drive Liam out to his vantage point. Ricardo made coffee for me. I could hardly hold the cup, I felt so weak.

'You need a doctor,' he said.

'I can't,' I said.

'A doctor would put you to bed, a hospital maybe.'

'I know.'

He went to the chopper and came back with a medical kit. He gave me some antibiotics and put aloe vera cream on my face.

'Some of those bites don't look good,' he said. 'There may be some infection in them. Take the two antibiotics every four hours. They are strong. Perhaps they will fight whatever badness is in your blood. Can you stay here on your own?'

'Where are you going?'

'I got a friend north of here I have to see.'

'I thought you couldn't fly in this weather.'

'I can fly on instruments, without them if I must.'

'What about Xabarra's pilot?'

'No. He won't risk his boss in this weather. He will wait. Who knows? Perhaps he is not a very good pilot.'

He flashed his teeth in what I thought was a smile. He was leaving, I thought. He had seen us bite off more than we could chew, and I couldn't blame him for leaving. If I had been stronger and had a gun, I might have put it to his head and made him fly us. But there was nothing I could do. I stood in the doorway watching the machine clatter into life and take off into the rain. I made it as far as my sleeping bag and fell into another troubled sleep.

Sonny did not wake me when he came back. When I finally came round, he had cooked up chicken soup on a camping gas stove.

'Eat,' he said. 'As good as medicine, the chicken soup.'

But I was still light-headed and when I heard the blades of the helicopter coming back, I thought of the buzzing of some monstrous insect. A few minutes later, Ricardo came in and placed a bundle of oily sacking on the floor. He unrolled it to show two Colt revolvers, an old Thompson sub-machine-gun, and a Lee Enfield rifle. Ancient weapons, but they were weapons. Liam in particular would love the Thompson.

'What about your rule?' I asked. 'No weapons in the aircraft?'

Ricardo looked at me.

'I'm not breaking my rule for you,' he said, 'I am doing it for the lady, Deirdre.' He held his hand against my forehead.

'You have a temperature,' he said. He pulled down my eyelids and examined my eyes. He turned to Sonny. I couldn't see the look that passed between them.

The afternoon stretched on. We heard nothing from Liam. I spent my time cleaning the guns. None of them were in great condition, some of the barrels were pitted with rust and the mechanisms needed gun oil. I improvised with light machine oil that Ricardo had for the chopper. When I had finished, I couldn't guarantee that they wouldn't misfire, but I was reasonably sure that they wouldn't blow up in our faces. Ricardo looked at me again and gave me another dose of antibiotics. I lay down again.

I woke to the sound of the chopper blades turning and Jesus shaking me by the shoulder.

'Liam called,' he said. 'Xabarra's getting ready to pull out.'

I got to my feet and almost fell. Jesus steadied me.

'I'm all right,' I said, steadying myself. I walked unsteadily outside. The rain had stopped and the cloud had cleared to the west, where the sun was sinking in a fiery conflagration. Ricardo was at the controls and ready to go. Jesus bundled me into the chopper. Sonny was already there. He looked apprehensive. As soon as I was aboard, we took off, flying west towards Xabarra's villa. We approached the small hill we had used as a vantage point before.

'Look.'

Jesus pointed. The navigation lights of a helicopter were visible above the villa, rising slowly and turning.

'Where the hell is Liam?' I thought. The other chopper swivelled in what seemed like a maddeningly casual fashion. We scoured the ground, but it was too dark. Ricardo got as close in as he dared, the chopper blades whipping storm debris into the air. I watched as the other chopper cleared the buildings and built up speed as it took a southerly bearing. It was Sonny who spotted Liam, waving his T-shirt in the air. I slid open the door and Ricardo went down low and fast. Liam dived in, and Jesus caught hold of his belt as Ricardo turned hard and started to climb.

'Deirdre's with them,' Liam gasped. 'Deirdre and Alva and Saul. They had a bag over Deirdre's head, tied on. Looked like Alva was arguing about it. She was trying to pull the bag off, but Saul and Xabarra stopped her.'

Liam's face was white and tense. As we cleared the hill, I peered into the distance, but I could see nothing. The chopper was gone.

That was the worst time. Ricardo calculated a probable course and altitude for the other craft and we flew south on that basis, our navigation lights switched off, while Liam pored over charts as if he could psychically track his sister across them. We worked on the basis that Xabarra had set a course for Oaxaca, but there were no guarantees that this was so.

'What do you want me to do?' Ricardo shouted.

'Keep flying towards Oaxaca,' Liam shouted back.

We sat alone with our own thoughts. Down below was complete darkness. No lights showed at all.

'Does anybody live down there?' I asked Sonny.

'Many people,' he said, 'many people.'

Sonny clambered forwards and sat beside Ricardo. He seemed deeply aware of his lapses in the past and he stared restlessly into the night, scanning the sky ahead. I lay back against the skin of the aircraft. I knew I wasn't well. I felt weak, almost incapable of movement. When I closed my eyes, my mind filled with unwanted images. Liam hanging upside-down, and worse images. Images from Bosnia at the darkest point of the war, images from Africa.

When I opened my eyes, the darkness began to be filled with ominous flashes of light.

'Lie down,' I heard Liam say, 'you've got a fever.' I was soaking in sweat and my head began to pound, but I was afraid to close my eyes. I remembered the families sitting in the graveyard, sharing meals with their dead. I remembered Liam's story. Once again, my own dead had come flooding into my mind, but this time I could not drive them away. I felt their hands reaching out and dragging me into the shadows.

The minutes passed. The hours passed. I had no idea of time. I woke and the helicopter was flying through the darkness and as far as I was concerned it had been flying for eternity. Then I slipped back into the bosom of the dead. A man I had never met, shot down as he chased me on a mountainside. A soldier blinded with oil, trying to defend himself from me in the enclosed space of a boat engine-room, except that now his eyes were open and burning.

At one stage, I was vaguely aware of Liam giving me an injection. Afterwards, I found out that it was adrenalin. In Mexico, you could buy any kind of drug over the counter, and people diagnosed their own illnesses. I started to come around a little, but I felt terrible. Liam told me that he was reluctant to do it, but he thought that he might need me to at least hold a gun and pull the trigger. We did not know it then, but the fight to come was a much stranger affair.

It started when we heard a hoarse shout from Sonny. I had been doubtful about the man, but now he was starting to justify Liam's intuitive trust of him. We looked down and far below, close to the ground and with no lights near by, we could see the navigation lights of a helicopter. Ricardo wheeled the Huey around and went down fast. As we came down, we could see that the helicopter was hovering just off the ground. It had its landing lights on, illuminating the whole area below. We moved to within a quarter of a mile of it, Ricardo staying a few hundred feet above the ground so that there was no chance of the light from the spotlight catching us. Liam slid open the door so that we could see out. He had the binoculars out. He swore softly under his breath, and I heard anger and the catch of fear in his voice.

'What is it?' I said.

He handed me the binoculars.

It took me a while to make sense of the picture I saw. The door of the chopper was open, strapped back. A figure was standing in the door, stooped almost double, painfully so, because the door was so small. I realized that the figure was Deirdre, still with the bag over her head.

'What's going on?' I said. 'What are they doing?'

'Standard interrogation technique,' Liam said quietly. 'They used it in Belfast. You put a bag over somebody's head so they can't see where they are. Then you put them in a chopper and fly about for a while so that they think that you're hundreds of feet up. Then you descend to six feet off the ground. You tell the subject that they are going to die. They expect to die. They're standing in the door of a helicopter that is way above the earth. Then you push them out.'

'Jesus, Liam. How can you get information that way?'

'It's not meant to get information. That comes later. It's part of a process of breaking you.'

'That's Deirdre standing there,' I said in horror.

'I know.'

I stood up, meaning to get to Ricardo, tell him to go in with all guns blazing, to get Deirdre and to put an end to Xabarra for once and for all.

'Wait.'

Liam grabbed my arm. His fingers were like steel.

'Liam . . .'

'Listen, Jack. We go in there, what happens? Whoever's flying that thing sees us, first thing he does is get the fuck away from us. You know how fast these things can climb. He takes off, flying hard, what happens to Deirdre? She falls from there, she's OK. She falls from thirty feet, she's probably dead. We have to wait, Jack. We have to wait until they push her out.'

He turned to Sonny.

'Tell Ricardo to inch in, get as close as he can without being seen. And be ready to go in as soon as they push her.'

Sonny did a lot of gesticulating in Ricardo's face and I think he had the same problem persuading Ricardo not to go in there and then. But my eyes were fixed on the figure standing in the door of the helicopter. I knew that Deirdre was brave, but this was something that went beyond bravery or cowardice. Painfully crouched, blinded, deprived of dignity. What did she feel? The vibration of the airframe. The terrible cacophony of the rotor blades. The void that opened below her. We moved ever closer. There was scrubland below us and I began to see that we were on a large plateau. As we got closer, the scrub began to die away and then I saw that there were buildings surrounding the area where our prey was hovering. I brought the binoculars to my eyes and realized that this was some kind of pre-European city. There were ruined buildings surrounding an empty plaza. At one end there was some kind of carved pillar. The place had been cleared but the jungle was encroaching from the margins. And the chopper hovered in the middle of the plaza. I wondered: did Xabarra have a sense of the melodramatic, or was it simply that it was a flat, isolated place?

We were at the edge of the plaza, as close as we could go without being seen. We could see Deirdre clearly now. She was swaying slightly, whether from the pressure of maintaining her stance or from fear, we could not say. Liam took the old Lee Enfield and trained its sight on the chopper. But I had a feeling that this would not be resolved by guns. Suddenly I was aware of a shadowy figure behind Deirdre and knew as he pushed her that it was Saul.

She seemed to fall for ever, dull, heavy and lifeless, as if she had already fled her body in acceptance of death. And then she hit the ground and crumpled and lay still, and I felt a shout forced from my throat and heard Liam shouting and the engine roaring as Ricardo swung so tight and hard that Sonny was almost pitched through the open door, Liam grabbing the back of his jacket as he toppled. And then we were crossing the sand of the amphitheatre, only feet off the ground.

The other pilot had seen us. I expected him to break for it as we tore towards him like a Valkyrie. I think I truly believed that our anger and righteousness would drive him off, send him fleeing into the darkness where he belonged. But the chopper turned towards us and held its ground, holding and holding, and Ricardo's face did not change as we came in hard and fast until at the very last moment he hauled desperately at the controls and our skids skimmed the other's blades and we flew over him and I saw why Ricardo had swerved away at the last moment. His hands gripping the controls and his eyes burning like dark coals, Richard Xabarra was flying the other chopper.

Ricardo pulled the Huey up in the air so abruptly, I thought we had hit something. I had no idea of the skills involved in flying a helicopter, but I knew this man was an adept. He swung us around again until we were facing Xabarra. The Ranger turned towards us, tail in the air, front end hanging low. And right underneath the front of the Ranger lay Deirdre, motionless, the machine hovering over her like a terrible raptor guarding its prey. Ricardo inched forward. Xabarra held his ground. We moved forward again. And again. Sand swirled around the two machines and over Deirdre, but she did not move. Sonny lifted a revolver. 'No,' Liam whispered, as if to speak out loud might disturb the terrifying equilibrium of the moment. 'If we bring him down, he could land on Deirdre.'

And still Ricardo moved forward, millimetre by millimetre, his face a mask. And still Xabarra defied him, until in the end it seemed to me that we were so close that the blades above our heads must be somehow synchronized, interlocking, and that a breeze, a breath, a movement of air from the wings of a nightbird, would send us all to oblivion. And still they held it, and I wondered what it looked like from above, the amphitheatre bathed in eerie light, the shining metal of the two duellists locked together, the two men seeming motionless, but minute movements of hand and foot holding them, locking them together. I looked for Saul, waiting for him to fire on us, but I realized that the door position of the Ranger meant that he couldn't get a clear shot when we were head to head. And still they held it. But edging imperceptibly upwards this time. It was impossible to tell, but I thought it was Xabarra who was forcing Ricardo upwards, trying to gain the psychological edge by bringing a new dimension to bear. And then, incredibly, still rising, still locked, the two helicopters began to rotate slowly, as if the point where the blades almost touched was an axis upon which they turned and this time I sensed that this was Ricardo's doing, countering the tactic of the other, forcing him into this taut dance. I don't know how long this went on, but when I looked down I realized that Deirdre was a long way down. Get up, I thought to myself, get up and run, but she didn't move.

It couldn't last. One man surely had to slip, or to concede. The terrible strain would tell at last, send one machine plunging into the other or reeling back, the man at the controls exhausted and beaten. But that wasn't what happened. The strain told elsewhere, as a sharp bang reverberated through the Huey. Almost instantaneously, Ricardo hauled back on the controls and feathered the blades.

'Tail rotor,' he yelled. The coupling had snapped and he had turned off the engine which would otherwise have spun us out of control, letting the machine drift downwards, the weight of the craft spinning the rotors and slowing our descent, though it didn't feel much like it. We yawed wildly from side to side. I was thrown to the floor and one moment found myself looking at the stars through the open door and next minute at the ground. But Ricardo seemed to let the spinning blades start the engine just as we were about to hit the ground. The craft hit the ground heavily, and I could feel the impact shooting up through my spine and shoulders, but we were down and alive. I threw myself towards the open door, Jesus and Liam after me. We were too far away.

Deirdre was on her feet. She was unsteady, disoriented, the bag over her head leaving her with no sense of where she was, or of where to run. We had landed near the carved pillar, about five hundred yards from the centre of the arena where Deirdre stood. She started in one direction, then stopped. We were all yelling at her, but the Ranger was directly above her and there was no way she could have heard us. But it did not stop us yelling. The chopper touched down just behind her and the sound of its engine at last gave her some bearings, gave her a danger to get away from. She started to run towards us, tripped and fell heavily, got slowly to her feet and started to run again. We were all quiet now, aghast at our own helplessness. Saul got out of the helicopter and ran after her. He grabbed her by the arm, but she resisted and when he pulled harder she fell on her knees. So he took her by the hair through the top of the bag that was over her head, dragging her behind him at a half-trot and when she fell he dragged her on her face until he reached the door of the helicopter. He picked her up and threw her in. I watched as the Ranger wheeled and turned in the air. The chopper gained height and seemed to hesitate in the air, and then it was gone, flying low and hard, heading south, and leaving us alone with our broken craft in the deserted arena. The sound of the aircraft's engine faded to a low drone, which seemed to me like the drone of a hideous beetle. I saw Liam and Jesus looking down on me with expressions of concern on their faces, and then I remember nothing more.

Seventeen

I had few memories of the next forty-eight hours. Some vague sensation of being carried, and then a jolting ride in a vehicle of some sort. And then having a sour-tasting liquid forced down my throat. Sometimes it seemed that I woke and I was in a dark, hot place, full of strange aromas. And when I slept I dreamed of the dead. Their fevered eyes, the mad chatter as they poured out the woe of the dead. Afterwards, I told myself that they were figments, fever dreams. But they were real to me then and even in the cold light of day I found it hard to dismiss them.

In the end, I woke at night. I could hear cicadas quite near but I was inside, lying on a steel-framed bed with a few crude blankets over me. I tried to move, but I was too weak. I tried to speak then, but only a croak came out. It was enough for a shadow to detach itself from the other shadows in the room. I saw it was an old man. He was wearing jeans and a T-shirt. He came over to me and lit a candle. He held some water to my lips. His face was old, brown and wrinkled, but the hand that held my head from the pillow was strong and his brown eyes were bright.

'You've had a bad fever,' he said, 'but the worst of it's gone. Doesn't mean you won't be weak for a while. My name is Miguel Fuentes. Your friends brought you here. I am the nearest thing they have to a doctor in these parts.'

The man's English was good, with a slight American accent. I looked around me. I seemed to be in a small cabin, open on one side to the elements, the gap half-closed by a kind of wicker screen. Various herbs were hanging up to dry around the walls. I realized that there was a drip attached to my arm.

'Saline solution,' Fuentes said. 'You were getting dehydrated. I am what you would call a herbalist, but I use anything that works. I want you to drink this,' he said, holding out a cup. 'It tastes like shit, but it works for fever.'

I took it. It tasted foul all right.

'What is it?'

'Some roots, some wild mushrooms, a few other bits and pieces. Go ahead, it won't kill you. It's got natural antibiotic properties. It's also an anti-diuretic, with some tonic properties. And on top of all that, it has some cabalistic shit in it. At least, I say the prayers.' He grinned at me. 'Sorry,' he said, 'I'm inclined to be irreverent about things that actually do deserve a little respect. My father would have said that all the power that used to belong to the old people who lived here resides in the ground, and that the flora and fauna are portals to that power. At least, that wasn't what he said, but it was what he meant.'

'And you?' I said, intrigued, despite the weakness and the dull throb in my head.

'Me? I used to laugh at him. Then I laughed at myself. Now I think the old people are probably laughing at me. There is something . . . power, knowledge . . . call it what you like, but I'm too old to learn much, so I just use the little bit that I know. And I have one advantage.'

'What's that?'

'I know about death. I was on Guadacanal. I know what it looks like, I know what it smells like. I can look in a man's eyes and tell you if he will live or die, and if he is to die, I can tell to the hour when it will happen.' For a moment his eyes were dull.

'There's no magic to it. It just takes experience. The experience of watching men die thousands of times over.' He shook his head.

'Anyway. That was then.'

I drank more of the thin, bitter liquid, almost choking on it.

'Where are my friends?'

'They brought you here from the holy ground. The one who used to be a policeman . . .'

'Sonny . . .'

'Yes. He had heard of me and he got you to me somehow. Just in time, too, I'd say. It wasn't the mosquito bites that gave you the swamp. There was some old pestilence in that swamp. I could smell it off you.'

I didn't like the sound of that. I thought of the dreams I had experienced, the faces of the dead.

'Where is everybody now?'

'They got their helicopter fixed and they flew on to the coast. They said you would know where they were going, and that you could follow. The Irishman said to tell you that they had a job that just wouldn't wait. He said you'd understand.'

And I did understand. Liam had gone after Deirdre. And it was time I followed. I tried to get out of bed, but all I did was fall on the floor, pulling the drip after me so that the old man had to catch it, moving quicker than I thought possible.

'I don't know what it is you have to do,' he said, 'but you're not going anywhere just now. There's also a soporific in the witches' brew I gave you. Knits up the ravelled sleeve and all that.'

Before I had time to wonder at a Mexican healer quoting Shakespeare to me in the middle of a sultry Mexican night, I could feel sleep stealing over me. Fuentes helped me into bed. I could feel that strength again, and just before I slipped into unconsciousness it occurred to me that if he had been at Guadacanal, he was in his late seventies at least.

I don't know if it was the fact that the fever was leaving me or if it was something in the brew that Fuentes gave me, but I slept without dreams that night and when I woke in the morning the sun was shining and a pleasant breeze blew in from outside. I stretched out on the bed and discovered that the pain in my head and limbs had gone. I didn't feel all that strong, but the terrible, debilitating weakness had gone. As I was about to try to get up, Fuentes appeared with a plate of huevos rancheros, refried beans and fresh corn bread. I realized that I was ravenously hungry and I barely thanked him before getting stuck in.

'Slow down,' he warned me. 'It's good for you to eat, but your stomach is still weak. When you are ready, there is a pool in the river just down the path which I use for bathing. You could do with it.'

Fuentes went off, whistling, and left me alone. I took a good look around the small shack he lived in and realized that I had taken the man's bed. There were a great deal of plants and herbs drying, and other odd organic shapes in jars that I didn't recognize. There were scales and mortars and pestles, the things you would expect a herbalist to have, but there was also a fair complement of modern medicines. Apart from that, the place was spartan. But when I got out of bed and finally got on my feet, I saw a photograph of a young Mexican in US Army uniform. He was holding a purple heart. His mouth was smiling but his eyes were melancholy. I found my clothes beside the bed. I grabbed them, tucked them under my arm and strode out naked into the sunlight. I looked up on to the roof and saw an iguana regarding me with reptilian superciliousness. I noticed that the animal was tethered by one leg. It was probably intended for dinner. Outside was a neatly tended and freshly watered herb garden. Squashes and potatoes grew beside the herbs and I heard the grunting of a pig from somewhere, as well as the rushing sound of the river.

I walked down the path beside the river. Wild flowers that I could not name grew close to the water. When I got to the pool, I saw that he had dammed the river to create a bath and that water poured over a chute into it as a rudimentary shower. There was a towel and, incongruously, a bar of soap sitting at the edge of the pool. The water was cold and fresh and scoured the feeling of sickness from me, although it still took both hands and a lot of effort to haul myself out of the pool. As I did so, I noticed that the river was channelled through mossy old stones further downstream, stonework that looked thousands of years old, but perfectly interlocking.

I had already decided to leave that day, but by the time I got back to the little house I was exhausted. Fuentes was working in his vegetable patch. He examined my eyes and my tongue. The sun had risen higher in the sky and was now beating down, oppressively, it seemed to me.

I told Fuentes that I had to go.

'At least wait out the midday,' he said. 'The heat of the sun will not be good for you.'

In the end, I consented to lie down on the bed and of course slept. It was late afternoon when I woke again. I jumped up, but the healer was there.

'You might as well lie down again,' he said. 'There is no way out of this place until the morning. A truck comes with the local people who have need of me. They will take you to a place where you can catch a train.'

I shook my head, trying to rid myself of the terrible debilitating fatigue.

'You need to rest a little more,' he said gently. 'I know that time is pressing on you, and I know that danger lies ahead of you, but you are not able to go now. I think that the person you are looking for is safe.'

'How do you know that I was searching for somebody?'

'You talked in your fever.'

'How do you know that she is safe?'

'Call it intuition if you like. My father would have said that the old people were talking to him.'

206

There was something sincere in his manner that made me believe him. When I was younger, I had read Carlos Castenada and other writers who concerned themselves with unlocking the doors of perception, but the years had left me sceptical. If you open the doors of perception, you had better be ready for the things that are on the other side wanting to cross your way.

'Do you have a car?'

He shook his head.

'It's fifteen miles of dirt track to the nearest road,' he said, 'and even then there's not much traffic on it this time of night.'

I knew then that I had to wait until the morning. I thought about what Xabarra had done to Deirdre.

'What is that place?' I asked him. 'The place where our chopper landed?'

'A minor settlement,' he said. 'Some say Zapotec, some say not. It is very ancient, whatever it is, and my feeling is that it predates the Zapotec empire. It's a place I don't like to go at night.'

I didn't ask him why. The duel between the helicopters might have been carried out with the most modern of hardware, but the almost suicidal rigour which had been applied by both men was redolent of ancient enmities. Equally, I was sure Xabarra knew what he was doing when he brought Deirdre there.

'Let me prepare some food,' he said, 'I don't often have company.'

His kitchen was a roofed-over area outdoors with a gas cooker and a table. I sat at the table and watched him prepare chicken with *mole*, the Oaxacan unsweetened chocolate sauce. He baked bread in a clay oven while the chicken cooked. As he did so, he told me his story. His father had been regarded as a shaman by the local people. He never claimed to be anything more than a healer, although he sometimes took peyote in order, he said, to gain a greater understanding of the world around him so that he could better perform his office. However, Miguel said, he greatly reverenced the peyote, and respected it. Miguel had been different, impatient, itching to see the world. When he was seventeen, his father had consented to let him go to Mexico City to work. When he was there, he got involved with a group of Americans who were interested in the works of Aleister Crowley and other cabalists. The name of Crowley sent a shiver through me. He was a showman and a manipulator, but I had seen some of his cabalistic drawings once, and I had no doubt that there was a genuine strain of the diabolic in his work.

Miguel had told them about his father and they had persuaded him to come back and learn what there was to know about how his father harvested and used the peyote. He had learned his father's trade, which had delighted the old man, but the old man would not reveal the secrets of the peyote. 'That comes last of all,' he would say.

But then one night his father had caught him at the jar which contained the dried plant, filling his pockets. Immediately the old man had known that his son's interest in his craft was a fake. Furiously he had denounced his son, and expelled him.

'What happened then?' I asked.

He shrugged.

'I went north of the border and enlisted. I never saw those people again. They had an interest in evil, I suppose, the interest of wealthy, well-fed people in the dark side of things. I saw the dark side of things on Guadacanal, flames and men shrieking like beasts in the night. I didn't need to see any more. When I came back, I realized that I should be my father's son. But he wouldn't let me come back, and he lived for many years after that, thirty years. So I travelled up and down the continent until the day he died. Then I came back and started to learn his trade.'

He sighed. 'I was too old for an apprentice really, and I had no master, but I do my best.'

As we ate the chicken, he told me all he could about the *indigena* concept of spirituality and cure, the idea that illness is a loss of

208

soul, about the Triqui witch doctors, Nakawe the fertility goddess, the *brujo* who would help you regain your soul. And there were older, less benign beliefs, the cult of the jaguar, the cult of human sacrifice, the cult of the serpent. His knowledge was formidable and convincing. But at the end of the meal, the tiredness took me once again and I had to sleep. He helped me to the bed and gave me another drink of the sour draught. Within minutes, I was asleep.

I don't know what woke me. Perhaps the fact that over the years I have acquired a feral instinct for danger. Or something in the place itself, which was, I believe, a place of healing, rejected what was happening. All I know is that my eyes snapped open and I saw cold steel above me. Instinctively I writhed sideways and the blade slammed into the bedding where my throat had been.

There was absolute silence. I rolled off the bed on to the floor. I was still weak. I could see legs in jeans, a pair of sneakers. Sitting on the floor, I desperately pushed myself backwards with my arms, scuttling like a baby. Long steel, I thought to myself, a long steel knife. Familiar, but archaic. I kicked the bed at the man to try to gain a little space to get on to my feet. He swiped it aside and I saw that it was Miguel, and that the steel in his hand was a World War II bayonet. And that I saw that the pupils of his eyes were no more than pinpricks. Peyote. It came to me in a flash that Miguel had been in too much of a hurry to gain his father's knowledge, and had tried to use the hallucinogenic as a shortcut. I didn't know if the man I had been speaking to in daylight was mad, but this man surely was.

I was on my feet now, backing towards the centre of the hut, and he was coming towards me, slowly, but with absolute certainty.

'Miguel,' I said desperately, 'Miguel, Jesus . . .'

In reply, I saw his teeth gleaming in the darkness as he smiled. My hands found the big table where he did his work. I picked up the heavy stone pestle and threw it at him. It glanced off his skull with enough force to down any normal man, but he seemed not to flinch and did not even lift a hand to wipe away the blood that streamed down his face. I turned and frantically tore at the flimsy wall of the hut until it collapsed under me. I fell and rolled forwards and waited for the blow of the knife between my shoulderblades. But Fuentes kept up the same inexorable pace. I picked myself up and ran, or tried to run, for I could only manage a trot, down the path that led to the river. The cicadas were silent and I was aware of my own breathing, and of the small rustlings and bright eyes that regarded me from the darkness on either side of the path. Then the rushing sound of the river drowned everything out. I looked around and Fuentes was behind me, not running, but walking in the same exact manner. He must have been running, a voice in my head murmured, he must have been running. I started into my stumbling jog again, my legs barely able to carry me. Red lights flashed in front of my eyes. The path followed the river, but after the bathing place, it became steeper and rougher, and I fell several times, picking myself up and running on. The first time I fell, I looked back and saw Fuentes still coming after me with the same untiring pace. After that, I didn't look back.

The path ran under some scrubby trees then, and I was in absolute darkness. I stepped on something hard and it writhed under my foot, and I drew in a sobbing breath as I realized it was a snake. A surge of adrenalin sent me down the hill, not running as much as falling, branches whipping my face, and then I hit one low root and went sprawling on my face.

I lay there for a moment and then the image of Fuentes coming down the path forced me to lift my head. I wished that I hadn't. The horror behind me was nothing to the horror in front of me. The taxi driver, Sonny, was tied to the trunk of a tree. He had been dead for some days. Wild animals had been at him and his empty eye sockets stared at me with a sense of hideous beseeching. There were other marks on his body as well, tears and gashes. But no animal had left the gaping wound in the centre of his chest, a wound with black-lipped edges that you could fit your doubled fists into it. This time I was beyond fear, and I did not have to force my weakened limbs into a run. I left the clearing behind without a thought of Sonny, or of the tired-faced pretty wife in Mexico and the two treasured children.

This time, I ran through the trees, ignoring the path, no longer worried about snakes or scorpions. My face was sticky with blood and it was as if I could no longer feel my legs, but I kept running.

And then I emerged into open space. Into a place I had been before. A sense of inevitability about it, as if the whole chase had been leading to this place, the carved pillar towering above me now, oil stains on the ground where the chopper had landed. And some part of me felt relief. It seemed that at least one of our company had got away in the chopper. I turned slowly around. Fuentes was there, as if he had known that I would be drawn to this place. I sank to the ground. I was exhausted. I would not be able to fight him. But he didn't move. He seemed to be waiting for something. And I waited with him. There was a sense between us that I was already dead, that my breathing was merely a formality, a charade that had to be maintained for some predetermined time. I took stock of the night around me. It was warm and somewhere in the distance an owl hooted and was answered by another nearby. I thought to myself, if I could at least see Deirdre again. I saw the moon rise above the buildings at the far end of the arena. The radiance flooded the whole place. I followed Fuentes's expectant gaze to the pyramid behind me. As I did so, a long shadow began to resolve itself, reaching from top to bottom of the pyramid. Then its outlines began to clear, delineated by the silvery light, and I saw that the shape of a serpent was cast in shadow from the ground to the top of the pyramid.

I had read that a similar phenonomen could be seen in the

Yucatan but I was unprepared for the majesty of it. The serpent seemed to be gathering the moonlight to it, devouring it.

Fuentes stood still as the shadow grew and took form. Something glinted in his hand and I saw it was a gold object, shaped like a claw. A jaguar's claw, I thought. He had told me earlier that day that such an object had been used for human sacrifice. I felt reality begin to drift away from me. It seemed to me that stocky figures had started to congregate at the edges of the arena, men with broad, unreadable faces and brown eyes, stepping, it seemed, from prehistory. They made no sound, but it felt as if the forest was teeming with them. They seemed to move silently forwards until they were standing behind Fuentes in some sort of approbation of his actions. As the moon cleared the small hills behind the amphitheatre, Fuentes's own shadow seemed to lengthen, falling on me so that I flinched away from it because it seemed like a pestilent thing. With a grunt of satisfaction, he stepped forward and I saw the golden claw in his hand glitter as he did so. I could think of nothing else to do but to put my hands across my face, more so that I did not see the darkness that was coming than to protect myself. And so I waited, until a guttural shout disturbed the silent and terrible equilibrium of the night.

I let my hands fall away. Fuentes had stopped as though uncertain. The shout came again and he shrugged and moved towards me. This time, the shout came from several throats and I realized that it had emanated from the men who had emerged from the forest. Fuentes stopped and turned towards them. He said something, gesticulating towards me. An indication that I was his prey, a warning not to interfere. One of the small men stepped forward then. He had the air of a leader. There was something earnest in his tone as he talked to Fuentes, almost pleading, and I could sense an air of triumph about him, as though this was an argument that he would win. The language was harsh and complex, possibly Zapotec, but I knew that I was the subject of whatever exchange was taking place. The small man spoke one last time. Fuentes was imperious. He waved the man aside with a gesture of the golden claw and the small men seemed to step back and wilt at the sight of the fearful thing. With a dismissive grunt, Fuentes turned back to me.

This time, the guttural voice had an air of command about it which surprised me, but Fuentes once more dismissed it with a gesture, not bothering to look back. But he should have looked back, because the leader of the small men had reached beneath his huelpe and produced an ancient but deadly looking Colt Peacemaker. He spoke now, rather than shouted, and his voice had a tone of a verdict arrived at and a sentence pronounced. This time, Fuentes did turn towards him, an expression of surprise on his face, just in time to receive a bullet in the rib cage. The bullet did not stop him. He walked towards the small man with the same jerky, inexorable stride that he had employed in his pursuit of me. The small man fired again. The bullet passed through Fuentes's chest. I saw long filaments of material from the back of his jacket drawn out four feet behind him as the heavy slug tore through the material. Fuentes's pace did not alter. The crowd of men behind their leader shrank back in fear, but their leader did not flinch. He waited until Fuentes was almost on him, the golden claw raised, before he pointed the gun at Fuentes's face and fired three shots. The air seemed filled with blood and matter and Fuentes went down fast and hard. The little man put his foot on the back of the mortally wounded man's neck and fired his final shot into his head.

I managed to push myself into a sitting position. All the small men had gathered around Fuentes now, staring down at his body. They didn't seem much interested in me. The scant consolation that I had was that the little man seemed to have used all his bullets. I tried to get to my feet and fell. The movement attracted the attention of one of them. As he came over to me, I saw that he had a machete at his belt. I started wishing that he had in fact saved a bullet for me. I tried to get up and failed again. The man watched me with seeming interest. Then he produced some leaves from a pouch at his belt. They didn't look like coca leaves and I didn't know if people used them this far north, but he mimed putting them in his mouth and I took a handful and started to chew. They were not unpleasant, pungent with a slight taste of aniseed, and the rush was almost immediate. Within a few minutes, I was on my feet. The man smiled and nodded. I took a few faltering steps towards where they had gathered around the corpse of Fuentes. They parted as I approached. Death seemed to have diminished him into what seemed like a pile of old clothes. He was further diminished by what they had done to him. They had hogtied him to a pole by pushing cords through the tendons of his feet and hands and, as I watched, two of the men lifted him off the ground and put the ends of the pole on to their shoulders. The leader looked at me and to my surprise broke into a gap-toothed smile. He clapped me on the shoulder and handed me something. It was the jaguar claw. He turned me towards the path back to Fuentes's place.

'*Adios*,' he said, giving me a push in the back. I didn't have to be told twice. I started towards the path. If they wanted their leaving of this place to be a secret, then I wasn't going to stand in their way. But as I went up the path, I met four of them coming down. They brushed past without looking at me.

I found what they had been doing when I had walked a few hundred yards further on up the path. The body of Sonny had been removed from the tree and there was a neat patch of freshly turned earth on the ground a few yards away.

I surmised that Liam had taken over after I had fainted. He had gone after his sister, but he had left the weakest member of the team behind to look after me. Perhaps Sonny had indeed known of the presence of a healer in the area. I wondered how he had faced his death. I wondered how long it had taken.

The small men had placed the contents of his pockets neatly on top of the earth. A cigarette lighter, a mobile phone, some holy medals and a wallet. Inside the wallet I found the photograph of his worn, pretty wife and two immaculate children. I couldn't bear to look at it, but I swore to myself that I would make sure that Stone found them and looked after them.

It didn't seem to take long to get back to Fuentes's place. As I reached it, the sun was coming up and some of the terror was seeping from the air. I did a quick search of the place. In an old tin box under the bed, I found some war memorabilia and writings by Aleister Crowley. It seemed that Fuentes had never dropped his connection to the Satanist. And there was another, more grue-some object. It has long been a practice of soldiers at war to collect trophies of their enemies, and many men came home from war with parts of their enemies' bodies. Ears strung together were a common trophy. In a culture of war and death, it made a kind of terrible sense. Fuentes had such a trophy. Many of the ears were old and dried, barely recognizable for what they were. But there were other, more recent acquisitions and on one pair the blood had barely dried.

I took them outside and threw them into the bush and I said a silent prayer for their owners. It was as much as I could do, and although I was fairly agnostic, only the foolish could have denied the presence of harsh deities around that place. Then I started to cast around. I had found a set of keys in the box as well, and it didn't take long to find a little lean-to containing the transport that Fuentes had denied owning. It was an old Kawasaki Z900, a triple-cylindered thoroughbred, with none of the civilizing chara-teristics of a modern bike, but a raw and untamed power which suited my mood.

In the house, I found a map. It didn't take long to find out where I was. A place called Dainzu, forty-five kilometres from Oaxaca. There was a legend indicating antiquities on the map, and underneath it was the representation of a courtyard and a ball court, and a tomb with a jaguar doorway.

The only weapon I could find was an old .45 revolver of indeterminate make. I stuck it in my pocket along with a couple of cases of shells. I took the jaguar's claw from the table and examined it. The fleshy part of the claw had been crudely made in gold with solder lines visible on it. But there was nothing amateurish about the actual claws. They were made of steel and were razor sharp. I wrapped it carefully in an old cloth and stowed it under my shirt. There was a pair of Zeiss binoculars hanging on the wall and I took those as well. I started the Kawasaki and it ticked over with that inimitable triple sound, full of promise and full of menace. I rolled her around to the front of the house and stood up in the saddle. I gunned the throttle and fired a shot from the old revolver into the air. It reverberated around the bare hills. I hoped that my rescuers heard it, and took it as thanks. I didn't know why they had killed Fuentes, but I suspected that he had become an abomination to them. Then I turned the bike, kicked it into first gear and hit the dirt road that led north.

The road was bad, and I took a pounding, as much from trying to save the temperamental machine by hauling it around potholes as anything else. It was only about five kilometres to the nearest metalled road, but I was exhausted by the time I got there. The first stretch of road was good and the bike came into its own. I hung off it into the corners and went flat out on to the straight, and the exhilaration helped for a while but I needed something more. At the first small town, I saw a *pharmacia* and stopped. I don't know what sort of sight I made going in. I had cleaned up a little, but I hadn't shaved for days and there was old blood on my clothes. They were polite but wary.

I saw what I was looking for straight away. There was a box of Benzedrex nasal inhalers on the counter. I bought four. I got milk in another little shop, and then a minor miracle happened.

Gathering dust on a shelf at the back of the shop was a single bottle of Redbreast whiskey. Two minutes later, I was on my way out of town with the bottle tucked safely under my jacket.

Once I was out of town, I stopped. I broke the top off one of the inhalers and took out the little cylinder of tissue paper in the centre which was impregnated with the active ingredients. I knew there was a lot of chemical junk in there, but there was also pure benzedrine. I tore the paper into little pieces, dipping it into the milk before swallowing it to help kill the foul taste. When I had eaten all the paper, I drank the milk to get the residue. Then I reverently unwrapped the foil on the bottle of Redbreast. I allowed myself one drink only, but as the malt flowed down my throat, it took me back to rainy days and greens and the earthy fortitude of the place it came from and washed the strangeness and perverted spirituality of the past few days clean away.

I was a more clear-minded man when I got back on the bike, albeit speeding on the amphetamine and subject to a worrying sense of invulnerability and a feeling that this time I wasn't going home until I had finished the thing.

Eighteen

In less than an hour, I was in light traffic, going through Oaxaca. It was a normal morning, and I felt like some barbarian from the outlands, smelling of blood and superstition. I threw the big bike through the traffic and something about the way I was handling it made the rest of the traffic get out of my way, even the most macho driver. On the far side of the town, I pulled up and examined the map. I knew that Xabarra's place was on a hilltop to the southern side of Monte Albán. I saw that there was only one hill which was served by a road. It had to be there. I took the turn for Monte Albán and turned off on to a narrow, well-surfaced road a few kilometres before it. The sun was up now, and was beating down mercilessly and I was glad of the breeze provided by the forward motion of the bike. I was convinced I was on the right trail. Minor roads like this one weren't well surfaced unless there was a reason for it, and what better reason than the presence of a wealthy and powerful man? I was even more convinced when I turned a corner and found the road blocked by a police cruiser. A policeman stepped out and held out his hand. He eyed me suspiciously for a moment.

'You can't go this way,' he said. 'Is closed.'

'How come?'

'Is closed,' he said. He stepped back, looking nervous now. I heard a sound in the distance. It could have been anything, an engine, or noisy mining equipment. That is, unless you had heard it before. And if you had heard the distinctive chatter of a Thompson sub-machine gun before, you could not mistake it for anything else.

I made a show of telling the cop that I thought I was on the road for Monte Albán and he became friendlier and explained to me in great detail how I had gone wrong. I gave him a cheery wave as I turned the corner. I had no doubt the man was there on Xabarra's orders.

I had passed a goat track leading up the hill. I went back to it. It was a path about two feet wide, going straight up, and the big Kawasaki was no trail bike, but I didn't have an option. The first time I hit the throttle, the back end slid out sideways and it was all I could do to hold the bike up. After that, I kept it moving with quick blips on the throttle. Hard on the engine and hard on me. Within minutes, I was soaked in sweat, but I kept going. On one bend, I slid again and the thorns of a cactus ripped the flesh on my arm. But I went on, one ear tuned to those three cylinders, all other senses intent on the rocky track. I prayed that the chain was well-maintained, that the coils were well insulated, that the tyres wouldn't puncture. About half-way up the hill, I stopped and turned off the engine. There was absolute silence and then I heard a rifle shot. I put my weight on the kick-start. The engine fired and died. I left it for a moment and tried again. Nothing. I forced myself to wait – one minute, two minutes. I heard another rifle shot, but if I flooded the engine, it was all over. I tried it again. It clattered, misfired and caught. It was a lesson, I thought. Keep the engine running.

After that, it was easier. The path widened as the vegetation thinned at the top of the hill. I found if I stood on the footpegs and leaned over the handlebars, the rear end would dance about but would find a grip somewhere. I covered the remaining ground in ten minutes. When I cleared the final ridge, the great bulk of Monte Albán loomed in front of me. And from far below came the sound of a Thompson sub-machine gun, like the cough of a wounded animal. I looked through the binoculars. The first thing I saw was the chopper. Its perspex was scarred and broken and the fuselage was peppered with bullet holes. About twenty yards from the Huey, a rough stone barrier had been built and there were three figures behind it. I saw Liam with the Thompson, Jesus with the rifle, and Ricardo prone on the ground. I thought for a moment that he was dead, but he stirred slightly and was still. They were in big trouble. Further up the hill, I saw the metalled road I had followed, and then a large villa with several hectares behind it covered with vegetation. That must be Xabarra's villa, I thought. I looked for the men who had pinned down Liam. They were on the road, beside a dirt track which led towards the bulk of Monte Albán. There were three of them besides Xabarra and Saul. They had two pick-ups with powerful searchlights, but they weren't attempting to shelter behind them. They didn't have to. Liam and Jesus's weapons didn't have the range to hurt them. In contrast, they had several sniper's rifles on tripods, and each of them had a high-velocity hunting rifle. They were relaxing in the sun and passing round a flask, for all the world like a hunting party. They were welcome to it, I thought. I hunted best alone.

I could follow the path down to the road or follow the slope of the hill, which was five hundred yards of scree. I hit the throttle and launched the Kawasaki on to the scree. I threw it sideways, turned the handlebars at right angles to the tank, stuck my left boot in the ground and let the slope carry me down, speedway style, the big rear wheel kicking shale thirty feet into the air. The slope was treacherous, the bike wasn't built for it and I was too old and too tired for stunts, but I got down the hill in twenty seconds, hit the road going hard sideways, doughnutted the back around until I was facing the right way and dug into the throttle so that the front wheel lifted off the ground and stayed off through second and third gear, the lethal three-cylinder whine kicking in.

When the front wheel touched down, I stuffed the .45 down between the brake cable and the handlebar where I could reach it, and went to war.

They didn't know what hit them. I took out the first gunman with the butt of the pistol, swinging at his head as I rode past, striking him so hard, I thought I had broken my arm. The second one got my boot, driven into his stomach and thrown back against one of the pick-ups with a hard, ringing sound. The third didn't get off the ground where he was aiming a shot. I wheelied the bike and slammed on the rear brake at the last moment. The bike came down on him like a guillotine, the sharp metal sump guard at the base of the engine falling like an axe against his lower back. He moaned and lay still. I rode on over him and turned in the road. Saul was behind the wheel of one of the pick-ups. I wasn't worried about him. I heard a shout from Liam down below and reckoned he could cut him off.

Xabarra made for one of the rifles on the ground, but I squeezed off a shot and he ducked back. But it was only a feint. His real target was the pick-up, which was facing me with its engine running. He dived through the door and hit the gas. I knew he was trying to make it to the villa. I knew that I wasn't letting him past, and I knew where I wanted him to go. As he sped towards me, I planted shots in the windscreen, deliberately spaced. No man can drive into that. The Jeep swerved wildly, straightened and headed straight down the track that led towards Monte Albán. As the Jeep slithered on the dirt track, I saw Xabarra's hand clearing the shattered glass from the windscreen. A few hundred yards down the track, the Jeep stopped.

I knew he was inviting me to follow him. I loaded the .45 carefully, then turned the bike. It was time.

Twenty minutes later, I was still following Xabarra up the dirt track. He drove fast and well, but not on the edge. He wanted to take me to a place of his own choosing. Great clouds of choking dust billowed out from behind the truck. My mouth felt clogged with it and I was worried about how the bike's air filters would hold up to it. Once or twice, I thought I heard a cylinder miss. My eyes and skin were stinging, but the gun was safely tucked inside my jacket. Every so often, the dust would billow away from me and I could see the top of Monte Albán, getting closer and closer. It was a weakness in him, that taste for melodrama. It suited me. I could do melodrama with the best of them.

In that searing, dusty ride into the hills, the sun's noon glare reducing everything to glaring bronzes and burned-out ochres, everything fell away, the fate of Paolo and his daughter, the death of Paul in the terrible cavities under New York, the agonies suffered by Liam and his sister at the hands of Xabarra. There was only me and Xabarra.

But I was still thinking. I reckoned I couldn't tackle the Jeep on the road. A stuntman might make the jump from the bike to the pick-up, but there was no way a tired, beaten-up ex-covert opera-tive was going to do anything except end up under the wheels of the Jeep. But I could at least seize the advantage. As we neared the great plateau that was Monte Albán, I made use of the dust cloud to get close behind the Jeep without being seen, sitting just off the driver's-side bumper. When the dust cleared enough for me to see something of the road, I gunned the bike past him. I almost didn't make it. As I got level with the driver's window, the middle cylinder missed and I lost acceleration. Xabarra saw me and swung the wheel viciously to the right. I think he might have clipped the rear mudguard, but the missing cylinder cut back in again and I was past. The cylinder kept missing on a regular basis and it was all I could do to stay ahead. Each time it died, Xabarra's bumper crept closer to the rear of the bike, only for it to cut back in again, the bike leaping forward uncontrollably. Then it died for good and suddenly I was coaxing every drop of power out of the remaining two cylinders in order to stay ahead, dropping the bike down, speedway-style again, to take the corners in a power slide. I knew I couldn't keep it up until we got to the top of the plateau a quarter of a mile ahead. I reached over the handlebars and grabbed the gun. As I did so, the front wheel struck a stone and did a tankslapper, the handlebars smacked at a right angle on to the bike, then slapped the other way. Nine times out of ten, a rider is pitched off. This time, I was lucky. I managed to straighten the forks. I had the gun in my hand. I fired backwards, aiming low. In the mirror, I saw a gout of steam explode from the front of the Jeep as the bullet hit the radiator. Momentarily blinded by the steam, Xabarra swerved off the track. His driver's-side front wheel hit a drainage ditch with a huge jolt. The next time I dared to look back, I could see that the wheel was buckled and badly out of line and that he was fighting to keep it on the road. I had my own problems, the Kawasaki was starting to sound even more ragged. I looked down and saw a fine spray of oil on my leg. I reached under the tank and smacked the middle coil with my hand. The middle cylinder caught, the bike leaped forwards, but the revs kept rising and as I hit the plateau, the engine note rose to a shriek and then died. The bike coasted over the last rise and into the centre of the great plateau of Monte Albán.

Even at that moment, it was impossible not to wonder at the human labour that had removed, by hand, the entire top of a mountain. As the bike coasted to a halt, there was an eerie silence. There was no one around. The sun hung above the ruined city, a great, blazing disc. The heat was palpable and no breeze stirred the white dust or the baked walls of the ancient structures of the ball court, pyramid and plaza. This was a place of last recourse, a place of judgement. The Jeep mounted the edge of the plateau and stopped, steam pouring from the bonnet. I lifted the gun to put another bullet in the engine. I pulled the trigger and the ancient barrel exploded.

It was a moment before I realized what had happened. The

sound of the explosion echoed across the plaza and the gun dropped from my hand. I looked down at my hand as if from a great distance and saw that the tip of my little finger had been blown off down to the first knuckle. Gouts of bright red blood pumped on to the dust and soaked in immediately, as if the ancient land was greedy for it. I waited for the pain and then it came. I tried to compartmentalize it, set it aside to deal with later. Through a haze of shock, I saw that the Jeep was empty. I looked around wildly but I couldn't see Xabarra. With my good hand, I got one of the Benzedrex inhalers out of my pocket and ripped the top off with my teeth. This time, I swallowed the roll of paper whole, half-gagging on it. I was going to need the stimulation, but I didn't know if my cardio-vascular system could take it. The speed hit me straight away and I looked at the top of my finger as if it belonged to someone else.

Then I heard Xabarra's voice. He seemed to be standing next to me and I spun round wildly.

'Jack,' he said again.

I looked down towards the end of the plaza. Xabarra was standing on one of the steps, about half-way up. He was five hundred metres away, but his voice was conversational and as clear as if he was standing next to me.

'It's very impressive, isn't it, Jack? The whole plaza is designed around this very spot. It is acoustically perfect. A priest could stand here and address a crowd of ten thousand people and not have to raise his voice.'

'Where are they, Xabarra?' I shouted.

My voice came out hoarse and cracked. I started to walk towards him. He seemed a long way away.

'The women are at my villa,' Xabarra said. 'I would say they're having lunch on the terrace just now.'

'Let Deirdre go. She's nothing to you.'

'Nothing to me? That's the crux of the matter, isn't it, Jack? She's nothing to me. But I'm nothing to you. What do you want from me?'

I didn't answer. I felt as if the sun were a great burning weight trying to drive me into the dusty ground.

'Blood,' Xabarra said. 'That's what you want, Jack. My blood. Look to your left. Look.'

In spite of myself, I turned to look. On the side of a tomb I saw dancers carved in a frieze, life-size, seeming to turn in an exuberant series of moves.

'Look at them closely. They aren't dancers. They are enemies in the act of being slaughtered. Look between their legs.'

I looked. Their genitals had been cut away and blood spurted from the wounds. I turned away from them and trudged grimly on. I looked up at Xabarra. I was close to the pyramid now and he was jumping lightly down towards me. There was a knife in his hand. I reached inside my shirt and drew out the jaguar's claw. I took off the bike helmet and held it in my left hand. The grip on the claw was awkward. I had almost forgotten about the severed finger. Then Xabarra was in front of me. He smiled at me mirthlessly.

'This is it, Jack,' he said, 'this is the end.'

Even with the speed, I felt weak, uncoordinated. I brought an image of Deirdre standing in the door of the chopper into my mind, tried to focus on it, to use the anger to keep me cold and dangerous. I gripped the straps of the helmet in my right hand so that I could use it as a shield, and brought up the hand holding the jaguar's claw.

It was the first time I had seen anything approaching uncertainty in his face. His eyes narrowed and he drew breath between his pursed lips.

'It really is a settling of accounts, isn't it, Jack? The old world and the new.'

'Looks like the old world is on my side,' I said.

'I wouldn't say that. I wouldn't say that all.'

He brought up the knife hard and fast, aiming at my belly.

I knocked it aside with the helmet and lunged with the claw, but I was far too slow and clumsy. I stumbled and Xabarra came back with a fast and deadly backswing that would have killed me if he had aimed it at my body, but instead he went for the face, the blade flashing across my eyes with millimetres to spare. I got the message. Xabarra wanted this to last. He was going to take me down slowly.

He was coming at me again, the blade flashing under the helmet as I tried to fend him off and pricking the inside of my arm. I slipped and went down on one knee. I tried the old knifefighter's trick of scooping sand off the ground into his eyes, but he had seen it before and he ducked back before the sand hit him.

Apart from that, I had nothing to offer. He kept coming towards me and I kept backing away, waving the jaguar's claw in the air, but it didn't offer any threat and he knew it.

'You never really got it, Jack, did you?' he said. 'You never really understood any of it. You have a weakness for the sentimental. Alva told me about Fiesole. A heartwarming picture, the man carrying the little girl. Look where it got you, Jack.'

I could feel the anger tighten in my throat. He was expecting me to react, and I did. I feinted forwards, but pulled back at the last moment. As he countered, I slipped sideways. I had the sun behind me now, so that it was in Xabarra's eyes. It was a small advantage, but at least it was my advantage. How small it was, however, became apparent when Xabarra slashed at me at waist level. I heard the swishing sound and looked down to see my shirt cut wide open and blood seeping out. I didn't know how bad the cut was, but I felt a wave of nausea at the thought of my stomach being opened. I had to push the thought out of my mind.

'I might be a sentimentalist,' I said, my voice sounding weak, 'but I don't get pleasure from torture.'

'Don't moralize at me, Jack. It doesn't suit you, and it doesn't suit your profession.'

Xabarra's tone was one of contempt. He came forward, slashing underhand. I backed away, almost running backwards at this stage, aware of nothing except the burning sun, the dust under my feet and the bright shining death that threatened me at every step. Xabarra switched hands suddenly and came at me with the left. I countered with the jaguar's claw. It deflected the knife but it glanced off and the hilt caught the severed top of my finger. Agony seared through me and I had to choke back bile. Xabarra grunted in satisfaction and came in for the kill, going for my belly with an underhand jab, but his haste was a mistake. I got the helmet in the way and the knife stuck in the padding on the inside of it. With one hand, I tried to pull the knife from his grasp, and with the other, I sank the claw into his inner thigh and dragged it back towards me, going for the artery. In a desperate movement, he got the knife out of the helmet and I fell backwards, scrambling away from him. I hadn't got the artery, but he was limping badly and blood gushed from his leg. I had my own problems. The heat, the blood loss and the poison in my system had weakened me to the point of collapse. I realized that I had my back against the base of the pyramid. Everything in my body was telling me just to get away from him. I thought that if I could get up a few levels of the pyramid, his leg wound might prevent him from climbing after me. Everything else fell away except for the need to escape, the need to survive.

I threw myself on to the first level of the pyramid, then the second. He followed me. He was slow and he winced as he swung the injured leg on to the stone, but he was still after me. I had no option but to keep going upwards, climbing in the searing sun. I could hear his breathing behind me, a thin hissing sound. The stone tore at my hands and still I climbed. Faintly, in the distance, I thought I heard voices shouting and an image came unbidden into my head of a story I had read as a child, of a noble Aztec youth climbing to be sacrificed, the crowd below shouting encouragement, the priest waiting with an obsidian knife.

In the end, there was nothing. Not even the man with a knife at my heels. There was just the sun and the ancient stone.

It was not my strength that gave out. Instead, it was the stone itself, the age-old mortar losing its coherence, a big slab coming away at the touch of my hand. Suddenly I was sliding down, dust and the rumble of stone filling the air. I know that I had hit Xabarra, and I heard his gasp of pain, and then we were both plunging downwards.

I believe I lost consciousness then, but it could only have been for seconds. When I came to, I was on the ground, sprawled across Xabarra. I tried to move, but pain shot through my body. I looked down and saw that the slab of stone lay across my right foot and both of Xabarra's legs. I realized that I still had the jaguar's claw in my hand. Xabarra looked dazed, but as I looked down at him, he turned and glanced at the golden claw, then looked right into my eyes. Then he spat at me and turned his head away so that his throat was exposed. It seemed I was being invited to bury the claw in his flesh.

It was then that I heard John Stone's voice. I looked up, trying to blink away the sweat. Through a haze, I saw John Stone standing on the low stone platform twenty yards away. Liam and Deirdre and Alva were with him. Around them, and scattered around the plaza, I could see Mexican military. Even through the blur of pain and confusion, I could see that they had no markings on their uniforms.

'Let him go, Jack,' Stone said. 'The women are both safe. It's time to end it.'

I was having trouble understanding what was going on.

Liam was standing with his arms folded, with that wry grin on his face, that Olympian detachment he achieved on matters of blood and death.

'Jack . . .' Deirdre said, her voice pleading, looking at me with something like pity in her eyes.

I was only half-listening. I knew that those uniforms with no markings meant something, that the men were special forces, which meant that someone probably had me in their sights. I looked down at Xabarra. He hadn't moved. It seemed for a moment in the heat and dust of the plaza that I could actually smell his blood, that I lusted for that warm metallic odour.

'Jack, for God's sake,' Deirdre cried out. 'Can you not see it? This isn't about drugs or any of your bloody spies and sneaking around. Xabarra is Alva's father. Can you not see it? It's what I was trying to tell you outside the cathedral. Look at the two of them.'

I didn't have to. I could see it in Alva's high-cheekboned face. The strangeness in her. I had left Europe behind and immersed myself in a world of drugs and violent death and thought I knew where I was and what I was doing. But I had ended up playing a much more deadly game, that of families, blood and kinship. The ties that had brought old men on a journey of forty years to wreak vengeance on an old woman, and a young man they had never met. The ties that had led Alva to abandon the man who reared her to seek knowledge of her own blood, a knowledge acquired at any cost.

Xabarra turned his face back to mine. It seemed that he was smiling.

I heard the sound of booted feet around me, then something hard hit me on the head, and I slipped into unconsciousness, falling away into a kindly oblivion.

PART III

Nineteen

The wind whipped the freezing grey water of the Hudson into peaks and blew dirty white foam on to the piers. It was a cold, unforgiving kind of day and I was glad to be out in it. The cold has its own dangers, but I felt I had left a psychic furnace behind when my plane climbed out of Mexico City two days before.

I saw John Stone standing on the end of one of the piers, seeming at one with the greyness of the day. He waited for me to reach him. My progress was slow. I had broken bones in my right foot and I wasn't strong enough to get up much speed on crutches. The fifteen stitches in my stomach didn't help either. And on top of everything, the place where the top of my finger used to be jarred with every step. When I reached him, he turned and patted me on the shoulders. An odd, almost paternal gesture.

'In a good film,' he said, staring out over the tide, 'this would be the moment when all the loose ends would be tied up.'

We watched a gull diving for some rancid scrap floating past on the river. We both knew that all the loose ends were never tidied up.

'Xabarra is one of yours, isn't he?' I said.

'How did you know?' he asked mildly.

'All that sensory deprivation stuff. He had to have learned that in the College of the Americas. Manual 30/15. Isn't that what you call the instruction book?'

'Most efficient form of extracting accurate information. Would you rather have sensory deprivation used, or physical torture?'

'Xabarra used physical torture as well. And Deirdre had nothing to give him. He threw her out of the helicopter for fun.'

And a lot of other nasty people came out of that academy for psychopaths the CIA had set up, I felt like saying, but it seemed that the liberal side of me had been stifled down in Mexico. I could still imagine the weight of the jaguar's claw in my hand.

'So why did you send me after Xabarra?'

'He'd decided to go freelance.'

'And why did you stop me killing him?'

'He'd decided to come back into the fold.'

'Simple as that?'

'These things are rarely simple. You know that, Jack. But you were indirectly responsible for him coming back. The thing in the tunnel had a lot to do with it. He rang me to say that he had a psychopathic Scotsman on his trail and would I help him shake you?'

'But you sent me after him . . .'

'Precisely. To be honest, I didn't think you would get as close as you did. Xabarra realized that no man is an island, and he came back into the fold.'

I was silent. I had been used as a means to regain Xabarra's loyalty. There was no point in feeling betrayed. That was what this business was about.

'He did have to pay a price, though.'

'What was it?'

'He had to hand over Deirdre. Alive. He wanted to keep her, you know. He likes to collect things. I always liked Deirdre.'

'What about me? And Liam and Jesus?'

I hated myself for asking the question. He looked at me with a minute lift of his eyebrows. I took it to mean that we had been on our own down there.

'To be honest, the whole thing seems too tortuous to be credible.' I said.

He shrugged.

'You get an instinct for what works and what doesn't work,' he said.

'And what do you get in the end?' I said.

'We get Xabarra. He is tough, intelligent, wealthy and has good political instincts. We also get the use of his heroin, which means that we control the supply and therefore the price. And when you control the price, you control the economy of the heroin-producing regions. Which means you control the power structures.'

'Which is what you want.'

'It's very satisfying. Tell me. How is Paolo?'

'He has recovered consciousness, but he doesn't know much about where he is, or who he is, for that matter. They say the memory will come back, but I'm not so sure. Did you know Alva was his daughter?'

'No, it surprised me,' Stone said with a disapproving air. He didn't like things to surprise him. I felt a cold drop of rain on my cheek.

'Apparently her mother left Xabarra and went to Italy. She met Paolo there when Alva was a baby. Paolo, I think, made sure that Xabarra couldn't find her. Then her mother was killed.'

'And Paolo sent you after her without telling you this?'

'We all have our faults. Paolo's is pride.'

'A very noble attitude to the whole thing,' he said drily. 'And she is staying with Deirdre now?'

'They stayed with me in hospital in Mexico City, then we all flew up together. Jesus has introduced her to his Narcotics Anonymous friends. They haven't got her in a twelve-step programme, but she is thinking about it.'

'Is she going to see Paolo?'

'She's going back to London with me.'

'What about Xabarra?'

'She's confused. She knows now what he did to Paolo. And to Deirdre and Liam. But he is her father. She hasn't seen him since.'

235

'Quite a family. There is one other thing.'

'What is it?'

'That piece of information you asked me for?' He handed me an envelope. 'I think you might find it surprising.'

I took the envelope and put it in my pocket. I was tired of talking. I wanted to ask him how they had found us in Mexico. I wanted to ask him if he had been talking to Xabarra the whole time we were stalking him. But I was weary of the whole thing and I wanted to go home. The salt smell of the river reminded me of my croft on the west coast of Scotland.

'I'm tired, John,' I said.

'Go home,' he said. 'It's over.'

I walked slowly back, the wind now driving the rain horizontally across the piers.

But it wasn't over.

That evening, I walked over to Irene's. I hadn't seen Jesus since we had come back, but Liam said he was in a dangerous, reckless mood. He had been taken in by the cops for questioning about the incident in his house. Apparently he had hit one of the cops and now he was out on bail on an assault charge. When I got to Irene's, I found that things had taken a more serious turn.

'I told him,' Irene said. 'I had to tell him the truth about his father.' I cursed inwardly. Her timing was bad, but maybe there was no good time to share such terrible truths.

I found Jesus at a bar on First Avenue. He was sitting at a corner table with a Coke in front of him. He got straight to the point.

'Did you know?'

'Yes.'

He slapped the table hard with the palm of his hand. He started to talk quietly then, but I could see the sinews in his neck standing out, tension simmering in him.

'You know,' he said, 'I think I could have handled what she did.

236

To kill a man? I've killed men. You've killed men. The man was my father. I think I could still live with it, find some way to fit it into my head, you know? But it's the fact that she didn't tell me. It makes something . . . something of shame for me to be here and alive. I can't get over that, Jack. And I've no one to help me get over it.'

His face was full of pain. I stayed with him for a little while longer, but there was nothing I could do.

I took a cab uptown to Deirdre's apartment. She was watching television in the darkened apartment. She had refused to discuss what had happened when we were in Mexico.

'Where's Alva?' I asked.

'Liam took her to the movies.'

I was glad. I could only take so much of tortured families. And I had the vague intention of helping Deirdre to her own peace. But she had her own ideas.

'I know you're here to talk about Mexico,' she said, 'and I don't want to talk about it. What happened with that helicopter . . . it took my old life away, made everything that happened before it seem unreal. I have to get used to the new life.'

'What about after that?' I asked. 'When you went to the villa.'

'I think Alva intervened. He was all charm after that. Sinister, but charming. He even apologized for tossing me out of the helicopter.'

'I wouldn't trust that charm,' I said, with a little too much heat.

'I didn't, Jack,' she said gently.

I realized that I was jealous and I think she realized it, too. She excused herself. When she came back, she was wearing her coat.

'Let's go,' she said.

We drove to Christopher Street, barely speaking on the way. When we got into the apartment, I reached for her. There was real hunger there, but there was detachment as well. I realized afterwards that I had been rough to the point of violence with her, and she had been pliant and uncomplaining. I started to speak, to say sorry, but she touched her fingers to my lips.

'It's all right, Jack,' she whispered. 'I'm not the only person had something terrible happen to them in Mexico.'

I dozed for a while. I woke to the sound of the apartment door closing. She was gone. I felt grateful that she had been there in the first place, but the place was empty without her. I turned on the television and watched Leno. Twenty minutes later, I heard the door open again. I went into the kitchen. Deirdre had placed several large brown paper bags on the counter.

'What's this?' I asked.

'Most people's spiritual selves reside in their soul,' she said, 'but yours resides in your stomach. And it needs feeding.'

'I smell fresh crab,' I said.

'*Carangrejo recheado*,' she said. 'Portuguese stuffed crab. There are Tiger beers in one of those bags.'

I poured a beer for each of us.

'Did Liam tell you what he is going to do? she asked.

'No.'

'He is going to Mexico with Ricardo. Something about *indigena* relief in Chiapas. I didn't ask too much.'

I grinned at the thought. It sounded much more like Liam than subcontracting in the Bronx.

It was after one before we finished eating. Deirdre got up to put the dishes away.

'Look,' she said softly. 'Look.'

I came to the window. It had started to snow, the outlines of the city softening, taking on the contours of some magical middle-European city from far in the past. We stood there for what seemed like an hour, not daring to make a sound in case we broke the spell. In the morning, the snow would be churned to slush, but for now all the possibilities of transformation that I had thought were gone for ever seemed to be contained in the frosty, alchemical city conjured by the falling snow.

I spent the next day making arrangements to get back to

Europe. Jesus rang me at eleven in the morning. He sounded in better shape, talking a lot. He said that he could sort things out between his mother and the men from Puerto Rica who were still in prison but were apparently due to be sent home any day now. It wasn't until later that day that I was to find out what Jesus had in mind and by then it was too late to do anything about it.

I contacted the hospital in London. Depressingly, Paolo didn't seem to have made any progress. They were hopeful that Alva's presence might make the difference. That was another problem. I couldn't seem to make contact with her. Not that she was missing, she just didn't seem to be available when I tried to get in touch with her. I was starting to have doubts as to whether or not she would come to London.

I booked the flights for three days' time anyway. Then I put in a call to Marie Regan. I hadn't forgotten the promise I had made.

I went over to Deirdre's place, to see if I could catch Alva. Much of the snow had indeed turned to slush, but there was still enough fresh snow to make the air bracing and clean-smelling. Alva wasn't there. I was drinking coffee with Deirdre when Liam came in.

'Has anyone seen Jesus?' he said.

'Have you tried his mother's?' Deirdre said.

'That's why I'm worried. She hasn't seen him all day, but you remember the rifle, the Martini Henry we took off the Puerto Rican? It was hidden there, and it's gone.'

'He can't get near the Puerto Ricans in prison,' Deirdre said.

A sudden terrible thought came into my mind.

I grabbed the phone and dialled a number from memory. John Stone answered on the second ring.

'Stone,' I said urgently, 'where is Xabarra?'

He hesitated.

'Come on, Stone,' I said impatiently.

'Actually, he's in New York. But I couldn't really tell you where.'

239

I hung up.

'He's in New York,' I said. 'Liam, call Billy E, see if he can help us find Jesus.'

As Liam was calling, I paced the floor. Jesus obviously knew where Xabarra would be. He had no special intelligence, so it had to be something gleaned from general knowledge.

'I think I know where he is,' Deirdre said, her voice shaking a little. She was holding a copy of *Vogue*. It was open at a page featuring a Chagall exhibition that had just arrived at the Guggenheim. It was opening that night.

Liam practically carried me down the stairs. His car was outside. We stopped for Billy E and Tonto, then sped towards the Guggenheim.

The space outside Frank Lloyd Wright's wondrous building was thronged with people attending the opening.

'I know somebody here,' Billy E said, 'an old junkie.'

The man was guarding a service entrance to the rear of the building. Billy E talked to him urgently for a minute, then the man stood aside and let us in.

The interior of the building was an enormous six-storey spiral with a ground-floor space in the middle and galleries leading off each turn of the spiral. We took a service lift to the top floor of the spiral.

'Shit,' Liam said, 'this is perfect sniper territory.'

'I'll stay here,' I said, 'I can't walk much anyway. Start working your way down the ramps.'

I thought that the top ramp was the most likely place, but the rest of the place had to be covered. Liam and the other two men hurried off. I scanned the top level. Then I looked down and saw Xabarra.

He came through the front door leaning on two canes. The slab of stone had crushed his legs as well as mine, and he had that terrible wound in his thigh. He was waving off the solicitous enquiries of the great and good with a wry, charming expression. He was wearing evening dress and looked perhaps a little thinner than the last time I had seen him, but apart from that he hadn't changed. Then I saw Alva in the crowd.

She was staring at him, as if by staring she could absorb the part of him that belonged to her, absorb it and connect to it, and find that the man she knew as her father was something other than the living nightmare he had shown himself to be. But I could see that it wasn't working. Something like resignation began to steal over her face. Then Xabarra saw her. His face was consumed by a wolfish expression and he beckoned to her with his crooked finger. I saw the tears start in her eyes for a moment before she buried her face in her hands and turned away in grief. Xabarra shrugged to himself, then turned away from her in an act of dismissal, as if she had never existed.

Moments later, I saw Jesus.

He was on the second ramp, four floors below me. He must have known that I was there because the minute I saw him, he looked up at me, waved and smiled. The smile was open and guileless, as though he had found some peace, and after that day, when I thought of Jesus, it was that upturned face that I saw. Then he looked away and his expression turned serious. He brought the Martini Henry up to his shoulder. I could see Liam and the others on the fourth ramp. I knew that shouting would do no good. So I watched the bolt being drawn carefully back, I imagined the brass shell easing its way into the chamber, the trigger mechanism gathering tensile strength as his finger tightened on the trigger, the deadly half-arc of the firing pin.

He fired straight and true and he hit Xabarra in the middle of the forehead, blowing him backwards across the foyer, spraying the crowd around him with blood and brains. There was pandemonium, screams, men and women running for exits, security guards with drawn guns running. And in the middle of it all, a point of stillness, the body of Xabarra lying on the floor, almost forgotten. Except for the small figure moving slowly towards him. For the first time, Alva looked like the child I had known all those years ago. As I watched, she knelt beside her father and lifted his head into her lap and smoothed his hair, sticky with blood, back from his face, and my heart was flooded with pity.

It wasn't over. I turned away from them, as though to watch was a terrible intrusion. Without thinking, I went into the gallery nearest to me. The room contained a Mark Rothko in black and grey, the work of a master at the end of his life, every brushstroke saying that beauty is a far more terrible and ambiguous thing than we ever expect.

I went to the window. It was snowing again fitfully. I saw Jesus running up the street, holding the rifle. I saw a cop get a shotgun from his car, saw his mouth open as he shouted a warning. He brought the gun to his shoulder. Jesus was running the way a child runs, with abandon, knowing that he is going to be caught and punished because that is the way of the world and he expects no more. The cop fired and I saw red bloom in the middle of Jesus's back. He staggered and fell and did not move. A small bundle in the snow, a Puerto Rican street urchin who flew too high and fell too hard.

Twenty

I waited in the departure lounge, keeping my hands in my pockets for warmth. The heating in this part of the terminal had broken down and I could see my breath in the air in front of me. I had an odd feeling of weightlessness, as if the things that made me, the experiences and memory, had been excised by the events of the past month.

I was on my own. I hadn't seen Alva since her father's death.

I had gone with Irene to the morgue to identify Jesus. When we came out, the three old Puerto Rican men were waiting for us.

'They will help me take my son home to Puerto Rico to bury him. We are family now.'

I wondered if this was what Jesus had meant about building a bridge between his mother and his father's family.

'This is the last time I will see you, Jack.'

I didn't know what to say. It was clear that, as far as Irene was concerned, I bore, if not blame, then responsibilty for what had happened. I couldn't argue with her. I bent to kiss her, but she drew away and offered me her hand stiffly. I took it, then she turned and walked towards the car where the three old men stood watching me without expression.

I was daydreaming and I missed my flight call. I felt a gloved hand slip into the crook of my elbow. It was Alva.

'We'll miss our flight, *caro* Jack,' she said.

The following morning, I was in London. I found it hard to look at my friend in a wheelchair, but Alva took to the task of caring for Paolo with a firm solicitude that surprised me. I wasn't sure if he knew me, and he looked at Alva with such unabashed pride and gentleness that I wondered if he mistook her for her mother. As soon as I could, I slipped away. If Paolo remembered anything of the mission I had gone on, he gave no sign. I stayed for two days to keep an eye on what was happening, but I was reassured when I went to the hospital on the second day and met them coming out of the park.

'What were you doing?' I asked.

'Alva was teaching me the names of the flowers,' Paolo replied in English. I left them then. There was nothing I could give.

Back in Scotland, my house seemed somehow shabby and uncared for. I lit a fire, and opened a good bottle of wine, but I couldn't seem to lift the gloom. I had one more meeting connected with the whole affair and I wanted it to be over. I took some prawns out of the freezer and cooked them badly, and then I waited.

At eight o'clock, a car pulled up outside the house. I opened the door to Marie Regan, kissed her cheek and took her coat. She sat down at the table. Her face was grave.

'I don't know what happened to you over there,' she said, 'but . . .'

'I'm sure you're anxious to know what I found out about this heroin,' I said, 'the stuff they're attributing to your husband.'

She sat forward eagerly. She was wearing a dress of blue crushed silk. I could smell her perfume. Her hair fell over her cheek as she moved.

I took the document that I had received from Stone out of my pocket.

'The heroin never belonged to Paddy,' I said.

'That's good,' she said. 'Thank you, Jack. Thank you. I didn't think he was into that, but sometimes you doubt . . . you know . . . and his memory can't defend itself, can it?'

'The heroin never belonged to Paddy,' I said slowly and deliberately. 'It belonged to you, Marie.' I read from the document. 'A substantial and serious effort has been made to construct a false trail as to the ownership of the consignment, but we are in no doubt as to its true provenance.'

She didn't say anything. She just smiled a slow, thoughtful smile.

'I was supposed to turn up the false trail, wasn't I?' I said. 'Let Paddy off the hook. You didn't want your children to think their father was a drug smuggler and you couldn't tell them the truth.'

'I'm sorry, Jack,' she managed in the end. She didn't sound very sorry.

'Something else,' I said. 'You never asked about Paolo. You remember Paolo? You were there when he had his legs blown off.'

'No,' she said slowly. 'I never did ask.'

Her eyes met mine. I could smell the perfume again, stronger this time. I was aware of her hand on the table next to mine.

'If you hurry,' I said, 'you can catch the last ferry at Stranraer.'

She got to her feet.

'Whatever happened over there, Jack, don't put it on me. I wasn't honest with you, that's true, but that's all.'

I didn't turn to see her leave. I heard the car engine start and the sound of gravel, and then it was gone. I felt defiled. I went to my case and took out the jaguar's claw. I took it down to the sea and threw it as far as I could. It glinted once in the moonlight, then fell silently into the sea. I went back to the house and set a bottle of Redbreast and a glass on the kitchen table.

Much later, the phone rang. I answered it. I was aware that my voice was slurring and my thoughts were uncertain.

It was Deirdre. We had hardly been able to look at each other in those last few days in New York.

I told her about Marie's visit. And then I told her that I had slept with Marie. She was more rueful than angry.

'Jack, Jack,' she said. 'I know her. I could have told you what she is.'

I told her about Paolo afterwards. I think it was then that I broke down. She let me go for a little while, then she talked to me with small, soothing words, talk of good memories, things that we had shared in the past, and gradually she brought me round and calmed me.

When she put the phone down, I was back on what passed for a level.

I looked at the bottle. It was almost finished.

I poured what was left into the glass. I raised it once to Jesus, and prayed that he had found his love in whatever place he had gone. And then I raised it to Paolo and Alva naming flowers in the park.

A memory of Mexico came back to me. Of a cracked and ancient Christ crucified with a badly repaired arm. I wished upon them the best that we could wish for, the imperfect peace that was the domain of a splinted Christ.